# MICHAEL MORPURGO
## Stories of King Arthur

EGMONT

# EGMONT

*We bring stories to life*

This collection first published in Great Britain in 2014 by Egmont UK Ltd
The Yellow Building, 1 Nicholas Road, London W11 4AN

*Arthur, High King of Britain* text © 1994 Michael Morpurgo
*Arthur, High King of Britain* illustrations © 2002 Michael Foreman
*The Sleeping Sword* text © 2002 Michael Morpurgo
*The Sleeping Sword* illustrations © 2002 Michael Foreman
The moral rights of the author and illustrator have been asserted

ISBN 978 1 4052 7127 1

1 3 5 7 9 10 8 6 4 2

www.egmont.co.uk
www.michaelmorpurgo.com

A CIP catalogue record for this title is available from the British Library

57381/1

Printed and bound in Great Britain by the CPI Group

MIX
Paper
FSC FSC® C018306

## EGMONT

Our story began over a century ago, when seventeen-year-old
Egmont Harald Petersen found a coin in the street. He was on
his way to buy a flyswatter, a small hand-operated printing
machine that he then set up in his tiny apartment.

The coin brought him such good luck that today Egmont has
offices in over 30 countries around the world. And that lucky
coin is still kept at the company's head offices in Denmark.

# Arthur,
# High King of Britain

*For Ros,*
*who helped me so much*
*MM*

# CONTENTS

# 1 THE BELL

THE BOY LEFT HOME AT FIRST LIGHT, ENOUGH food and drink in his rucksack to last him the whole day. It was something he had always promised himself he would do – if ever he had the chance, if ever the circumstances were right. He told no one of his plans, because he knew his mother would worry, his little sister would tell on him, and his father would try to stop him. As far as they were concerned he was going shrimping off Samson. He would be getting up early to catch the spring tide just as it fell, so that he could walk the sea-bed from Bryher to Tresco and from Tresco over to Samson. That was what he'd told them. Everyone did that, but what no one had ever done, so far as he knew anyway, was to walk over to the Eastern Isles and back again. Everyone said that it could not be done in the time. His father was quite adamant about it. That was partly why the boy was determined to do it.

He had worked it all out. He knew the waters around the Scilly Isles like the back of his hand. He had lived there all his twelve years. From the deck of his father's fishing boat, he had learnt every rock, every sandbank. He knew the tides, the currents and the clouds. He could do it. The spring tide would be the lowest for years. The weather was settled and perfect – red sky the night before – and the wind was right. So long as he left the Eastern Isles by half past twelve he would have enough time to make it back to Bryher and home before the tide rose and cut him off. He knew precisely how fast the tides came in. He knew there would be places where he would have to wade shoulder high through the sea. And if the worst came to the worst he could always swim for it. He was a strong swimmer, the best in his school. He could make it. He would make it.

He stood on Green Bay looking out across Tresco Channel, the cold mud oozing between his toes. He checked his watch. Just before six. A pair of oystercatchers busied themselves in the shallows, and were interrupted by a gang of raucous gulls fighting over a crab. They took off, piping their indignation. The sea was fast draining away in the Tresco Channel. It was a windless, cloudless dawn. The boy hitched up his rucksack, and began to trot out towards Tresco. As he had expected, the sea was still running fast through the channel. He splashed out into it, the force of the current soon reducing him to a walk. He took off his rucksack, held it above his head and waded in deeper. The cold of the water took his breath away. He thought that maybe he had set out too early, that he might have to turn back and wait for the tide to ebb a little further; but a few steps more, and he was through the deepest water and then out of it altogether. He clambered up over the dunes and broke into a run, passing Tresco church by quarter to seven. He was on time.

As he came down to the harbour at Old Grimsby, the whole sea-bed was open to the sky. It was as if Moses had been there before him. The sea still ran through in places, but he could see his route plainly – Tean, then over to St Martin's and along the shore towards Higher Town Bay. And there were the Eastern Isles still surrounded by sea, the Ganilly sand-bar already a golden island in the early morning sun. The sand-bar would be his only way in and his only way out. In less than two hours, by his reckoning, the sand-bar would be a brief causeway to the Eastern Isles. He would have to hurry. He ate his breakfast on the move, a couple of sausage rolls and a jam sandwich. He gulped it down too fast and had to stop to wash it down with water. Biting into the first of his apples, he headed out towards Tean. With the tide still going out he knew this was the easiest part. It would be on the way back that he would have to race the tide home to Bryher. The return must be timed perfectly, to the minute; so the sooner he reached the Eastern Isles the better. Once there, he would have just a quarter of an hour to eat his lunch and rest. With this in mind, and only this in mind, he reached St Martin's and ran along the beach, trying to keep to the wet sand. It was easier on his aching legs than the softer sand near the dunes.

The sun was high now and hot on his head. The rucksack was chafing at his shoulders, so he hooked his thumbs into the straps to relieve the soreness. When the beach became rocks he turned inland and followed the track through the bracken towards Higher Town. He was passing the school gates when he saw Morris Jenkins coming down the track towards him. He was about the last person the boy wanted to meet. Morris would want to talk. He always wanted to talk.

'What're you doing over here?' Morris shouted.

'See you, Morris,' said the boy as he ran by, breathless.

'Flaming marathon, is it?'

'Something like that.' And then he was out of sight and heaving a sigh of relief. He slowed to walk. His legs felt heavy. He was tiring. He longed to sit down, to rest; but he dared not, not yet. He thought of Morris Jenkins. He had resisted the temptation to tell him where he was going, what he was doing. He'd only have scoffed. When the time was right, when he'd done it, then he would tell anyone, then he'd tell everyone. There'd be those who wouldn't believe him, of course, Morris amongst them, but he didn't mind that. He would know and that was all that really mattered. He bit into another apple and pressed on towards the Eastern Isles.

By noon the boy was sitting in triumph on the highest rock on Great Ganilly, the largest of the Eastern Isles. There were a few other walkers out and about now, shrimping the sea-bed around St Martin's; but he was quite alone on the Eastern Isles, except for a solitary seal bobbing in the open sea and a few shrieking terns that were diving at him, trying to drive him off his rock. He sat where he was, ate his lunch and ignored them. In time they gave up and left him

in peace. He finished his last jam sandwich and checked his watch. He had ten minutes to spare. He'd rest for a minute or two and then be on his way. Plenty of time. He lay back on the rock, head on his rucksack, his eyes squinting in the glare of the sun. He closed them, and wondered how the Scilly Isles had been when they were one entire island, before it tipped fifteen hundred years ago and let the ocean flood in. Had there been an earthquake, or a tidal wave perhaps? No one knew. A mystery. He liked mysteries, he liked the unknown. Lulled by warm stillness and more exhausted than he knew, he slipped into sleep.

When he woke, the sun was gone, the sky was gone, the sea was gone. He was cocooned in thick fog. The foghorn from the Bishop Rock Lighthouse sounded distantly, echoing the fear that was taking root in the boy's heart. He scrambled down through the bracken. It would be clearer down on the shore. It must be. It had to be. If he could see the sand-bar, then he could find his way back to St Martin's. It was all right, it was all right! There was the sand-bar stretching away into fog. All he had to do was follow it and he'd be safe. Only then did he think to look at his watch. Twenty-five to one. Just five minutes behind time. He'd have to hurry. He ran out on to the sand-bar, his eyes straining for some shadow in the white-out that might be St Martin's. It had to be that way. It had to be. He was running through sandy pools, and then the pools were suddenly not pools any more, but the sea itself. He could go no further. The ocean was closing in around him. He could hear the sea running now, rippling in over the sand-bar to encircle him. He stood frozen in his fear and listened. A sudden wind came in off the sea and chilled him to the bone, yet it gave him the only hope left to him. He was stranded. Great Ganilly had vanished, St Martin's was invisible. Only the wind could save him now. If the wind would only blow away the blinding fog, then at least he could find his way off the sand-bank, and swim back to Great Ganilly and safety. So he stood in the wind and watched all about him, waiting and praying for the fog to thin.

Bewildered, disorientated and frightened now for his life, he found the highest place he could on the sandbank. He felt a strange calm over him, a detachment from himself. He wondered if this was the beginning of dying. When he cried out it was only to hear the sound of his own voice to be sure he was still alive; but once he'd begun he did not stop. He shouted, he screamed until his head ached with it, until his throat was raw. His words were at once muffled and lost. There was no hope. He sank to his knees in the sand and gave up. The sea would take him, drown him and grind his bones to sand.

A bell sounded from far out across the water, a ship's bell. Whilst the boy was still doubting his own hearing, it ran out again. Muted in the fog, there was no resonance to it, but it was real. He was not imagining it. The boy was on his feet and running across the sand calling out. 'Over here! Over here! Help! Help me!' He stopped to listen for the reply. There was none, only the bell ringing from somewhere out at sea, distant, faint, but definitely there. He splashed out through the shallows and was soon waist-high in the sea. He stopped now only to listen for the bell, to fix his bearings, to reassure himself each time that it was no illusion. The bell was closer now, sharper. He was out of the sea and running on stones, his feet slipping, sliding. More than once he stumbled to his knees, but always the bell called him to his feet and gave him new hope, new strength. It was beckoning now, helping him, guiding him – he was sure of it. 'Where are you?' he cried. 'Where are you?' The bell answered him again and he staggered on towards it. When he found himself wading out into the sea again, he did not stop. He had no choice, he had to follow the bell. When the water came up over his chin and he could walk no more, he began to swim, pausing every few strokes to listen for the bell, but each time he stopped the bell seemed further from him. He was being swept away. He kicked hard against the current, fighting it; but he knew he was fighting a losing battle. He cried for help, and the salt water came into his mouth and choked him. His strength was fast ebbing from him. The cold of the sea gripped his legs and cramped them. His arms could no longer keep him up. He cried out one last time and the sea covered him. His last living thoughts were of his mother. She was clutching his wet rucksack, hugging it and crying, the rucksack he must have left behind on Great Ganilly. At least she would know he had got that far. Seaweed tugged at his arms and held him down. He hoped there was a heaven.

Heaven was warm and the boy was glad of it. He shivered out the last of the cold and looked about him. He was lying in a vast bed and covered with skins. The fur tickled his ear. A great roaring fire burnt beside him and a man in a long grey cloak was poking at it with a stick, sending showers of sparks up the chimney. The boy had often tried to picture heaven when he was alive. This was not at all how he had thought of it. He was in what appeared to be a huge hall, lit all around with flaming torches; and in the middle of the hall was the biggest table the boy had ever seen, round, entirely round, with maybe a hundred chairs set about it. At one end of the hall was a staircase hewn out of the rock, winding its way upwards into smoky darkness. The boy coughed.

'So,' said the man, straightening up and turning

towards him. 'So you are awake at last.'

The boy found his voice. 'Are you God?' he asked.

The man put his head back and laughed. His hair and beard were white and long, but the face and eyes were those of a man still young – too young to be God, the boy thought, even as he asked it.

'No,' said the man, and he sat down on the bed beside him. 'I am not God. My name is Arthur Pendragon. I live here, if you can call it living.' He leant forward and whispered. 'Year in, year out, they keep me shut up down here in this cave. Even a hibernating bear comes out after the winter, doesn't he? Be patient, they say. Be patient and your time will come.'

'They?'

'There are six of them, six ladies. They brought me here. Only when the fog is down and I cannot be

seen, only then will they let me out. I am supposed to rest, but for some years now I have not been able to sleep as I should. I have had dreams and my dreams tell me my time is coming, that I will soon be needed again. I wait only for a messenger.' He spoke now in greater earnest. 'You are not the one? You are not the messenger? You were not sent, were you?'

The boy shrank back in fear.

'No, of course not. You couldn't be. You didn't ring the bell, did you? When he comes, he will ring the bell, they have told me so.' The man smiled with his eyes, and the boy knew he had nothing to fear. More than that, he realized suddenly that he might still be in the land of the living. But he needed to be quite sure.

'I'm not dead then?' he ventured.

'Not you, nor I,' said Arthur Pendragon. 'But you nearly were.' A carpet by the fire stirred and became a dog, a deerhound. The dog yawned, stretched and came padding over to the bed.

'Meet Bercelet,' said Arthur Pendragon, and he scratched the dog's head. 'My only companion in my long confinement. The ladies who brought me here don't talk much. They're good enough to me. I want for nothing, but it's like living with shadows. Still, now we've got you, for a while at least. It was Bercelet who heard you first, you know. Like me, he longs for the fog, so we can escape for just a few hours from this tomb of a place. Nothing he likes better than a good run. They heard you too, my six ladies. "Do nothing," they said, "or you will betray yourself." "Do nothing," I said, "and I will indeed betray myself, and that I will never do, never again." So I rang the bell, but you did not come. I rang it and rang it, and still you never came. Then I heard you calling again, and you were closer this time. So I went looking for you. I found you just in time, I think.'

'You pulled me out?'

Arthur Pendragon nodded and smiled. 'They are not at all pleased with me, my ladies, my keepers. But you are here now and there is nothing they can do about it. And at least I have someone to talk to, someone from the real world. I talk to Bercelet, of course, and to myself – oh, I talk a lot to myself. Do you know what I do? I tell myself all the old stories again and again, so that I won't forget them. Stories, like people, die once they are forgotten. If they die, then I die with them. I want people to know how it was, how it really was. I don't want us to be forgotten.'

The boy sat up suddenly. He looked at his watch. The face was misted over. He listened to it, but it had stopped. 'How long have I been here?'

'You slept half a day and a whole night.'

'But I must get back,' said the boy. 'They'll think I'm dead.'

'No, they won't,' he said. 'We'll get you back home soon enough, once your clothes are dry. The ladies wanted to send you back straight away, all cold and wet; but I wouldn't have it. "We'll send him back warm and dry," I told them. And so I will, I promise you; and this king does not break his promises, not any more.'

'A king? You are a king?'

'I told you. I am Arthur Pendragon, High King of Britain, hibernating these past centuries here in Lyonesse.'

The boy had to smile a little despite himself. The old man nodded knowingly, and went on. 'You don't believe me, do you? Well, why should you? But believe I took you from the sea. Believe I carried you in here. Believe those are your clothes drying by the fire. Believe you are lying in my bed. Here, feel my hand. Flesh and blood like yours.' The hand that touched the boy's face was warm and rough, rough like his father's fisherman's hands. 'See?'

'But King Arthur – it's all just stories, a myth.'

'A myth, you say! A myth! Do you hear that,

14

Bercelet? Your master's a myth.' He turned to the boy again. 'You *have* heard of me then?'

'Yes,' said the boy. 'A little. The sword, in the lake.'

'Excalibur. Is that all you know? Well, whilst we're waiting for your clothes to dry, you shall hear the rest. It's a long story, a story of great love, of great tragedy, of magic and mystery, of hope, of triumph and of disaster. It is my story, but not only my story. In those empty chairs you see about the Round Table, there once sat a company of knights, the finest, bravest men this world has ever seen. And they were my friends too. I'll tell you about them, I'll tell you about me. Lie back now and rest.'

He patted the bed beside him, and Bercelet jumped up and stretched out beside the boy. He sighed deeply and licked his paw. 'I know, Bercelet, you've heard it all before, haven't you? And besides, you were there – for most of it anyway.' The dog closed his eyes and sighed again. 'Well, the boy hasn't heard it, so you'll just have to put up with it. I'll begin at the beginning, when I was a boy and not much older than you are now.'

Arthur Pendragon sat down by the fire, stared into it for a moment, and then began.

## 2 NOBODY'S CHILD

I LOOK AT YOU AND SEE MYSELF AS THE CHILD I
once was, a dreamer, a wanderer. I have to strain to
remember the castle where I grew up, the bed I slept
in, the table I ate at. But I can still see clear in my
mind the wild forests of Wales and the wind-blasted
mountains above them where I passed my early years.
And they were carefree, those years. I had a mother
for my best friend, and a father for my constant
companion and teacher. He taught me how to hunt,
to stalk silently, to kill cleanly. From him I learnt how
to handle a hawk, to sweeten in a fox, to hold a bow
without a tremble as I pulled it taut, and to use a
sword and a spear as a knight should. But from my

mother I learnt the great things. I learnt what is right, what is wrong, what should be and what should not be – lessons I am still learning even now, my friend. I never in my life have loved anyone more than my mother, and I think I never hated anyone more than my elder brother Kay.

Kay was six years older than I was and the bane of my young life. Time and again he would foist the blame for his own misdeeds on to my shoulders, for ever trying to turn Father against me – and in this he often succeeded. I would find myself banished to my room or whipped for something I had not done. I can see now the triumphant sneer in my brother's eyes. But with Mother he was never able to taint me. She would never hear a word against me, from Kay or from Father. She was my constant ally, my rock.

But she died. She died when I was just twelve years old. As she lay on her deathbed, her eyes open and unseeing, I reached out to touch her cheek for the last time. Kay grasped my arm and pulled me back.

'Don't you dare touch her,' he said, eyes blazing. 'She's my mother, not yours. You don't have a mother.' I appealed to Father and saw the flicker in his eye that told me that Kay was speaking the truth.

'Kay,' he said, shaking his head sadly. 'How can you say such a thing now, and with your mother lying still warm in death? What I told you, I told you in trust. How can you be so cruel? And you a son of mine.'

'And me?' I said. 'Am I not a son of yours too? Was she not my mother?'

'Neither,' said Father, and he looked away from me. 'I would have told you before, but could never bring myself to do it.'

'Then,' I cried, 'if I am not yours, and if I am not hers, whose am I? I can't be nobody's child.'

He took me by the shoulders. 'Dear boy,' he said, and he suddenly looked an old man, 'I cannot tell you who you are. All I know is that you were brought here as a newborn baby by Merlin. It was Merlin who made me promise to keep you, to protect you and to bring you up as I would my own son and this I have done to my very best. If there have been times when I was hard on you, then it was because I always had that promise to fulfil.'

'Merlin?' I asked. 'Who is this Merlin?'

Kay scoffed at that. 'Do you do nothing but dream? Everyone knows who Merlin is. He's the maker of the old druid magic, a weaver of spells, a soothsayer. He knows what will happen, long before it does happen. He knows everything that has been and everything that will be. Why he bothered with you I can't imagine.'

I turned to Father. 'Is this all true? I was brought here by this Merlin? My mother is not my mother? You are not my father?' He nodded and I could see the pain in his face reflecting my own. But Kay had to rub more salt in the wound.

'So you see,' he crowed. 'You are a bastard, a foundling. You should be grateful we took you in.'

At that my blood was up. Small though I was, I felled him with one blow and I would have done him more damage had not Father pulled me off him.

'That is not the way I have taught you, Arthur,' he said, still holding me back. But I broke free of him and ran off into the forest. There I wandered for days and days like some wounded animal, maddened with pain.

I found myself sometime later in a hidden valley covered with a purple mist of bluebells, and a stream running softly over the stones. Faint with hunger and thirst, I lay down and drank my fill. And as I drank, I thought. I had heard of old men and old women who have no longer the will to go on living, who would seek out just such a hidden place and lie down to die, to be eaten by wolves, and to be picked clean by crows. There on the bank among the bluebells I decided to lie down and never get up again. I closed my eyes and began the sleep of death. I was not afraid.

I would join Mother and leave the misery of this world behind me.

Deep in my troubled dreams I heard the approach of an animal picking its way through the bluebells, splashing through the stream. I felt hot breath on my face, and knew I was not in my dream any more. I braced myself for the shaking and tearing I knew I would have to endure before I died. I opened my eyes, curious to see the wolf that would finish me. He stood over me, his tongue drooling, his great grey eyes blinking lazily. It was no wolf but a deerhound; and then a voice was calling him off. An old man in rags, a beggarman he seemed to be, was fording the stream, barefoot on the stones and leaning on a staff to steady himself against the current. I struggled in my weakness to push the dog off me.

'You're a new smell,' said the beggarman. 'Don't worry, Bercelet will not harm you.' And he came and sat down heavily beside me. 'Have you anything to give a poor beggarman?' he asked. I shook my head, for I had nothing. He went on. 'Then at least give me some of your time. Time costs nothing and a young man like yourself has enough of it to spare. You have a long life ahead of you, longer than you know, longer even than you may want. Since the High King Utha died I have wandered this land from end to end. I see

around me nothing but ruin and desolation. Everywhere I find greed and famine, hand in hand and prospering. I see a kingdom divided and weakened. I see lords and kings squabbling like sparrows amongst themselves. And, as they fight, the Picts and the Scots come down from the north country, pillaging and burning at will, and the Irish and the cursed Saxons pour in their hordes from across the seas and we are defenceless before them. They take our towns, our villages, our farms. They burn our churches, they enslave our people and we can do nothing, for the heart has gone out of us. We are a people entirely without hope.' He looked around him. 'You see this valley of bluebells? It all began here a thousand, two thousand years ago maybe, with just one fine bluebell that grew strong and proud. And then one by one others sprang up around it and a valley of thicket and bramble was turned into this paradise on Earth. You can grow to be just such a flower, and then others would follow you. It only takes one. Think no more of dying, young man. Look around you, and wonder what one flower can do and know then what one man can do. All Britain could be as fine as this wood. You may be the first bluebell, you may be the one.' He smiled gently at me out of his dark eyes and ruffled the hair about the deerhound's neck. 'I need only look into a man's eyes and I can see his soul. I see in you the seed of greatness. Let it grow.'

After we had talked some more together he put his head back against the tree and we slept. When I woke he was gone and the dog Bercelet with him. At first I thought that the beggarman must have been part of my dream, but then I saw the bluebells flattened where he had sat and his staff left behind, leaning against the trunk of an ash tree. I was on my feet at once, the staff in my hand and calling after him. But only the cackle of a mocking jay answered me.

I stayed for some days more in the hidden bluebell valley, hoping the beggarman and his hound might return. But they did not. I fed on the brown trout that bunched in the shady shadows of the stream, offering themselves for a meal. I ate greedily, and as my strength returned, my spirit too revived. I left the wood behind me and made for home.

I had been gone for a month, maybe it was more, and they had given me up for dead. Father clung to me and cried. 'Never again think you are not my son,' he said. 'Kay I bred, and love him as a man must always love his son. But you, I *chose* to love and I love you both as a son and as a friend also.' But even as he hugged me, I saw the steely glint of envy in Kay's eye and I knew I had no friend for a brother, nor ever would have.

The years passed and I kept always in my mind the meeting with the beggarman among the bluebells – I kept his staff too – and I heard more and more of those marauding Saxons who were driving our good people from their homes and how there was no one king strong enough to stand against them. Those they did not kill they harried and chased into the valleys and forests of Wales. The people came with nothing but the clothes on their backs. They had nowhere to shelter, no food to eat. We did what we could for them but it was never enough. I heard tales of fire and slaughter and terrible cruelty. Only the south of Britain and Wales itself still stood out against the invader. But for how long? I wondered.

For me there was a new urgency in my battle training. Daily I sparred with sword and spear against Father, against Kay, against anyone who would teach me more. In these mock battles, Kay sought often to provoke me – always when Father was not there, I noticed – calling me his 'bastard brother', but I turned aside the jibes with a smile, as a shield might glance away a thrusting sword.

One winter's day when I was about fifteen, word came to the castle that the Lord Archbishop of Britain was calling every knight in the kingdom to London. Here it would be decided at last, once and for all, who should be the High King of all Britain and lead the struggle against the Saxons. It was the last chance for all of us, Father was convinced of it; and far though it was to travel, and dangerous too, we had to go where we were needed. 'And you will come with us, Arthur,' said Father. 'Though you are not yet a knight, I should like you with us.'

'He can ride as our servant then,' Kay mocked. 'Can't he, Father?'

'Will you never learn to curb your wicked tongue?' Father said. 'Must you shame me every time you open your mouth?' He turned to me. 'No, Arthur, you come as our squire, not as our servant. It will be your first time away from Wales, and your first time in London.'

And so we all three came to London the week before Christmas and took lodgings not far from the great Abbey church. I saw little of Father, who was always away meeting the Archbishop and the other kings and knights and lords. During the day, Kay kept me so busy grooming the horses and polishing the armour that I had no time even to see the city. Kay was true to his word. I was no squire to him, but rather the meanest of servants. He showed me off amongst his friends. If I wasn't his 'bastard brother' I was his 'bastard servant'. Father was rarely with us, so there was no rein now on his viciousness.

Father would return each evening to the lodgings and the story was always the same. They could not agree. Each king, each lord, each knight had his own faction, and the past bitterness left no room for harmony. They howled at each other like tomcats. It was hopeless, Father said.

Christmas day came and a hard frost with it. The bells of the great Abbey ran out over the city, drawing us all to Mass. There in the Abbey we kneeled and prayed together for deliverance from the Saxons. The Archbishop prayed for all of us: *'Jesus, Son of God, defend us and keep us. We pray you provide for us, find for us a leader, someone who will bind us together and give us heart to fight. Give us, dear Lord, the faith to hope again. Give us a sign. Help us, sweet Jesus.'* And the chorus of 'Amen' echoed in unison through the Abbey. I looked at the bowed heads around me and thought of the bluebells in the hidden wood in Wales so far away, and of the beggarman whose staff I had always kept beside me ever since. I had it with me then.

I came out of the Abbey after Mass was over and saw a large crowd gathering at the far end of the churchyard under a great yew tree. I was intrigued and began walking towards them, when Kay and some of his friends came running past me, blundering into me and knocking me to my knees. 'On your feet, bastard brother,' he called out. 'Get back to the lodgings at once and prepare my armour and horse, as a servant should. Bring them to me at the tournament field by three o'clock. And don't be late.' Then he was gone into the crowd, his belly-laughing cronies with him.

I left the Abbey behind me and joined the bustle of the city streets. Everyone, it seemed, was making for the Abbey churchyard. I was like a trout swimming against the stream. As I walked back to our lodgings through the crowds on that Christmas Day, I yearned for the wild woods of Wales, for peace and quiet, for larks and bluebells. I lay on my bed in my room and dreamed I was there again, the beggarman beside me with Bercelet, his great drooling hound, and the silver stream running softly over the stones. I fell into a deep sleep.

I was woken by the bells of the Abbey ringing out – one, two, three – three o'clock. It's always the same. When you're in too much of a hurry, horses never do as you want them to. They would shift about as I saddled them. They trod on my toes, blew out their stomachs so I could not tighten their girthstraps. I lashed Kay's armour on to his horse, mounted mine and set off. More than once his horse broke free of the leading rein; and more than once his armour fell off and I had to stop to pick it up again. I galloped the horses through the empty streets and we clattered over the bridge. I could hear ahead of me the roar of the crowd. The tournament had already begun.

Kay was waiting for me at the gate, his friends gathered around him. His face was dark with anger. 'Where have you been?' he demanded.

'I'm sorry,' I said. 'I was sleeping.'

'Sleeping! You're late, damn your eyes. You're useless, even as a servant you're useless, a useless bastard.' And with that he began to arm himself, his friends helping him with his buckles, and he chiding me all the while. Suddenly he stopped and looked around him. 'My sword!' he cried. 'Where in God's name is my sword?'

I had forgotten it. In my hurry I had forgotten it. I had to confess it.

'Then you'd better fetch it, hadn't you!' shouted Kay. He slapped my horse on its rump, so that he reared up and nearly threw me. I rode off, their mocking laughter ringing in my ears. But I made up my mind there and then that I would take my time. I rode slowly back to the bridge.

As I passed by the Abbey, I heard a bird singing loudly, a robin I thought, a cock robin, but I could not see it anywhere. I was looking over into the churchyard when I saw something that had not been there before – or if it had, I had not noticed it. Under the yew tree there stood a massive granite-grey stone. Suddenly the sunlight came through the clouds and the stone shone like burnished steel. It shone so brightly that it hurt my eyes to look at it. Strange, I thought, and I dismounted. At first I supposed it was the frost on the stone that glittered so, but I soon saw that it was not the stone itself that shone. It was a sword, a sword stuck incongruously into the stone. And there, at last, was the robin I had been looking for all the time. He was sitting on the pommel of the sword, singing his heart out. As I came closer, the robin stayed where he was, eyeing me. I was so close now I could almost reach out and touch him, but when I tried he flew off and up into the great yew tree. My hand was resting now on the sword hilt. Only then did I think of Kay and the sword that I had left behind at the lodgings. Why not? I thought. Kay wouldn't notice the difference. This sword looked much the same as his. It would save me the journey back to the lodgings. I'd borrow it and put it back later. I looked around to see if anyone was about. The churchyard was deserted. I glanced up at the robin. 'Don't tell,' I said, and I grasped the hilt and pulled it.

It came free of the stone easily enough, much more easily than I had expected. It was a fine sword, heavy but well balanced. It fitted my grasp as if it had been made for me. Sword in hand, I said goodbye to the robin and left.

As I approached the tournament field for the second time, I saw Kay and his friends waiting for me, and stiffened myself to endure their barbs. I handed the sword to Kay who snatched it out of my hands. 'About time,' he snapped. He never even looked at it. He turned his back on me and strode off towards the field.

I tied up my horse and followed some distance behind. It was my first tournament and I walked around it in a daze of wonder. Flags of every colour flew everywhere, lions, unicorns, lilies, castles, all dancing in the wind. Tents, gold and white in the sun, covered the field. And ladies – such ladies. Every one of them looked to me like a princess. I moved amongst them, my heart pounding with excitement. They looked at me as though I were not there, but I did not mind. I gazed on their long white necks, their shimmering dresses, their glittering jewels, and I was in love with all of them instantly.

The noise of the crowd drew me away to the tournament itself. I stood for some time on my own and watched. There were thirty or forty knights busy in mock battles, hacking and thrusting fiercely at each other. The crowd roared them on, laughing and whistling whenever a knight retired hurt and limped from the field. Then I saw Kay being helped away, cursing as he came, his shield in two, his fingers dripping blood.

I found him sitting on the ground spitting blood from a cut lip. Father was there too. 'You'll be all right,' he was saying. Kay threw down his sword in a fit of temper. 'Lousy sword,' he said. 'Blunt as a staff.' Then he saw me. 'You didn't sharpen it, did you?' I said nothing. Father had retrieved the sword and was turning it over in his hands.

'This sword, Kay,' he said, 'this is the sword from the stone in the Abbey churchyard. I am sure of it.' There was a sudden hush and people began to gather around. Kay got to his feet. He glanced at me, a puzzled frown on him, and then his face lit with a sudden smile. 'Of course it is, Father,' he said. 'I thought I'd surprise you, that's all. I couldn't get a proper grip on it. So I went back later, on my own, and I tried again. It came out, just like that, with no trouble at all.'

Father was looking at him hard. 'You took the sword from the stone?'

'And why not?' Kay was offended. 'Why should it not be me? Am I not good enough?' All this time I said nothing. I could not understand what all the bother was about, nor why it was that Kay was claiming that he had taken the sword from the stone. Why should he be confessing to such a thing, boasting about it even? Thieving was bad enough, but thieving from a churchyard! If Kay wanted to brag about it, let him. I'd keep quiet.

'There is only one way to settle this, Kay,' said Father. 'We will go back to the Abbey churchyard, replace the sword in the stone and then see if you can draw it out again. Agreed?'

As we rode back across the bridge I felt Kay's eyes always on me, and Father too kept twisting in his saddle to look back at me. Somehow he already knew Kay had been lying, that it was I who had pulled the sword from the stone. I looked down to avoid the accusation in his eyes. How could I explain to him that I had just borrowed it, that I was going to put it back? He wouldn't believe me, and neither would anyone else.

Once in the churchyard again we gathered round the stone in silence, our several steaming breaths misting the frosty air around us. Father took the sword and thrust it deep into the stone. A bird sang suddenly and shrill above my head. I looked up. It was my robin again, his red breast fluffed up against the cold.

'Well, Kay,' said Father, standing back, 'go on then. Pull it out.'

Kay stepped up. I could see he did not want to go through with it, but he had no choice. He grasped the hilt with both hands, took a deep breath, and pulled with all his might. The sword stayed firm in the stone. He heaved at it. Red in the face now, he shook it. He wrenched at it. It would not move.

'That's enough Kay,' said Father quietly. 'You lied. You have always lied. You have shamed me yet again, and this time in front of the world. Step down.' And he turned at once to me. 'It is your turn, Arthur. Everyone else has already tried.'

I looked around me. The churchyard was packed now, everyone pushing, jostling, craning to see.

'Don't bother,' cried someone. 'He's only a boy.'

'And a bastard boy at that,' cried another.

Father took my hand and helped me up on to the stone. 'Go on Arthur,' he said. 'Take no notice.'

The robin sang out again as I took the sword in my hand. I drew it out as I had done before, without effort, smoothly, like a knife from cheese. Sunlight caught the blade, and the crowd fell suddenly silent.

Some crossed themselves, others fell at once to their knees. And then I saw Father kneeling too, his head bowed. 'Father, don't!' I cried. 'What are you doing? Why are you kneeling to me?'

He looked up at me, his eyes filled with tears. 'I know now,' he said. 'It was for this that you were brought to me by Merlin all those years ago.'

'But for what?' I said. 'What are you saying?'

'Kay,' said Father. 'Tell Arthur what is written on the stone. Read it aloud for him, so that Arthur may know who he is.'

Kay did not have to read it. As he spoke, his eyes never left my face. 'It says,' he began hesitantly, reluctantly, 'it says, *"Whoever pulls the sword from this stone is the rightful High King of Britain"*.'

'Quite so,' came a voice beside me. The man I found at my side was a head taller than I was. When he put back the hood of his dark cloak I saw his face was parchment-white and etched with age. His hair was long to his shoulders and shone silver in the sun. He put his hand on my arm. 'You remember me? You remember Bercelet?' he said.

I knew then it was the voice of the beggarman from the bluebell wood, and beside him was Bercelet, the shaggy deerhound I had once thought was a wolf.

'Merlin!' the crowd whispered. 'It is Merlin.'

'Then the sword in the stone is nothing but a trick,' said one of Kay's friends. 'Just one of his magician's tricks, and not a sign from God, as the Archbishop said it would be.'

'Not true.' It was the Archbishop himself, speaking as he came through the crowd. 'It is from God that Merlin has his great powers. It was God alone who set this stone in the graveyard, and it was God alone who put the sword in it. And the words written round it are written by God Himself. I tell you it is God Almighty who had chosen this boy for our king.'

'He can't be,' someone shouted. 'He's Kay's bastard brother. Everyone knows it. Besides, he's just a boy.' And furious arguments broke out all around the churchyard.

Merlin held up his hands to calm them. 'Hear me.' He spoke softly, but everyone seemed to hear him. 'This boy you see before you is Arthur Pendragon, and he is the rightful High King of Britain. His father – and he himself does not yet know it – his father was King Utha Pendragon, and his mother the Lady Igraine. He is born to greatness, born to save this realm, and chosen by God himself. When he was just a babe in arms I took him from his mother and father. I took him for safety's sake, for I knew the king had enemy spies all around him, who would murder both the king and his heir, if they could. And I was right, was I not? Was not King Utha poisoned? This boy, this prince, this king I saved. And I saved him for you, and for all Britain. He was brought up in deepest Wales as Sir Egbert's son, and as Sir Kay's brother, but he is neither. He is your true born High King. This stone and this sword are the proof of it. But so that no man should ever afterwards challenge him, we will leave the sword in the stone until Pentecost. Anyone who wants may try to draw it out. I tell you now, though, that no one but Arthur Pendragon, King Arthur himself, ever shall.' And the crowd knelt again before me and I felt Merlin's firm hand on my shoulder.

For three months after I had drawn the sword from the stone I stayed in London, and Merlin tutored me day and night in the arts of kingship. King after king, lord after lord and knight after knight came to the Abbey churchyard and tried to draw the sword from the stone, and every one of them failed. Some went away in a fury, vowing they would never serve under any beardless boy king; but most came to me and knelt before me and swore their allegiance.

It was some time before Kay could bring himself to do it, and when he did he could not look me in the face. He asked pardon for all he had done. 'If only I had known,' he said. 'If only I had known, I should not have done what I did, I should not have said what I said.'

'What is past is past,' I replied. 'Stay beside me, Kay. Be steward of all my lands.' I would never afterwards be able to trust Kay, I knew that; but I thought it wiser to have him near me where I could see him.

Merlin had taught me much already. He was always at my side, my mentor, my teacher and my friend too. He was there with me in the Abbey at the Coronation, as the Archbishop crowned me King, setting the golden circlet of kingship on my head. It was light enough to wear, but I knew even then, as I wore it for the first time, that the burden of kingship would grow heavier with each passing year. I should have been happy that day, but I was not. I was not overawed. I was not frightened. I was numb. Even then, after three months, I still could not believe what was happening to me.

At the feasting afterwards Merlin leant across and spoke to me quietly. 'So now it begins, Arthur. With these good men and with others still to come, you will build the Kingdom of Logres, God's own kingdom on earth, here in Britain. And it will flourish gloriously, for a while at least.' He sat back in his seat. 'A tree, however fine, cannot last for ever. Your tree too will one day wither and die, but from it a single acorn will lie dormant under the earth, until it is ready to grow again.'

As he spoke Bercelet came to lie down at my feet. Merlin smiled. 'Remember the beggarman in the bluebell wood?' he said. 'Remember the robin in the Abbey churchyard? I have the power to change nmyself into whatever I like, whomever I like. And I can divide myself too, Bercelet is not just a dog, you know. He is my eyes and my ears. He is part of me. From now on, always keep him with you. Keep him and you keep me. Together, we will guide you and protect you.'

Then Egbert, my dear foster father, stood and raised his cup to me, and everyone stood with him. 'To Arthur, our king, High King of all Britain. May you bring this poor country and her people out of darkness and into the light.' And all around the hall they thundered their applause.

Under the table, I pinched my leg to be sure I was not dreaming all this. Bercelet shoved his great shaggy head into my hand and gnawed at my finger. His gnawing turned to biting. It was no dream. Arthur Pendragon was indeed High King of Britain. The tooth marks on my knuckles told me so.

# 3 EXCALIBUR

AFTER THE FEAST WAS OVER, MERLIN AND I SAT
alone in the hall watching the fire dying. Bercelet lay
stretched out at my feet, his nose in the embers and
twitching in his sleep. We were silent in our own
thoughts. After a while Merlin stabbed the fire with a
stick. A few lazy sparks joined the smoke, floating up
the chimney.

'You see this fire?' he said. 'This is your kingdom,
all that is left of it.' He prodded it again. 'There is life
in it still, but it is hard to find amongst the ashes. A
spark or two is all that remains.' He looked at me hard
and held my eyes. 'The spark has to be kindled to a
flame, Arthur, and the flame to a roaring fire, such a

fire that will drive out all our enemies, and burn off the pestilence that stalks this land. It is you, Arthur, and you alone that can kindle this fire. I will use all my powers to help you, but the powers of evil ranged against us are at least as strong. Your three half-sisters will not rest until they have destroyed you. The youngest of them, Morgana Le Fey, will stop at nothing to recover the kingdom she thinks you have stolen, and believe me, she has the dark powers to do so. We must be brave enough, cunning enough and wise enough to overcome them. Through it all, you must never flinch from your course. Your kingdom is a land where cruelty and greed are rampant, where no man, no woman may live out their lives in peace and happiness. Everywhere, in every hamlet, in every town, there is fear. Warlords and brigands roam the countryside burning and pillaging at will. Mad with their own power and lust, they do as they please. The people everywhere are trampled and cowed, and those that resist are butchered. They have no protector. No people ever needed a king as much as these. In their hovels, they long for you. In their churches, they pray for you. It is for them and for God that you must fight, Arthur, never for yourself.' He grasped me by the arm. 'Have you the stomach for the fight?'

'If you are with me,' I replied.

'I shall be with you, but only as long as you need me,' said Merlin gazing into the fire. 'Some day I will have another place I must go to, someone else I must be with. But you will always have Bercelet.' He reached forward, plucked out the last charred stick and began to draw on the floor a jagged triangular shape.

'What is it?' I asked.

'Your kingdom,' he replied. 'Or rather what should be your kingdom. For the present, you rule in almost none of it. You are surrounded on all sides by your enemies, Saxons here – more Saxons there. Picts here and Irish here. Many of your knights have joined them already and will fight against you, out of envy, out of greed. And even those loyal to you, those few who feasted with us tonight, have never in their lives tasted victory. They are brave men, fine men, but they are used to losing. They need to win, Arthur. Rout the Saxons just once, and you will do it again and again. Give every man a horse, and it will happen as I say. This much I promise you.'

When you are young, everything seems possible. Self-doubt comes only with age, and I knew none of it then. With Merlin beside me, and every man on a strong, sturdy horse as he had commanded, I rode out to meet the Saxons in battle. We were a motley band and we were just a few at the beginning. But as we rode through the country, our numbers swelled. Every village we rode through added a woodcutter, a farmer or a charcoal burner. Some came with axes, some with rusting old swords, some even with the short swords from the days of the Romans, others with pitch forks. How the Saxons must have laughed when they saw us, a beardless boy-king and his rabble army. But what they could not know, what they could not see, was the new steel in our hearts, and the fierce, fiery anger inside us.

At Mount Bladon they came against us with the unthinking confidence born of arrogance. For all their long swords and their great shields, we rode them down and cut them to pieces where they stood. They did not even know how to save themselves. Say all you like about a Saxon, but he is no coward. They bled their blood into the soil of Britain and stained it for ever. Wherever you find the earth red, there you may know the Saxons stood and died.

Merlin's promise was kept. My army was on the march for three years, and I never in all that time doubted our invincibility. Every victory brought us new strength and new support. Each brave man we

lost in battle was at once replaced by two, then three, then four, till we were more than twenty thousand strong, battle-hardened and every one of us on a fit horse. The Picts melted into the forest and went back home without a fight. The Irish too learnt how we had dealt with the Saxons and ran for their ships. But the Saxons had not finished with us yet. They gathered a fearsome army and came over the water from the south west, thinking to take us by surprise. But Merlin warned me in time and we were ready for them. There is a swathe of red earth all across the West Country to mark the place where we met them, hunted them down and destroyed them.

I take no pride in the blood we spilt, nor any pleasure in it either. In those three years I saw more savagery than can be good for a man's soul. A terrible anger spurred me on so that I became careless for my own safety. Others called it courage, but I knew it for what it was. Sometimes, in the heat of battle, a red mist would come before my eyes. As I hacked and thrust and slashed, I became as someone else, someone I do not care to remember. I tell you, to kill a man is easy, all too easy. To enjoy killing is easy too, and I came perilously close to it. Only Merlin's firm counsel kept my face heavenward and kept my heart from hardening.

Our victories, and the so-called courage of the 'Boy-King Arthur' brought lords and knights, and kings too, flocking to my court at Camelot. I had built there a hilltop castle, surrounded by marshes and safe from the world; and here I returned to rest after the Saxon wars. I was still only eighteen years old. I was the idol of my people, the conqueror of the hated Saxon invader. It was enough to turn any young man's head, and it turned mine, even with Merlin beside me.

In my innocence, I thought that the fighting was over, that with the Saxons gone I might now fix my mind on what Merlin always called 'a king's proper work' – the welfare of his people. But now there were new dangers I had to face. New enemies rose up around me, those kings who had allied themselves with the Saxons, who still would not accept me as their rightful king – King Lot of Orkney, King Nantes of Garlot, King Idris and several others with them. They banded together and laid siege to Bedegraine, my great fortress in the Midlands. If once they took this, they would have a foothold in the heart of my kingdom. Merlin would not let me rest – they had to be driven out.

So, tired as I was in body and soul, I set out again with Merlin, my victorious army behind me. The march was long and my knights wilted in the summer heat. We came to the top of a ridge and looked down over the forest towards the castle of Bedegraine where a great army was drawn up and waiting for us. I looked at my men, and I could see that not a man amongst them wanted to fight. I knew it and Merlin knew it, for these were not Saxons but our own people; and besides, we were tired, tired of killing.

'Let the men spread out all along the hilltop,' Merlin declared, 'and let them draw their swords and bang their shields and shout until, the heavens echo.' And so we did until our voices grew hoarse, until our shields were dented, but by that time most of the army below us had turned and run. A few stayed to defy us – King Lot and King Nantes amongst them. The battle was terrible in its violence, but at least it was swiftly over. The two rebel kings fled the field, leaving their dead behind them. That evening, the battlefield was dark with feeding crows. Several of the enemy knights came afterwards to beg forgiveness. Merlin said I should be kingly and kind, and forgive them. 'One more friend,' he said, 'is one less enemy.' So I swallowed my anger and did as he advised. They swore allegiance to me there on the battlefield, and joined our army.

\*   \*   \*

With the fighting done, we celebrated that night in the castle at Bedegraine. We talked of little else but home and peace. But even as we sat there, word came to us that King Rience of North Wales was attacking the castle of King Leodegraunce of Camelaird who had fought alongside me so bravely against the Saxons. I could not abandon him; and war weary though they were, I knew my knights would not want me to. Rience was known as 'The Wild Man of Wales', a bloodthirsty savage who flaunted a many-coloured cloak, trimmed with the beards of all the kings he had conquered and killed. So I sent a defiant message that my beard was hardly worth the fighting for, but that he could have it if he could get it. We rested for a few days, and then reluctantly set out westwards into Wales.

We rode down on him from the hills of Snowdon and his army broke like sheep at the first charge. We harried them into the valleys, where most were happy to surrender. Rience did not, and paid the price. I found his cloak on the battlefield and wore it over my shoulders as we rode towards Camelaird.

For some reason Merlin kept trying to persuade me to sleep elsewhere that night, to turn back towards Camelot. He was insistent, but I was high on victory and I longed to see King Leodegraunce again. Besides,

I knew there would be a great feast waiting for us, and I loved nothing better than to see my people smiling and happy about me. We clattered over the bridge to be greeted ecstatically by King Leodegraunce and his people. At the feast that evening I threw Rience's cloak on the fire. The flames licked up around it and ate it greedily, and the hall rang to the rafters with cheers of joy and relief.

Afterwards in my room, high on our victory and heady with drink, I lay back on my bed and listened to the sweet music of a harp echoing through the castle. I had not heard so wonderful a sound since my mother last played for me, only weeks before she died. Drawn as if by a magnet, I went through the great hall and across the courtyard beyond, the music coming ever closer, ever sweeter. I stopped at a lighted window and looked in. Sitting alone in the room was a girl – no, rather a woman – and beside her a harp. As I strained to see better, I slipped noisily on the wet cobbles. But so intent was she on her playing that she did not hear me and she did not look up. Her fingers plucked effortlessly. It was her fingers, long, white and dancing, that I loved first. Her hair was the colour of honey, of gold washed in milk. It fell over her face so that I could not see her. But I did not need to, for I knew already she would be perfect. I felt a hand on my shoulder.

'King Leodegraunce's daughter.' It was Merlin. 'She is not well and has kept to her room.'

'What's her name?' I asked.

'Guinevere,' he answered. 'That is Guinevere.'

As he spoke, she stopped playing and looked towards us. I had been right. She was quite perfect, with a face of sweetness and strength in equal measure. She was pale though, too pale. Her smile, when it came, was easy and warm. And her dark eyes smiled with her.

'Merlin,' I said softly. 'That is the girl I shall marry.'

He tried to turn me away. 'There are other fish in the sea,' he said.

'Not for me,' I answered. 'I shall speak with her.' But still Merlin held me back.

'No, Arthur.' He spoke firmly, almost fiercely. I tried to pull myself free, but he held me fast. 'Marry her and you will bring yourself nothing but misery. Marry her and it will spell your ruin, and the ruin of your kingdom, too. I know what I say.'

'And I know what I feel,' I retorted, angry with Merlin for the first time. 'Haven't I always done what you wanted of me? Haven't I freed my country from the invaders? Must I always do what you advise? Am I a king or a puppet?'

Merlin sighed and turned away from me. My blood was up. I could not, I *would* not bring myself to call him back. When I looked in at the window again, Guinevere was gone. I closed my eyes and held the vision of her beauty in my head. I promised myself then, faithfully and in Jesus' name, that I would look at no other woman, and that when the time came I would marry her – whatever Merlin said. I said it out loud so that I should hear my promise myself, so that I should keep it.

Promises, promises. Those you want to keep, you keep, the others are more difficult. I make no excuses for myself except that I was young and foolish.

Within a few weeks I had already broken the first of my promises. I was in my castle at Caerleon. Merlin was not with me. Hurt by my anger, he had left me on my own. For the first time in my life I had no one to turn to – no mother, no father, no Merlin. Had he been there, it would not have happened as it did. He would not have let it happen, and if it had not happened . . .

She came, it seemed, from nowhere, a stranger from out of the stormy night, seeking shelter. She dined with us; and when she laughed, I laughed with her. Bercelet growled and showed his teeth, but I ignored him. The truth was that I liked her, and I saw her eyes adoring me and I liked that too. She was twice my age – but to a young man of eighteen, such things do not matter. She was a woman. That evening – and I am ashamed to say it even now – I did not give Guinevere a thought. It was not the howling of the storm outside that kept me from sleeping that night. It was the memory of the stranger, of the way she moved, of the warm scent of her hair, of the invitation in her eyes. When she came into my room, I pretended to be asleep. But when she climbed into my bed, I could not pretend any longer. Bercelet growled thunderously.

'You must choose,' she said. 'Either that dog goes or I do.' I did not have to think twice. Bercelet gave me a last baleful look. I knew they were Merlin's eyes looking at me, accusing, disappointed, yet somehow at the same time resigned. I shut him out and returned to my bed.

That night at Caerleon – though I was not to know it then – I sowed the seed of my own destruction.

When I woke in the morning she was gone. And then, only then, did I think of Guinevere and about how I had betrayed my love for her, how I had broken my promise. For days afterwards I rode out hunting in the surrounding countryside, trying to forget what I had done, but I could not put it from me. Angry at myself, I turned to drink for comfort; but I found none there, only a heavy head and a heavier heart. I longed to see Guinevere again, even though I knew how hard it would be for me to look her in the eye after what I had done. I longed too for Merlin to return so that I could make my peace with him.

Early one morning I was up for the hunt, when a young squire came riding into the castle courtyard. He was leading another horse, a body hanging limp over the saddle.

'Who did this?' I demanded.

'King Pelinore,' he said. It was a name to tremble at. Of all the renegade kings and warlords still defying my kingship, Pelinore was the most feared, the most ferocious. 'He murdered my master,' he went on, 'and for no reason. We were no more than five miles from here. We had travelled for weeks to join the young King Arthur.'

'Well, you're here now,' I said. 'And I am the Arthur you are looking for.'

The squire dismounted and fell on his knee. 'My Lord Arthur,' he said. 'My name is Gryflet. My master came to serve you, to follow you, and died before he could do so. Let me serve you in his place. I want to see King Pelinore dead in the dirt where he belongs.

Let me do it, my lord. Give me my knighthood, arm me and I will avenge my master's death.'

He was younger even than I was, with a boyish bloom still on his skin; I could not send him out to fight Pelinore. He would not stand a chance. I would have denied him at once and gone myself – that was what I should have done. But his eyes were eager and pleading; and besides, if I am honest, I was more than a little reluctant myself to face this Pelinore.

'Very well,' I said, 'but be careful. Ride against him only once. If you are unhorsed, then you are not to fight him on foot. There are few better warriors than King Pelinore. You promise me now?' He promised, and I could see he meant to keep his word.

So I knighted him there and then. We armed him and he went on his way. It could not have been more than a couple of hours later when a horse came meandering wearily into the courtyard, Gryflet swaying in the saddle, his face twisted with pain, blood oozing from his side. He was trying to hold it in, but he could not. It ran through his fingers and dripped on to the ground at my feet.

'I kept my promise, my lord,' he said, trying to smile through his agony.

We helped him from his horse and into the castle to have his wounds tended. Stung to anger, there were plenty of us now who wanted to go out after Pelinore, but I chose to go myself. It was pride that made me do it, pride and a little shame too perhaps. So, armed with sword and spear, with Bercelet padding along beside me, I rode out over the bridge and down the narrow forest road. I had not gone far before I found Pelinore's pavilion by a well, and his horse drinking; but there was no sign of him – only his shield swinging from the branch of an old oak tree.

'Pelinore!' I called. 'Come out from hiding. You may be able to whip small boys. You won't find me such easy meat. Come out if you dare!'

From the shadows beneath the trees strode a towering man, his helmet under his arm. 'You have killed one man today,' I went on, 'and wounded a young boy, and for what?'

'I joust with everyone who passes this way,' King Pelinore replied. 'I am my own master. I do what I please, where I please and how I please; and it pleases me to knock people off horses.'

'In that case,' I said, bristling at the man's arrogance, 'in that case, you'd better get up on your horse, because it also pleases me to knock people off horses, people like you.'

He smiled, swung nimbly up on to his horse and settled in the saddle. 'Well,' he said, 'what are we waiting for?'

We rode away from each other a short distance, turned and couched our spears under our shoulders. I felt my horse gathering himself under me. I touched him with my heels and unleashed him. He sprang forward. I pointed my spear at the centre of Pelinore's shield, and braced for the shock, all of me clenched. Both spears splintered at once on impact.

'You're good!' he cried, as he turned, his horse snorting and prancing. 'You're very good, but not good enough. We'll do it again, shall we?' And he called for more spears. That was when I noticed Bercelet walking off purposefully into the forest. I wondered for a moment what he was doing, where he was going.

'That's a sensible dog you have,' King Pelinore scoffed. 'He knows when to run. You want to go with him?' I took the spear I was offered.

'You're full of talk.' I cried, 'Come on!' And we charged again. Again the spears disintegrated. But this time, I was nearly unhorsed and I knew I had met my match. A third time I pounded towards him, shield held tight to my body, leaning over my spear, every fibre of my strength concentrated on the point of my spear, and the point of my spear at the centre of his shield, at his heart. Maybe my horse swerved at the last moment, maybe I over-reached myself. Who knows? Either way, I was caught off-balance. He lifted me clean out of my saddle and dumped me in the dust, the breath knocked out of me. Spurred to fresh anger at this indignity, I was on my feet at once, sword drawn and waiting for him. He dismounted, whipped out his sword and came at me like a wild thing, driving me back and back. I countered all I could, fending him off with my shield, but then my shield flew from my grasp. There was blood running down my neck and I knew suddenly that I wasn't fighting any more to win, I was fighting for my life. Desperate now, I whirled up my sword and brought it crashing down on his helmet. I had split many a Saxon in half with just such a blow, but this time it would not bite into the steel. Instead, it shattered and I was left holding just the hilt of my sword. I never even saw where the blade went. Before I knew it he had knocked me over and pinned me to the ground, his sword pressing into my neck. I thought then of Guinevere, and how I had now broken both my promises. First I had betrayed my love for her, and now I would never marry her. I would never even see her again.

'Beg,' he cried. 'Beg for mercy, and maybe I'll think about it.' Losing was bad enough, but surrender was unthinkable. Maybe it was the thought that I might never see Guinevere again that gave me new strength. I don't know. I twisted away from under him, rolled over, sprang to my feet and hurled myself at him. I wrestled the sword from his grasp and we fought like animals in the dust. But always he was too strong for me, too heavy. I was losing and I knew it. My will was weakening all the time. On my back, his fingers round my throat, I saw Bercelet come running out of the woods, barking at me, barking *for* me perhaps. Either way, it was too late. King Pelinore had his sword in his hand again. It flashed in the sun and I closed my eyes so as not to see my death blow. It never came. When I opened my eyes I saw his raised arm frozen in the air.

'Enough.' It was Merlin's voice. 'Kill him, Pelinore, and you snuff out at one blow the hope of Britain. This is Arthur, your king.' And he stretched out his arm and took the sword from King Pelinore's hand.

'You are Arthur?' King Pelinore breathed. 'What have I done? What have I done?' And at that his eyes closed and he crumpled to the ground beside me. Merlin helped me to my feet.

'How did you find me?' I asked.

'Haven't I told you?' he said gently. 'Bercelet is my eyes, my ears. Even when I am not with you, you are never out of my sight, nor out of my mind.' And when we embraced, I remembered that he must have already witnessed the wickedness I had done that night in Caerleon.

'I missed you,' I said. 'I should not have said what I said. I should not have been angry with you. But I loved Guinevere then, and I love her still.'

'I know,' said Merlin. 'And I know too there is nothing I can do about it. Sometimes it is hard for me, knowing what is to happen. So much of it I do not want to happen, and so I try to stop it, even though I know I cannot! The quarrel was as much my fault as yours. If that is what you want, then you shall have Guinevere for your queen!' He held me at arm's length and shook his head. 'But I can see you need more than Bercelet to protect you when I am not here. It is time for Excalibur.'

'Excalibur? What's Excalibur?'

'You'll see,' said Merlin.

'And what about Pelinore?' I said. 'We can't just leave him here. I may not like him much, but he's a fine fighter. No one has ever beaten me before.'

'And he wouldn't have beaten you, Arthur, had you not drunk yourself to sleep these last few nights and so weakened yourself. It's no bad thing – to lose is a lesson to learn. There is always someone faster, fitter, stronger. It is true that there are not many who will ever better you, but there will be some. There is one in particular, strong like a lion, who will come to be the bravest of your knights and the best of your friends – for a while, at least. And there will be another of your knights, even stronger than he, whose strength will come from his goodness, from his purity.'

'Tell me no more, I beg you,' I said. 'What I do not know, I cannot grieve over. When I want to know, I will ask. Promise then you will always tell me the truth. And promise you will tell me nothing more unless I ask.'

'You are wise beyond your years, Arthur,' said Merlin. 'Very well then, I promise I shall tell you nothing of your future unless you ask, but what I do tell will always be the truth. And do not worry about King Pelinore. I have not harmed him. In a few hours he will wake from his sleep, so ashamed he ever took up arms against you that he will become one of your great allies, one of your most trusted friends. I am much more worried about you than him. We must have these wounds seen to at once, and after that we shall find Excalibur.'

For three days I rested with Merlin in a hermit's cave deep in the forest, until my wounds healed. I was still stiff with my aches and pains when Merlin said the time had come to leave. With Bercelet leading the way – he always seemed to know where he was going – we went deeper, ever deeper into the forest. We followed the deer tracks, and came into wild open country, to a place I had never been before.

It was a still, warm evening and the flies were down, when we came at last to a great lake and could go no further. Herons croaked in alarm at our approach and lumbered off across the water to the wooded hills beyond. Tail circling, Bercelet went in after the ducks in the reeds and put them up. They took off and flew low over the water, leaving the lake silent behind them, the falling mist already shrouding the treetops around the shore. Merlin called Bercelet back, and he came reluctantly, shaking himself dry all over us.

'Now, we wait,' said Merlin.

'What is this place?' I asked.

'This lake separates life from death, Arthur. Beyond the mists is the Island of Avalon. Those who live there are not living, neither are they dead. They live in a half-life. They are people not of this world, yet they can come into this world. They have earthly powers and unearthly powers, powers for good and for evil. Yet the lake is just a lake, like any other.'

'Where is this Excalibur?' I asked yet again. 'And what is it anyway? Can't you tell me?'

'Oh, be still with your questions, Arthur,' said Merlin. Suddenly he leant forward and pointed. 'Look.'

I looked, but could see nothing at first. But then as I looked I saw the surface of the lake shiver and break. And, to my amazement, up out of the lake came a shining sword, a hand holding it, and an arm in a white silk sleeve.

'There,' Merlin whispered. 'You have your answer. That is Excalibur. It comes from that half-world of Avalon, the blade forged by the elf-kind, the scabbard woven by the Lady Nemue herself, the Lady of the Lake, and my lady too.' And as he spoke her name, his voice faltered. 'See, here she comes.'

And out of the mists came a figure in flowing green, walking across the water. Yet the water seemed undisturbed beneath her feet as if she was walking on air. She came towards us, holding a scabbard in both her hands, and a swordbelt hanging from it. From the way she looked at Merlin and from the way he was looking at her, I could see there was an old love between them, a love still strong. There was a secret smile in her eyes and it was all for him. But when she spoke, she spoke to me.

'My Lord Arthur, I have made this for you. It is woven from the gold of Avalon. Keep it always with you. *Always*, you hear me?'

'But the sword?' I said. 'How do I get the sword? Do I have to swim for it?'

'You will not need to,' she said, and she smiled gently. As she spoke, I saw a boat lying in amongst the reeds. Where it came from, and how it came to be there I do not know. 'Get in,' she said.

I did not hesitate. The moment I stepped down into the boat, it moved, gliding with scarcely a sound through the dark waters out towards the arm in the middle of the lake. As we came nearer, the boat slowed and paused, only just long enough for me to reach out and take the sword by the blade. The arm withdrew into the lake. I watched until the last finger vanished.

I sat down in the bottom of the boat and examined the sword on my lap. The hilt was encrusted with jewels and gold, and fitted my grasp like no other I had ever held. The blade was broader than any I had seen before, yet it felt as light as a feather, as if it was part of my arm and not a sword at all.

The boat reached the shore and I looked up. Merlin was waiting for me, the scabbard in his hand. The Lady of the Lake was nowhere to be seen. I slid the sword into the scabbard and Merlin buckled the swordbelt around my waist. He stood back to look at me. 'So, now you have Excalibur. Which do you prefer, Arthur, the sword or the scabbard?'

'The sword, of course,' I said, drawing it out for the first time. 'A scabbard without a sword is useless.'

'Not this one,' said Merlin. 'I tell you, Arthur, if you do as the Lady Nemue said, if you have the scabbard round your waist, then you will never lose a single drop of blood. Excalibur may bring you victory and glory and honour; it may scythe down your enemies like so much ripe corn, but the scabbard will always keep you safe. Never be parted from it, Arthur, never. She made it specially for you, as a favour to me. That woman is the love of my life. One day,' he went on, musing, 'one day, I shall go to her, but not yet.' When he turned to me, his eyes were filled with tears. 'I must be with her. She is always in my head. I think you understand what I mean, don't you Arthur?'

I understood, only too well. 'How much longer will you stay with me, Merlin?' I asked.

'A little while yet,' he said. 'A little while. And besides, I will never leave you quite alone, you know that. You will always have Bercelet.' And Bercelet came up beside me, and shook himself again, showering me from head to toe.

'Oh, a comfort,' I laughed. 'A great comfort.'

So we came home with Excalibur to Camelot. That evening I passed Excalibur round the table, so that all the knights could see it and hold it. Each of them kissed it reverently and passed it on. Pelinore was there, come to ask forgiveness and to become one of us, as Merlin had foretold. I said that he could stay with us, only if he first made his peace with Gryflet. He and Gryflet embraced warmly in front of the whole company, and the hall resounded with cheers. After that no two knights were ever greater friends than Pelinore and Gryflet.

We heard, only weeks later, that King Lot and King Nantes had again raised another army and were marching south against us. 'They have seen their last spring,' Pelinore cried. 'Let me go after them, my lord.' I hesitated, still not sure of him.

Merlin leant over and spoke to me softly. 'Trust him, Arthur. Let him go.'

So Pelinore took Gryflet and a hundred good men from the army and rode out the next morning. They had been gone a month when a messenger returned with the shields of King Lot and King Nantes. Pelinore had ambushed them, killed the two kings with his own hand and scattered their army. He was even now harrying the remnants northwards.

That evening in the courtyard I was leaning on my staff and gazing up at the shields of the two kings hanging on the walls, when Merlin came out to join me. He didn't say, 'I told you so'; but he was thinking it. I could see that from his smile.

'The staff I gave you,' he said. 'May I borrow it for a moment?' And with that, he took it from me and plunged it into the ground. At once a tree sprung up, a sapling first and then a great oak tree, spreading until it was towering over the courtyard. 'When you sit in its shade, Arthur,' said Merlin, 'remember me, and think what I told you once about acorns.' At that he bent down and picked up a handful of acorns and gave them to me. 'Keep them,' he said. 'You have made me proud, Arthur. I could not be more proud if you were my own son. And how I wish you were.'

I looked at the old man walking away, and an aching sadness welled inside me. I knew now that he would soon leave me, and I knew also how alone I would then be.

# 4 GUINEVERE

YOU SHOULD HAVE BEEN THERE, THE DAY
Guinevere came to Camelot to be my queen. As she
rode up towards the castle, the people came running
out of their houses to welcome her. They threw
flowers in her path, they cheered, they clapped. From
the ramparts I looked on, my heart brimming with
love and expectation, hope and happiness. I
remember, she caught a flower, a foxglove it was, and
waved it at them, and they cheered her all the more.
They loved her already. One look at her and you had
to love her.

I had practised over and over again what I would
say to her, but when we met in the courtyard, I was

tongue-tied and awkward. She gave me her foxglove, and with such a smile that she set me at once at ease. For the week before the wedding, we rode out together whenever we could. It was the only way to be alone, for Camelot was fuller every day as the guests gathered from all over the land. There were faces I had never seen before, family I knew of, but had not yet met.

In that short week before the wedding, Guinevere and I came to know each other, soul to soul. She hid nothing from me – I was quite sure of that – and I hid nothing from her, nothing but the shame of that one night at Caerleon and the promise I had broken. We went on talking long into the night when the castle was quiet. Bercelet, I noticed, now ignored me completely. He lay at her feet, his great eyes gazing up at her in adoration. You may laugh at me, but I was pricked to jealousy – the first jealousy I had known – and by a dog.

We were quiet before the fire that last night, our talking done. Guinevere was stroking Bercelet in between the eyes where he liked it best, when I dared to tell her. I took her hand and turned it over in mine. 'I loved your fingers first,' I said.

'And I loved your eyes,' she replied. She looked away, suddenly downcast.

'What is it?' I asked.

She sighed. 'I want to be your wife, Arthur,' she said, 'but I do not want to play the queen. I know I must, and I know you must play the king, but I wish it were otherwise. I am afraid we will learn to play the parts so well that we shall forget ourselves and forget each other.' She touched my cheek and kissed me.

'I shan't forget,' I whispered. 'I shall never forget.'

'No,' she said, and she smiled through her tears. 'No, I don't think you ever will.'

The next morning I was up early. I met Merlin on the ramparts. He was looking out over the mist-covered marshes. There were three horses, plodding slowly along the causeway, legless in the mist. 'Look,' said Merlin sadly. 'They have come. I feared they might.'

'Who are they?' I asked. As they came closer, I noticed that one of them had a child riding in front of her.

'Those are your three half-sisters, Arthur, your mother Igraine's daughters by Gorlois, children of her first marriage. I have told you about them before. Elaine and Margawse have come to make their peace with you, I have no doubt. But do not trust them. Remember, neither Elaine nor Margawse have any great cause to love you. Your half-sisters they may be, but both are widowed, and by you too. Pelinore might have killed their husbands, King Nantes and King Lot, but it was in your name that he fought them. Take care. Take care.'

'So the third must be Morgana Le Fey,' I said, 'the youngest.' Merlin's eyes narrowed and a shiver came over him so that he had to lean against the ramparts to steady himself. 'I hoped never to see her here in Camelot,' he said. 'Of all the people on this earth, she is the one who most threatens you. She may look like an angel, but she has the soul of the very devil, and all his evil powers too, powers that I can no longer stand against. In my youth I might have done, but not now, for my own powers are waning. Sometimes I think they are almost gone. Beware of her, Arthur, beware of her, I tell you. She would have your kingdom for herself and, if she cannot have it, then she will do all she can to destroy it, and you with it.'

'Who is the child?' I asked, but Merlin did not seem to want to answer. I asked again.

'You do not want to know,' Merlin replied, and he looked away quickly. 'Not on your wedding day. I will cast no dark shadows on such a day.'

As I looked at the three riders I was filled with a sense of terrible foreboding. 'You promised me once, Merlin,' I said, steeling myself, 'that you would never tell me the future unless I asked you to, nor deny me the truth if ever I asked it. I have never asked what shall become of me, or of my kingdom – although I know you could tell me. I do not want to know, for if I once know the end of it all and how I will get there, then there would be little reason to live my life through. If that child is part of my future, then tell me. Tell me at least who he is.'

Merlin nodded slowly, 'Yes,' he said. 'You have a right to know. Every man has a right to know his own son.' He looked me straight in the eye. 'Yes, he is your son. He is called Mordred. His mother is Margawse. She came to you that night at Caerleon. I tried to warn you, but you put me out of the door, remember? She came, not of her own accord, but was sent by her sister, Morgana Le Fey, to seduce you. Margawse had no love for you in her heart that night, Arthur, only revenge. Her son is the weapon Morgana Le Fey will use against you.'

'But Margawse is my half-sister,' I cried, still unable to believe what I was hearing. 'Surely I couldn't have done such a thing. I couldn't have.'

'You were not to know it, Arthur,' said Merlin, taking me by the shoulders. 'There is no blame on you. You are a man like any other. You were enchanted, bewitched. Morgana Le Fey planned it all.

Mordred is your Judas, Arthur. He will betray you. It is for that he was conceived, and it is for that he will live his life. Never forget that he is the creature of Morgana Le Fey, and that she is determined to destroy you. Take my advice. Keep him near you, keep him under your eye where he can do you the least mischief. It is your safest way.'

They were below us now in the courtyard, and Margawse was looking up at me and smiling, a knowing smile, a loveless smile.

I remember little of the wedding ceremony itself, except the light touch of Guinevere's hand on my sleeve as we stood before the Archbishop and took our vows of fidelity. After the blessing her father, King Leodegraunce, led me away into the great hall of Camelot. There, set in the middle of it, was a great round table – yes, this very same one – and as you can see, on each seat was written in gold, the names of my knights.

'My wedding gift to you, my lord,' said Leodegraunce. 'Merlin made it with his own hands for your father King Utha Pendragon, and then after his death it fell to me to look after it. Now the Round Table is back where it rightfully belongs, at the court of the High King of Britain.'

'Here at this table,' said Merlin, putting his arm round

my shoulders, 'here will sit all those great men, who will help you build the fair Kingdom of Logres in this land. Some are here already, and so you will find their names already written on their seats. Many are not yet with you, but I know who they will be. Their names will be written for them when they come. Lancelot will be one, son of King Ban of Benwick, and it will not be long now before he comes. Another will be Percivale, Pelinore's son, still only a child. His time will come too. They will all have their places at the Round Table.'

'I need to know no more, Merlin,' I said. 'I shall know them when they come.'

'There is one you will not know,' and he pointed. 'Read what is written on that seat.'

'It says, "Perilous". Why Perilous?' I asked.

'Because if any man but one sits in it, it will be the death of him. Only one knight may ever sit there. It will be on the day the Holy Grail comes to Camelot. He will be the last to come and he will be the best of you all.'

'Tell me no more, old friend,' I said, clapping a playful hand over his mouth. 'Let me live for now, for this happy moment; and let the future look after itself and fall out as it will.'

Merlin laughed, and led me away to my place at the Round Table.

So the knights all found their seats at the table and their ladies on the canopied dais at the end of the hall; and in the midst of them all, sat Guinevere, my queen and my wife, her face glowing with happiness. I did not like to look up towards her too often, because on one side of her was Margawse and on the other was Morgana Le Fey. But when I did, and when our eyes met, the smile she sent me was of pure love. It was, I tell you, it was love in the beginning, and trust too, complete trust – a trust I had already betrayed.

Merlin sat beside me at the Round Table. He said little and, like me, he ate little. Bercelet's head rested heavy on my foot as usual, a permanent reminder he was there, quite deliberately, so that I should not forget him. He ate a great deal more than I did that evening.

And yet, in spite of all the joy about me, I was uneasy in my heart. So much, it seemed, was expected of me. In the bright eyes of the knights sitting with me at the Round Table that evening, I saw a burning hope and a fierce loyalty. Gawain was there, the bravest of the brave, loud in his drink already. Gaheris, his younger brother, sat beside him; and beside him was Kay, my brother and my steward, puffed up as he ever was with self-importance. Beyond him were the twin-brothers, Balyn and

Balan; then Bedevere, Gryflet and Bors – over a hundred of them in all. And they all had such faith in me. None of them doubted that one day and one day soon, we should together make a heaven of this land, that we should between us give birth to the Kingdom of Logres. I knew I must be the only one there that doubted it, and I knew now that there was only one way I could rid myself of those doubts.

As I sat there, I had it in my head that I should go upstairs there and then and smother Margawse's son, my son, before he could grow up and do me or my kingdom any harm. I pushed back my chair to go, but Merlin's hand gripped mine and held me. 'It is not the way, Arthur,' he said. 'Have I not taught you that evil can never destroy evil? Only good can do that.'

At that moment, a sudden hush fell about the hall. A lady stood in the doorway. I saw at once it was the Lady Nemue, the Lady of the Lake, who had walked across the lake and brought me the scabbard for Excalibur. Merlin stood up slowly, older suddenly than I had ever thought him to be.

'She has come for me,' he said. 'I must go with her, Arthur. She will take me to my long rest. But Bercelet will stay with you, to comfort you and to look after you. A part of me goes, and a part stays behind. Be true to yourself, my Lord King, and keep your face always heavenward. We shall meet again when the time comes, but it will be a long, long time in coming.' And he put a hand on my shoulder and left me for the last time. As he walked away, I wanted to cry out, to call him back, to beg him not to abandon me; but the king in me would not allow it. At the door, with the Lady Nemue at his side, he turned and spoke to everyone.

'You no longer have as much need of me as I have of this lady. You have Arthur. With him at your head, and now with his Guinevere at his side, you must fight the long fight to expunge the evil from this land and make it at last a fit place for your children. There will be those who will seek to divide you and corrupt you. Listen always to your king. There never was such a king on this earth, nor never will be again.'

The pair did not walk out of the door, but vanished like smoke in the air. It was the last I ever saw of Merlin. Bercelet started up after him, but when he saw there was no one there to follow, he came back and sat beside me, and I stroked his head where he liked it. 'He's gone,' I said, softly, my voice all but breaking. 'We're on our own now.'

For some time afterwards, the spirit of the feast seemed dulled; but Guinevere took her harp and played it, and at once the music seemed to soften the pain of Merlin's going. It was a small sound, yet it filled the great hall and brought everyone crowding in from all over the castle. When she had finished, the hall filled with applause and the feasting spirit was suddenly renewed. But my heart was not in it. I had something else on my mind. I slipped away and climbed the winding stairs to the tower. I found Mordred where I thought he would be, in a side room, his bed by the window. There was a white screecher-owl eyeing me from the window ledge. It did not fly off as I expected, but glared at me, unblinking. The child lay on his back, looking up at me. There was no murder in my heart, not any more.

A voice spoke from behind me. 'You would not harm him?' It was Margawse.

'No,' I said. 'He is my son. I could not harm him.'

'He needs a father,' she said. 'You are his father. Let him stay here with you and be king after you.'

'Never,' I replied. 'If he stays, he stays as my nephew, not as my son. Do you hear? Say anything of what passed between us that night at Caerleon, say I am the boy's father, and there will be no end to my anger and my vengeance upon you and upon your sisters. We will look after the boy here at Camelot; But I never want to see you again as long as I live, nor your sisters. Tell that to Morgana Le Fey, and now go. Leave me in peace.'

She left, and shortly afterwards Bercelet came looking for me. The owl heard him padding up the steps and lifted off the window ledge into the night, leaving behind a terrible screech in the air. Bercelet snuffled at the child, a rumbling growl in his throat. I pulled him away, and we went down together to join the feasting. I tried not to glance up at Guinevere, for I feared I might not be able to hide my shame. When at last I did venture to look, I saw she was laughing gaily with Morgana Le Fey, who at that moment turned her gaze on me. Morgana still laughed on, but her eyes were full of hate.

Early the next morning, I took off into the hills to hunt the stag. There were just the three of us: myself, Acalon – who knew hounds better than any man alive – and Uriens who had asked himself along. I never much cared for him but, with Morgana Le Fey for a wife, I felt sorry for him. I didn't mean to be away from Guinevere for more than a day.

Soon enough, the hounds picked up the scent of a stag and we followed. There we had sight of him, bounding over the rocks ahead of us. We chased him and chased him, but could not close on him. On and on we galloped, down from the hills into the forest, our horses lathered white now and groaning under us with exhaustion. Acalon's horse was the first to go down, his great heart broken. Acalon rode up on mine for a while, and then mine too sank to the ground and could go no further. At that, Uriens' horse lay down and died, as if in sympathy. The hounds were baying well ahead of us and out of sight. We followed on foot through the forest, Acalon leading the way, until at last we broke into a clearing by a lake. There lay the fallen stag, the hounds tearing at his throat. Suddenly a horn sounded some way off in the forest. The hounds did not hesitate. Before we could stop them, they had disappeared into the forest towards the sound of the horn, leaving us standing by the lake, Acalon still bellowing after them to come back.

Uriens touched my shoulder. I turned, and saw a ship gliding towards us over the lake. It grounded just a few paces from where we stood. It was as if it had been sent for us. We could see from where we stood that the decks were strewn with deep cushions, and the masts were hung about with fine flowing silks of all the colours of the rainbow. Yet, wonderful though it was, my soul still drew back. It looked all too convenient, too comfortable, too perfect. I sensed a trap. I turned away, but Uriens spoke up.

'Come on, my lord,' he said. 'Where's your sense of adventure? This ship has come here for a reason. Let's find out what it is. We'll never know otherwise. Besides, it looks so inviting, the cushions so soft. There's no one there. There can't be any harm in it, can there?'

It was darkening already. We would never make it back to Camelot by nightfall. I was too tired to argue; and beside, Uriens was right, those cushions looked all too tempting.

Once on board, we found there was indeed no one there. As we stretched out on the cushions, we felt the ship move under us and found ourselves floating out towards the middle of the lake, the tiller moved by an unseen hand. Acalon laughed nervously.

'What's going on? What's happening?' he cried. And as he spoke, all the torches along the side of the ship lit up simultaneously, so that it seemed as if the whole lake was on fire around us. Whilst we were still marvelling at this, we discovered we were not the only people on board. Up from below came five, ten, twelve girls, each one as beautiful as the other, for they were all exactly the same, dressed in black, with the same dark hair, the same pale skin. They said not a word, but poured us wine and laid out our food – and such food, such wine. While we ate, they sat and played us sweet music on their harps. So, tired from the hunt, lulled by the music and the wine and the gentle rocking of the ship, I fell asleep.

When I woke, there were no cushions beneath me, no music. I was not in a ship at all. I was lying on the floor of a damp, dark dungeon; and when I sat up, I saw that I was not alone. Several men stood around me. 'Acalon? Uriens? Where are my friends?' No one answered me. 'Where am I?' I asked.

One of them spoke at last. 'You are in the castle of Sir Damas. And you are here for the same reason we are here. There are twenty of us, and some of us have been shut up in here for years, and I'll tell you why. This Damas has stolen his brother's share of his inheritance and kept it all for himself. Ontzlake, the brother, doesn't care to be cheated, and so he claims his inheritance back by right of arms – that's his right. But this Damas isn't just a thief, he's a coward too. He himself won't fight. He wants it decided by champions. He's asked every one of us to fight for him, but none of us will, because we are all Ontzlake's friends and we know the justice of this cause.'

As he was speaking, I realized my sword belt was gone, my scabbard with it, and Excalibur too. I remembered the ship. I remembered the wine, and I knew then that this was all part of some devilish enchantment of Morgana Le Fey. It had to be.

The dungeon door opened, and standing in the shaft of light was a young girl. I was sure I had seen her somewhere before, but could not think where it was. 'I am Sir Damas' daughter,' she said. 'You may either lie here and rot with these others for however many years are left to you, or you may fight today as my father's champion against my uncle Ontzlake's champion. What do you say?'

Then I saw who she was. She had the same dark hair, the same pale skin. She was one of the creatures from the ship, one of Morgana Le Fey's witches. I decided I would play along with her game.

'Well,' I said, getting to my feet, and brushing myself down. 'I'm not staying here for the rest of my life. I'll fight him for you, but on one condition. If I win or if I lose, all these good knights go free. Without that promise, I won't do it.'

She went away and came back a short time later, and said what I had hoped she might say. 'My father agrees. If you fight for him, the knights all go free. My father promises it.'

'Then I shall fight,' I replied, and with my companions' earnest good wishes ringing in my ears, I went up the steps after her into the bright sunlight of the castle courtyard. There I found waiting for me all I needed – a horse, armour and a sword, but it was not Excalibur. I was without the protection of my scabbard and I was without Excalibur. To win against a good champion, I would have to be at my best. I was weak from the cold of the dungeon and wondered if I had strength enough for a fight. As I rode towards the field, my visor down against the glare of the sun, I knew this would be a fight to the death, because if Morgana Le Fey had arranged all this – and I had no doubt she had – then it was my death she wanted, and nothing less. I would either kill or be killed.

Ontzlake's champion was ready for me. We saluted each other from opposite ends of the field and came together with a clash like thunder. I found myself on my back on the ground and struggling to get to my feet, my head whirling. I saw the two horses gallop off, and knew then that I had at least unhorsed him too. I was relieved at that, but my relief was to be shortlived. The first time his sword struck mine, I knew I was doomed. As the blows rained down, it was all I could do to stand on my feet, such was the force behind them. Every blow he dealt me could have been my deathblow. My shield was shredding before my eyes. Wounded in my side, I staggered back and almost fell. He came at me again and slashed me down my arm. The blood ran hot into my hand so that my sword slipped from my grasp.

'Pick it up,' cried Ontzlake's champion. 'Pick it up or I will kill you where you stand.'

As he backed away, his sword red with my blood, I saw some movement in the crowd and a lady stepped forward. I thought at first she might retrieve my sword for me, but she did not. She simply pointed at the champion's sword, and then suddenly turned her wrist. The sword flew from his hand and fell at my feet. She looked at me, and when our eyes met I knew at once who she was. It was the Lady Nemue, the Lady of the Lake.

'Pick it up,' she said. 'It is Excalibur.' And at once I saw she spoke the truth. I looked at Ontzlake's champion before me and saw my scabbard, Excalibur's scabbard round his waist. With one flashing stroke from Excalibur, I cut away the belt and the scabbard fell to the ground. Enraged, the champion bent down, picked up the sword and came at me. But now I had Excalibur and he could not stand against me. I drove him back and back, until I dealt him a blow that laid him out flat on his back, blood pouring from his neck. One glance told me he was a dying man. He looked up at me. 'Who are you?' he whispered.

'Arthur, I am Arthur, High King of Britain,' I said, and at that he turned his head away and wept.

'Oh, Arthur, oh my king. I could have killed you.' He could scarcely speak. 'And now you have killed me.' I knew the voice and I knew the man. It was Acalon. I knelt down beside him and took off his helmet. He pulled me closer. 'I did not know it was you, my lord, I swear it.'

'Oh Acalon,' I said. 'I know that, but how did you come by Excalibur? Was it Morgana Le Fey?'

He nodded slowly.

'I knew it,' I said. 'I knew it.'

'Then know this also, my lord. I have loved her secretly all these years and have told no one, not even her, but she knew. She played on my love, and what a game she played. What a fool I've been, such a fool.'

'Don't talk,' I said. 'Tell me later.'

'I must,' he whispered. 'There'll be no later for me. 'I woke up from my sleep and found myself by a well in some courtyard.' He spoke so softly that I had to bend closer to hear him. 'Her dwarf was there, and in his hands he held Excalibur. He told me he had come from Morgana Le Fey, that some foul knight had insulted her, had even threatened her life. He said that she wanted me to kill him for her; that if I really loved her, I would do it. He gave me Excalibur. He told me you had lent it to her, and I believed him, I believed him! My lord, you were not in your own armour. I did not know it was you.' Acalon looked up at me and clung to me with his last strength. 'What else was

I to do?' And with that he closed his eyes and died in my arms, before I could offer him any words of comfort.

Blind anger staunched the pain of my wounds. Still faint with loss of blood, I had Damas and Ontzlake brought before me and gave them my judgement. Damas would forfeit all he had to his brother. The knights in his dungeons would be released at once, and Damas himself would have nothing from his inheritance for he deserved nothing. 'And have the knights in the dungeon carry Acalon back to Camelot. Show the body to Morgana Le Fey, so she can see which one of us she has murdered. I will follow on later when I am strong enough. Tell her from me that, if I find her still there on my return, I will see her burnt at the stake for her crimes, sister or no sister.' And then the world turned inside my head and I could not stop myself from falling into a faint.

When I woke I found myself lying in bed in an ancient abbey. I could hear chanting from the chapel and a bell ringing softly somewhere in the distance. There was a nun by my bed. She leant forward. 'Are you better, my lord?'

'My sword!' I said. 'My scabbard! Where are they?' What Morgana had tried once, she would try again –

I was sure of it.

'At the end of the bed, my lord,' she said. 'Look.'

'Give me Excalibur,' I said. 'I'll have it in my hand, just in case.' She gave it to me. I grasped Excalibur tight, and then sank back into a deep sleep.

As I slept I dreamt. Morgana Le Fey stood by my bed, smiling down at me. She tried to wrench Excalibur from me, but I held on with the grip of a dead man and would not let go. When she saw she could not take it from me, she moved to the end of the bed. She lifted the sword belt and caressed the scabbard. 'Fine work,' she said. 'I shall take this instead then. Without it, you will bleed, Arthur, like any man bleeds; and one day I will watch you bleed out your life's blood. Your kingdom will at last be my kingdom.'

I woke, and at once looked for the scabbard hanging at the end of my bed. The sword belt was gone and the scabbard was gone. Horrified, I called out and the nun came running back.

'Did someone come in here?' I asked.

'Only your sister, my lord.' She said. 'She was so upset. She said she had to see you. She was your sister – I didn't think you would mind. She's only just left, a few minutes ago, her ladies with her.'

Ontzlake was there to arm me and set me on my horse, and then we rode out together after her. For days, for weeks, it seemed, we trailed them down forest tracks, along dry river beds, over mountain passes. Wherever they went, we followed. This, I knew, would be my only chance to recover the scabbard and to rid myself once and for all of Morgana Le Fey and her wickedness. In spite of all Ontzlake's protests I would not stop to rest, only to water the horses and feed ourselves.

And then one morning, we saw them – Morgana and her evil witches – ahead of us and riding out across a wide open plain. We had them now. I spurred my horse on for one last effort. But as we rode, a fog came rolling over the plain towards us. Morgana and her witches disappeared into it, and then we too were swallowed up and blinded by it. When we emerged at last into the sunlight again, there was no sign of them. We found ourselves in amongst a circle of great standing stones. We searched the ground and found hoof marks but they stopped here and went nowhere. It was as if Morgana Le Fey and her witches had vanished into the earth itself. Then, as I looked about me at the stones, they seemed to me not to be stones at all, but dancing maidens, cavorting in their triumph. I understood what had happened. 'They have turned themselves to stone,' I said. 'There is nothing more we can do. I have lost Excalibur's scabbard for ever.' And I stood in the centre of the circle of dancing maidens and called out. 'Leave me be, devil sister. Never show your face to me again or I swear I will kill you!' But the stones mocked us with their silence. We turned our horses and rode home, for Camelot.

Some weeks later, still weak from my wounds, we came at last to Camelot. Guinevere came running out to meet me, Bercelet at her side, barking his welcome. She held me as if she would never let me go. 'Oh stay by me, Arthur,' she whispered. 'Never leave me again like that. I cannot be without you, I cannot.'

Before I knew it, Gawain and Bedevere had hoisted me on to their shoulders and I was carried up into the great hall where all my knights were gathered. When at last they set me down, I sat by the fire and told them all that had happened.

Bedevere spoke first. 'So that was why your half-sisters left so suddenly,' he said. 'Morgana Le Fey came back and took the other two away with her at once. She was gone before they brought back poor Acalon. We buried him with all the honour you would have wished my lord.'

Guinevere put her cool hand on my brow. 'We

knew some of it already,' she said. 'For Margawse came to see me the night before she left.' My heart filled with a sudden dread at what Margawse might have told her. 'She said that Morgana Le Fey had made her do things she did not want to do. She said you would know what kind of things she meant. I asked, but she would not tell me any more. She left us her son, she left us Mordred. She asked us to be father and mother to him, and to bring him up as if he were our own son. I couldn't say no, could I? She says you will never see her again, nor any of your half-sisters. She promised.'

'Well then,' I replied, breathing again, 'I am well rid of them, and so are we all.' I looked around me at all my friends and felt cocooned in their warmth and love. They brought food for me by the fire. Bercelet had most of it, of course, but I had enough. I sipped my scented wine, put my head back and closed my eyes. I was home, and I was safe.

Bercelet rose to his feet with a growl. The great door flew open. We thought at first it was just the wind. Then we could make out a bent figure walking with a stick. As it came towards us, I saw it was an old crone dressed in mud-spattered rags, her feet bare.

'Is this the court of King Arthur?' she asked, her

voice thin and tremulous.

'It is,' I said. 'Come in, come in out of the cold.'

'I have brought you this,' she said, and she held out a black moleskin coat, trimmed with fox fur. 'I trapped the moles myself and the foxes too and I skinned them. I used only the soft belly fur. Only the best for my King. I made this especially for you, my lord. I have worked on it these last ten years.' She came up to me. 'Here,' she said. 'Take it and wear it, and may God bless you, my Lord Arthur.'

I reached out to touch it, but found I could not move my arm. Someone was holding me back. I thought at first it was Guinevere, but it was not. It was the Lady Nemue. Where she had come from, how she came to be beside me, I did not know.

'Don't Arthur,' she said. 'For this cloak is sent to you by Morgana Le Fey. Wear it and you die. Believe me, I know what I say.'

'How can you be so sure?' I asked.

'Let her wear it,' said the Lady Nemue, 'and you shall see.'

At this, the old crone began to screech and back away. Kay and Gawain seized her and brought her back. Gareth it was, who took the cloak from her and, in spite of her screams and struggles, wrapped it round her shoulders. At once, as if from inside her, she began to burn. Flames licked from her mouth, her eyes, and her ears, and in a few minutes, all that was left of her and her coat was a pile of smouldering ashes.

The Lady Nemue turned to me. 'I cannot be with you all the time,' she said. 'You must be more watchful. Remember that even though Morgana Le Fey has gone back to her castle, she can still reach you. Remember always what Merlin once told you: she will destroy you, if she can, if you let her.'

'Is Merlin well?' I asked.

'He rests,' she said. 'He sleeps in a deep cave beneath a hawthorn tree that blossoms all year round. He is old and he is tired. He has asked me to watch over you, and I shall do my best.' She looked down at Bercelet, who was sniffing nervously at the ashes, and she smiled. 'And you still have his eyes and his ears, don't you? God bless you, my lord, and keep you.' And she drifted away towards the doors, passed through them and was gone. Bercelet went after her and scratched at the doors. I was calling him back when I heard the sound of a child crying upstairs and an owl screeching about the tower.

'He cries all the time,' said Guinevere. 'He is such a troubled child. He frowns all the time. He never smiles at me and I wish he would. I must go to him. I must.'

When she came to bed later that night, she slipped

in beside me quietly. 'He is such a sad child, a strange child,' she said. 'The way he looks at me sometimes, he almost frightens me.' I took her in my arms and held her close.

'Still,' she said, 'you're back home, and I love you and you love me. That's all that matters, isn't it?'

'Yes,' I replied, 'that is all that matters.' But all that night the owl shrieked around the castle and would not let me sleep.

# 5 LANCELOT

WHEN I LOOK BACK OVER MY LIFE – AND I HAVE had a good many years to do it – I often find it difficult to recall the exact sequence of events or the speed of the passage of time. Memory, like the tide, ebbs and flows. Sometimes it is so sharp and clear that I can close my eyes, roll back the years and be at Camelot again. And that is just how I remember those early years with Guinevere.

We had been married for some time now, and we were happy together; but there was already a ghost of a shadow between us, a distancing. We had no child of our own, only Mordred. As he grew, he became an even more uncomfortable presence, reminding

Guinevere constantly that she was, as yet, childless; and reminding me always of the guilty secret that lay between us. Guinevere longed to bear our child and I longed for it too. Neither of us ever said as much. We did not need to, for we knew each other so well.

As my queen, Guinevere was all I could possibly want. Like me, everyone at Camelot worshipped her. She was everything they wanted her to be: beautiful, kind, even-handed, in every way a perfect queen. And, alone together, we were always good friends, trusting friends. Her counsel was wise, her loyalty absolute, her insights acute. But, as the years passed, we spoke less and less to each other about ourselves. We talked of the knights, of their adventures, of the court, of the kingdom, and of Mordred, always of Mordred. I don't think she really liked him any more than anyone else did. Maybe she just felt sorry for him, I don't know. But she began to lavish on him ever more obvious signs of affection, despite his endless whining and wheedling. If she and I ever argued – and it was rare – it was always over Mordred. Blind to his faults, she would defend his temper tantrums, and accommodate all his whims and fancies. She would deny him nothing. Mordred was slowly becoming a blight on our lives.

Yet, around us, Camelot flourished as never before.

From all over the kingdom knights came to offer their services to their king. And do not imagine these knights of the Round Table were all young men in the prime of their strength. Many were, of course, and as full of ideals and dreams as I was; but most were brothers-in-arms from the Saxon wars, and many of them gnarled by time and wise in their old age. They were determined, now that the land was ours again, to rid it of all evil, and to make it a place fit for their children and their children's children. From Camelot, they sailed out north, south, east and west, into the remotest corners of the kingdom; and whenever they went and wherever they went, they brought justice and peace to the people. Many did not come back and often, too often, seats fell vacant about the Round Table. But always there were knights to fill them and fresh faces at the feasting. Not a week went by without some knight returning to tell us of his adventures. Some were better storytellers than others, and it is true that hyperbole was not unknown at Camelot. But oh, those were heady, happy times, for we all knew so clearly why we lived each day, what we were fighting for and what we were fighting against. Come what may, we would build God's kingdom here in Britain, and bring about the Kingdom of Logres. We were all so sure of ourselves.

It is not easy being a king, even with such a queen as Guinevere beside you. I had no Merlin to guide me any more; the occasional look of approval, or disapproval from Bercelet was of little help or comfort – although he was a constant companion to me, and I do mean constant. He had even taken to sleeping on the bed with us – something Guinevere did not care for at all. He just would not be removed, not that I tried very hard. He was one of the reasons, I'm sure, that Guinevere would sometimes sleep in her room in the tower. Another was Mordred. He cried a lot at night and she said she needed to be nearer to him. Bercelet, though, kept his distance from Mordred. Whenever he saw Mordred he would growl, which was hardly surprising, as Mordred would pull his tail or tweak his ears at every possible opportunity.

Of all my knights, Gawain was always the closest to me, I suppose. He was a kind and good man although he could be hot-headed and sometimes too quick to anger. Somehow though, I never felt I could confide in him. Bedevere was wise, but weak; and my old foster-father, Egbert, was now too old and too infirm to be of any great help. Kay never grew up to become my friend, as I still hoped he might. Although he always tried to hide his feelings, I don't think he could ever quite forgive me for pulling the sword from the stone all those years before. So, in spite of family, in spite of good and loyal friends all about me, in spite of a loving wife and a perfect queen, I was more and more alone – until the day Lancelot came to Camelot. That was a day that is as clear to me now as if it were yesterday.

I was woken one morning by a commotion in the courtyard below. When I looked out, I saw four men carrying a litter in through the gateway. On it lay a knight still dressed for battle, crying out with pain as they set it down. A crowd was gathering, and I could see the knight struggling to get up, waving away anyone who tried to help him. I called down, 'Give him some air, let him breathe.' I dressed and hurried out into the cold of the courtyard. When I reached him, he was lying back, ashen-faced, his eyes rolling in his head. I did not need to ask his trouble. Embedded deep in his leg was the rusting blade of a sword, and a terrible gaping wound, already yellow with decay. I knelt beside him.

'My Lord Arthur,' he said, reaching up to touch my beard, 'I have one chance to live. You must help me. I am a dead man if I cannot find the knight who can draw out this blade and heal me. I have travelled for days to be here. The hermit who sent me said I had no hope unless I could find the best and the bravest knight at King Arthur's court. Only he can save me, for only he can draw out this blade and heal my weeping wound.'

I had him carried at once into the warmth of the castle, where Guinevere bathed his wound, and gave him what little food and drink he would take.

'You are kind, my lady,' he whispered, 'and I thank you. But it neither food, nor drink, nor kindness that will save me.' Then he fainted away into a deep sleep and I could not wake him.

I called in the knights of the Round Table, one by one, Gawain first – for I was sure he must be the most likely choice. I had always thought of Gawain as the best of us, both in strength and in integrity too. But he could not pull it out, and neither could anyone else. Each of us took hold of the jagged blade and tried to ease it out. I tried myself, but none of us could even move it. He groaned and cried in his sleep as the pain of it reached him. Some while later, he came to himself again.

'Every one of us has tried,' I told him. 'I am sorry, but there are no other knights here. Your hermit must have been mistaken.'

He shook his head violently. 'If he is not here, then he will come,' he insisted. 'I tell you, he will come. He must come.'

I had seen enough mortal wounds, enough drawn, grey faces, to know he was dying, and to know these were the last desperate ramblings of a man clinging on to any hope. Guinevere knew it too. She sat beside him and played her harp to help him pass away in peace. After a while I left him with her, for the smell of death always turned my stomach.

I was pacing under the tree outside when I heard horses coming. Two riders came clattering into the courtyard. I saw at once that one of them was the Lady Nemue and ran towards her, to help her dismount. The young knight who accompanied her sprang down from his horse and fell on his knee before me.

'My Lord Arthur,' he said. 'At last.'

'Who are you?' I asked.

'He is Lancelot,' said the Lady Nemue. 'He is my own foster child, the son of King Ban of Benwick, who fought alongside you at Mount Bladon.' The young man was looking up at me with a gaze so open, so direct that I had to look away.

'I remember King Ban well,' I said. 'A brave knight and a good friend.'

'You remember then that Merlin said there would come one day a knight, stronger, better, braver than any other, one who would be your friend? Well, this is he. Merlin brought him to me as a boy, to prepare him for you, to prepare him for this moment.'

'Perhaps,' I replied, 'perhaps then, he has come at just the right moment. I shall put him to the test at once. Follow me.' And I led them up from the courtyard and into the great hall of the castle, where Guinevere still played softly on her harp and the wounded knight lay deathly still on his bier.

'How is he?' I asked.

'He has little time left,' said Guinevere.

'We have this one last hope,' I said. 'This is Lancelot.' At that, Guinevere looked up and saw the young man. The music stopped at once and the hall fell suddenly silent around us.

'Heal this knight,' I said to Lancelot, 'and I will know you are indeed Merlin's chosen knight, and at once I will acknowledge you to be the best knight amongst us.'

The Lady Nemue put a hand on Lancelot's shoulder. 'He is not yet a knight, Arthur,' she said. 'Make my foster son a knight, and I promise you, the poor man will live.'

There were some murmurings at this. 'I thought a knighthood had to be earned in combat,' Kay protested, 'that a man had to prove himself to be a knight.'

A fine one to talk, I thought. I said nothing, but laid the flat of Excalibur first on the young man's shoulder, then on his head, then on his other shoulder. Lancelot thanked me, and again those eyes were burning into mine, not with defiance or any hint of arrogance, but with such strength, such assurance. He came over to the bier, knelt beside it and prayed for a moment, his eyes closed. Then he reached out and took the blade between thumb and forefinger and drew it out smoothly. As he did so, the wound closed behind it, the livid colour left it and the leg was whole again. The man's eyes fluttered open and he looked about him, the colour flowing back into his cheeks already. Lancelot held the blade up in front of him and offered it to him with a smile.

'Yours, I think,' he said, as the hall erupted with joyful cheering. Guinevere was laughing with her eyes, as she always used to when I first knew her. Lancelot was hoisted up and carried around and around the hall. But I still wondered even then if he could really be everything the Lady Nemue had said, for he was not a large man, a head shorter than I was, at least. If he was the strongest of us, as she had said, then his strength must lie inside him. I looked for a trace of pride in his smile as he was feted, but could find none. When at last they lowered him to the ground, he came and knelt before me. 'My Lord Arthur,' he began, 'I have two brothers, Lionel and Hector. They should be here tomorrow. They too will want to join you and serve you. Will you knight them, as you did me?'

'If they are fit,' I replied, and I turned to Guinevere. 'It is your birthday the day after tomorrow,' I said. 'We shall hold a tournament to celebrate it. Then we shall see both their mettle and Lancelot's. Some of us around this table are becoming a little rusty, a little idle. Gawain eats too much, and drinks too much – and he's not the only one. Gaheris sleeps too much, and Bedevere dreams too much. So, we shall hold a tournament for the Queen's birthday, and we shall soon see if Lancelot is as good as the Lady Nemue promises.'

Tournaments at Camelot were not just for fun. They were for sharpening up, for training, and sometimes for settling scores without anyone getting really hurt. People might be bruised and battered, but usually pride was all that was damaged. When, the next day, Lancelot first rode out on to the field, every neck craned and an expectant hush fell over the crowd. Gawain took him on first, then Pelinore, then Balyn, then Lancelot's own brothers, Lionel and Hector, and then me. We were all good, or we thought we were until then, but we all ended up the same – unceremoniously, humiliatingly deposited in the dirt at the first pass. Lancelot knocked down over fifty of us in that one afternoon; and when he had finished and came before me, all smiling, he had scarcely broken into a sweat. I had never seen jousting like it, and nor had anyone else. It was masterly and effortless. 'Not bad,' I said.

'And how are your bruises, my lord?' he asked, with a twinkle in his eye.

'Not bad,' I replied.

That night in bed, I was blue all down one side and stiff in every joint of me. But I did not mind and nor, I think, did anyone who had suffered the same at Lancelot's hands, for we knew then I had the champion of all champions at Camelot. And I knew too, that I had found at last a kindred spirit, a friend I could trust.

'I think,' said Guinevere, as she lay beside me, 'I think perhaps he's a man that you mustn't like too much.'

I wondered what she meant by that. I was still wondering when I fell asleep.

For the weeks and months that followed, Lancelot, Guinevere and I were scarcely ever out of each other's company. We hunted together, we hawked together.

We played chess (which he won all too often) and we talked together, long into the night. We talked as good friends do, at ease with one another, not bridling, not seeking to impress, not striving to persuade. In all that time, he never once presumed on his friendship to advise me as king, unless I asked it of him. We spoke of other things, of flowers in the meadows, and he knew every one of them. We spoke of the birds by the river; he could imitate all their songs. He could run his hands under a sleeping salmon and lift it, still sleeping, out of the river.

I remember once lying back in a meadow, head on my hands. Guinevere and Lancelot beside me. She was making a chain of buttercups. Bercelet was gambolling through the long grass, when a lark rose in strident alarm and hovered above us. Suddenly, it fell dead to the earth. Two boys came scampering through the grass. It was Mordred with one of his friends, triumphant at their kill. Mordred carried a sling in his hand. Lancelot caught them both by the scruffs of their necks, and made them pick up the bird to look at what they had done. He pointed up at another lark still rising. 'See what you have stilled with your stone,' he cried, and he banged their heads together and sent them off. When he turned to us, his eyes were filled with tears. 'If you could only teach the children,' he said. 'Then you could really change the world, then you could have your Kingdom of Logres, but not otherwise.' He stopped, thinking he had gone too far. 'I am sorry, my lord, but with you and your queen, I must speak what I feel.'

'I wouldn't want it any other way, Lancelot,' I said, and looked at Guinevere. I had expected her to protest at Lancelot's treatment of Mordred, but she had not. Instead she was looking at Lancelot in open admiration, her buttercup chain dangling from her hand. Lancelot took it from her and laid it gently on her head. 'A crown fit for the loveliest of all queens,' he said. For just a moment, it seemed as if time stood still, the three of us in such harmony with each other and with the world around us. I don't think I have ever before or since known such complete contentment.

He was with us for only a few days after that, and then one morning he was gone. He had said nothing to me, nor to anyone else. He had simply vanished.

The seasons came and went. Year followed year, and still Lancelot did not return. I sent out Bors, Gawain, Percivale and a dozen others to look for him. His brothers, Lionel and Hector, went too. They all came back with no word of him, no home. Guinevere begged me to send out more men to find him. She became ill and thin with worry, keeping to her room in the tower for days on end. Her harp stayed silent now; and when she did come down, she sat by the window, gazing sadly into the distance. I comforted her all I could, but somehow I was never able to find the right words. Like her, I was mourning the loss of the best friend I had ever had. I did not tell her so, but I was sure by now that Lancelot would never come back – he had been gone too long. Had he still been alive, there would have been some sighting, some rumour at least, I was sure of it. Our lives had become empty. Not only that, but the heart had quite gone out of Camelot.

We were at supper one evening, the autumn sky darkening with thunder outside, when Mordred came running into the great hall. 'It's Lancelot!' he cried. 'Lancelot's come back! Bors is with him. He's found him.'

Even as he spoke, a great thunderclap crashed above us, and shook the castle. The horses in the courtyard outside whinnied in terror and a great gust of wind blew open the doors. Two men were standing there, their hoods thrown back. Bors, whom I recognized, was supporting another man with long grey hair who looked vacantly about the hall until his eyes came to rest on me. He shook off Bors' arm and walked slowly, unsteadily towards me. Only when he came close did I see that it was indeed Lancelot. Even then, I knew him only from his eyes. The face was gaunt, the black hair gone to grey. He tried to kneel, but could not. I put my arms round him and held him to me.

'My dear lord,' he whispered. 'You will wish you had never seen me again.'

'How can you say that?' I said, as I led him to a chair.

He was looking around him, nervously. 'The Queen?' he whispered. 'Is she here?'

'Upstairs,' I replied. 'She has not been well. I will send for her.'

'No, please,' he grasped my wrist and held it tight. ' I haven't the strength to meet her, not yet. And besides, I must speak to you first, and it must be alone.' He sat down, holding his hands out over the heat of the fire. He waited until everyone had left the hall, and then he began his story, his voice so weak that it was unrecognizable.

'Since I last saw you, my lord, I have been to heaven almost, and I have been to hell.'

He seemed uncertain as to how to go on, unwilling almost. 'I will start at the beginning, from the first day

I left Camelot. I needed to be alone, and you will know why soon enough. I was riding along, not many miles from here, when a hermit came out of the woods waving his staff at me. I thought he was a madman at first. But then he called me by my name, so I listened. "Lancelot," he said, "come with me, I beg you. There is a dragon that stalks the land around the castle of King Pelles, at Corbenic. He will let no one in and no one out, and the people starve. Many good knights have tried to destroy him, but all were burnt to ashes. Only you can do it." I would have gone back to Camelot for my armour, and to tell you where I was going and what quest I was following; but I could not face you, nor the queen.'

He spoke now, with his fists clenching all the while, his head lowered as if in deep shame. He seemed quite unable to look me in the face.

'I went with him, my lord, not to save King Pelles or his starving people, not even to kill the dragon. I wanted only to meet my death in the fire of this dragon. I had inside me such a dark and terrible secret that I no longer wished to live with it.'

I tried to interrupt him to ask what his secret was, but he would not let me. 'After several weeks of travelling through the Wastelands,' he went on, 'we came at last into a forest so dense that there were not even deer tracks we could follow. But somehow the hermit seemed always to know the way. For days I breathed in only the bitter stench of scorched earth, until at last I came out of the forest into the light; and then I saw the reason for it. As far as the eye could see, the land was blackened, the trees reduced to smouldering stumps. The charred remains of beasts and birds lay scattered everywhere. The hermit pointed to the far distance. "The Castle of Corbenic," he whispered. "See what the dragon has done?"

'"Where is he?" I asked, too loudly it seemed.

'"Hush," said the hermit, finger to his lips. "Or you will wake him. Tread lightly too. Dismount and wrap your horses' hooves. Your only chance is to catch him asleep. Once he has woken, no man can stand against him. I will come no further. I dare not. God bless you, Lancelot." And with that, he disappeared into the forest.

'So I dismounted and walked on, my sword ready on my hand. For half a day, I walked through this devastation looking for the dragon, the sun beating down on my head. I was so faint with thirst that I must have missed my footing. I stumbled and fell. At once, I heard a roar like a hundred angry bears; and up from the ground close to the castle there reared a great rust-red dragon, wings outspread, spitting fire as

he came at me. My shield shrivelled at the first blast of his breath; but I went gladly on to my death, my sword whirling above my head, screaming defiance at the beast. With his second breath, I smelt my skin cooking. The third breath would be the end of me. I darted forward and hurled my sword like a spear. I expected it to bounce off his scaly hide. I expected death at any moment, but my sword flew through the air like a javelin and speared him through the throat. He crumpled to the ground, screaming, his tail flailing in his death agony. By the time I reached him, he was quite still. I drew out my sword and with one blow struck off his head. From the castle walls above me, I heard cheering, wild cheering; and then the bridge came down and they were streaming out to welcome me. A conquering hero, I rode into Corbenic, the dead dragon hauled behind me by horses. King Pelles, crippled from an old wound, was carried down to me, his daughter, Elaine, at his side.

'"Now God be thanked," King Pelles cried. "My people can eat once again. The corn will grow again, the birds will sing, and the black smoke of death will no longer hide the sun. You have given us new life. Come in, come in, Lancelot."

'"You know me?" I asked.

'"The hermit said you would come," said King

Pelles. "You were the hope we all lived for, we all prayed for. We knew no one else could kill the dragon, except Lancelot – the hermit told us as much. And now you are here and the dragon is dead."

'Warm as the welcome was, I did not want to stay, for it was still in my mind to seek my death and I wanted no part of any feasting or celebration. It was his daughter, Elaine, who persuaded me.

'"Come," she said, taking my hand in hers. "You are hurt. You are tired. Rest with us for a few days only – just until you are better, if that is what you want. Then you can journey on." I had neither the heart nor the will to refuse her.'

Lancelot looked up at me, his eyes full of pain. 'You see how weak I am with a woman, my lord?' Sighing deeply and shaking his head, he went on with his story.

'So I stayed. I bathed away the grime of the battle and the blood of the dragon and came down later into the hall, my burns still smarting. There was little food and no wine, but the hall was filled with joy and laughter. Coarse bread and spring water had never tasted so fine. After we had eaten, King Pelles turned to me. "This is little enough reward for all that you have done for us, Lancelot. But you shall see something now that no other knight of King Arthur's court has ever seen. Had you not come when you did, the dragon you slew would have killed us all, my dear daughter, too. But it was not for us that he came, it was for this."

'As he spoke, the hall filled with a light so bright that it hurt my eyes to look. Yet, in spite of that, I could not look away for I did not want to look away.'

Lancelot's grip tightened on my arm. 'Do not think me mad,' he said. 'But it was the Holy Grail. With these eyes, I saw it, my lord. I saw it carried into the hall by a lady all in white, the very cup our Lord Jesus Christ drank from at the Last Supper. It was not of silver, nor of gold, but of olive wood; yet around it shone a halo of light and a light that filled me with such joy, such peace. King Pelles told me as it passed us by that the cup was passed down to him through his family, the family of Joseph of Arimathaea, who brought it many years ago to Corbenic. He said that, one day, the Holy Grail will come here to Camelot, that knight after knight shall leave here to seek it, myself amongst them, but only one of us will ever find it – he did not say which. And, my lord, he said, more. The day we see the Holy Grail at Camelot will be the beginning of the end for you, and for all of us here.'

'That is your terrible secret?' I said. 'I tell you, King

Pelles is no Merlin. He has no eye, as Merlin had, to see how things may be. These are the ramblings of an old man. Pay them no attention. And, as for the Holy Grail, we do not even know that it exists. No one I have spoken to has ever seen it. What you say you saw may have been an illusion, some sorcery of Morgana Le Fey and her witches.'

'Believe me, my lord, it was no trick, no sorcery.' Lancelot leant forward and looked me full in the face. I knew from his eyes that he believed he spoke the truth. 'I saw it, I tell you. I saw the Holy Grail.' He sat back, breathing hard. Then he lowered his head again. 'But this was not my secret, my lord. Now you shall hear the worst, how Lancelot betrayed the love and the trust of his king and his friend. When you know it, banish me, have me put to death if you will, but tell no man, for it will be the ruin of your kingdom if you do.' For some moments he said nothing more; and when at last he did speak, he spoke so softly, almost as if he did not want me to hear him.

'I have a love, my lord. Since I first set eyes on her, I have been able to think of little else. She is another man's wife, and that man is the best friend I ever had.'

A cold dread passed through me as I tried not to understand the meaning of what he was telling me.

'She knows nothing of it,' he went on, 'and besides,

she loves her husband. I have no hope of her. Now you see, my lord, why I left you suddenly, why I wanted to die. But I found myself at Corbenic, alive and loved by everyone. And Elaine is fair and kind and good, and she is everything a man could want in a woman. I stayed months at Corbenic, Elaine constantly at my side. She soothed my burns with her camomile potion, and cured me. She sang to me, she made me smile again. She loved me. She did not say so, not then; but I knew it well enough. I knew too that I could never love her as she would have liked, because I loved somebody else. I wanted to love her. I wanted to forget, but I could not. Elaine had an old nurse – Brissen she was called – who could see what was happening. She told me I was cruel to lead Elaine on, that if I could not return her love then I should go before I broke her heart. She was right, but I stayed. I stayed, my lord, because a strange thing was happening. As the days passed, Elaine seemed to me to become more and more like Guinevere – there, I have spoken her name at last. It is done. It is said. She laughed like Guinevere, she tucked her hair back behind her ear in just the same way. I looked at her now, and I saw Guinevere, and I began to love her.'

I could not listen to any more of this. I got up and began to walk away. He took my arm and held me back. 'No, my lord, hear me out. Hear the rest, hear all of it, while I still have the courage to tell you. One night I came to her room and we slept together. But yet I did not sleep with Elaine. In my head, in my heart, I was with Guinevere. I woke in the morning and found Elaine lying beside me. I realized only then what a terrible thing I had done. So as not to be seen, I left by the window, jumped down and ran. I did not know where I ran, and I did not care. In time, I no longer even knew who I was. Maddened by guilt, tortured with self-pity, I wandered through the Wastelands. I slept wherever I lay down. I ate nothing but berries and mushrooms. When robbers attacked me and stole my clothes, I did not even fight back. I was happy to die. I was longing to die. But winters passed and summers passed and still I was alive. And then came another summer. I found myself again close to a castle I thought I knew. As I stood there, a wild boar came out of a thicket and charged me. I did not try to escape. He pinned me up against a tree and drove at me again and again, until one of his tusks snapped off in my thigh and he ran off leaving me bleeding on the ground. I crawled away into a shady place where I lay down on the soft grass to die – or so I thought, so I hoped. When I woke, I was in a great bed and there were two faces looking down at me, a small boy I did not know, and with him was Elaine.

'"You came back," she said, her eyes so loving. "I knew you would." And she kissed me tenderly on my forehead. "This is your son. I called him Galahad. He's five years old now. You have been gone for so long, Lancelot. First they said you were wandering mad in the forests. Then they said you were dead, but I knew all the while you were not." She turned to the child. "I told you, Galahad, didn't I? I said your father was a good man and a fine man. I said he would come home, didn't I?"

'Elaine was good to me, my lord. Again she nursed me back to health and saw to my every need. She told me she loved me. She begged me to stay with her and marry her. So did Brissen and King Pelles, and so did everyone I met, for I was still much loved there, still the great dragon-slayer, the saviour of Corbenic. Even little Galahad asked me to stay, but I think he already knew that I would not. I remember we were together on the river bank, watching the kingfishers darting upstream straight as arrows, when he asked me. "You won't leave us, Father, will you?" he said. "You won't, will you?" So I promised to stay. I could not disappoint him. And I did stay – for a while.

'But then my thoughts turned again to you, to Camelot and to Guinevere, always to Guinevere. I loved her still. I could not stay at Corbenic, nor live out a lie any longer. One night, while all the castle slept, I stole away into the darkness. I wandered into the forest and became lost. In time, I gave up all hope of ever finding Camelot again. I found a cave and lived there as a hermit, away from the world; and the longer I stayed, the longer I thought about it, the more I knew I could never return to Camelot. To do so would bring nothing but pain and misery. I would stay a hermit all my days. And I would have done so. But then one day Bors found me, half-starved, in my cave. He had been looking for me all this time. I told him I could not, I would not go with him back to Camelot, but he insisted. The king had sent him out to find me, he said, to bring me back; and he would drag me back if he had to. And so here I am, my lord, the shell of the Lancelot you once knew.'

As I stood looking down at him, I felt my fingers curl round the hilt of Excalibur. A terrible jealousy and fury took hold of me, and had he not looked up at me when he did, I know I would have struck off his head where he sat. But as I looked down into his sad, sad eyes, my heart went out to him. The echo of a night long ago in Caerleon sounded in my head. Had we not both weakened when we shouldn't have? Was his crime any worse than mine? Hardly. He loved

Guinevere. In my heart I had known it for a long time. And how could I blame him for it? Why should we not both love the same woman? He had not touched her. He had loved her only in his mind. If he had betrayed me, he had betrayed me only in mind. And he had told me. He had been honest with me. I helped him to his feet and embraced him. 'You are home, Lancelot. There is nothing to forgive, only much to forget. I, like you, have a child I should not have had – Mordred. But, unlike you, I have never had the courage to speak of it to anyone, until now. No one knows, except you, not even Guinevere. And she must never know, never.'

From outside, I heard the tolling of the chapel bell, and the sound of running feet and crying women. The door opened. Bedevere stood there, pale and speechless for some moments. 'My Lord Arthur,' he said, at last. 'You must come. You must come. Down by the river.'

'What is it?' I asked.

'I cannot speak of it,' he said, unable to control his tears. 'Just come.'

I asked no more questions, but followed him down through the water meadows to the riverbank, the bell tolling behind us. Everyone was there, but no one spoke, no one moved. With Lancelot beside me, I came through the crowd, and saw a barge coming in towards the bank. A young boy stood by the mast, and at his feet lay the body of a woman, dressed all in white, as if for a wedding. She had flowers in her hair, violets and primroses, and the whole barge was covered from end to end with lilies of the valley.

Lancelot leant on me heavily and whispered. 'It is her. It is Elaine.' As the barge grounded, the boy stepped out on to the shore and walked up to Lancelot, his face red from crying. He carried a letter in his hand.

'She told me to bring her to you. She believed you would stay. But she didn't blame you, and nor do I. She wanted you to see her, Father,' he said, 'in her wedding dress.'

Lancelot took the letter and read it. He handed it to me. I never read sadder words in all my life.

*Dearest and best,*

*I wanted you to be the last on this earth to see me. Forgive me, and if you loved me only a little, be mother and father to Galahad. Bury me where I can be close to him, and close to you. Think of me sometimes and pray for me.*

*Your loving Elaine.*

\*　　\*　　\*

Lancelot turned to me. 'I have no tears left to cry,' he said. And taking Galahad's hand, he walked away.

We buried Elaine that same afternoon by the chapel. Even the birds had stopped their singing. On one side of the grave, I stood with Lancelot, and Lionel and Hector, his brothers. On the other side was Guinevere and the two boys, Galahad and Mordred, Lancelot's son and mine, each holding her by the hand. I looked up and saw Mordred smiling at me. He was enjoying it. It was then I noticed Lancelot was no longer looking down at the coffin in the grave. He and Guinevere were gazing full into each other's eyes. From that moment, I knew she loved him as much as he loved her. But it did not trouble me. Lancelot was a true friend and he would never betray me. Guinevere was a true wife and she would not betray me. That is what I thought. That is what I believed. She turned her gaze to me. She knew I knew. Nothing was hidden. We three trusted each other utterly, because we loved each other utterly. So the two boys grew up together at Camelot, Mordred, the older, becoming ever more unlovable as the years passed. He teased Galahad. He bullied him mercilessly. Galahad was always gentle and quiet, and not at all rumbustious as boys often are. Galahad never once replied in kind. He simply ignored Mordred and walked away, as I had walked away from Kay all those years before. Often, as I lay awake at night, I wished it were Galahad who was my son, and not Mordred. But a father cannot choose his child any more than a child can choose his father.

# 6 THREE OF THE BEST

'BUT YOU'VE HEARD ENOUGH OF ME AND MY troubles,' said King Arthur. 'I am like an old dog with a thorn in his foot, like old Bercelet there. He licks it and licks it. It doesn't help, it only keeps the wound open. Better to leave it alone and let the poison come out when it will, and the thorn with it. But then, my thorn is in so deep and the pain of it still throbs all these hundreds of years later.'

Bercelet sighed deeply on the bed beside the boy, stretched himself and sighed again. 'That's his way of telling me I'm a maudlin, self-pitying old fool, and of course he's right, he's always right. So, no more of me, for the moment anyway.' He pointed to the Round

Table. 'You shall hear more about them, about my knights, my friends. At one time, in the golden years of Camelot, there were a hundred and fifty of us round that table. Some I knew well, like Gawain, like Lancelot and Bedevere. Some stayed only for a short time, left and I never saw them again. But we heard of them. The stories of their adventures came back to us at Camelot. The harpists sang of them, and their fame spread like fire all over the kingdom. I could tell you such stories – and they'd all be true – about each one of them. But you'd be here for ever, and you can't stay for ever, can you? Which of the stories to tell you, that's the question.' He thought for a moment, and then smiled suddenly. 'I know,' he said. 'You must choose. Get up out of that bed. Go on, up with you.' He clapped his hands. 'Climb up on the Round Table. Walk round and choose. You choose three names and I'll tell you their stories. How would that be?'

King Arthur whipped back the fur rug and helped the boy to his feet. He stood on the seat marked 'Percivale', and then climbed up on the Round Table. 'Three,' said Arthur. 'Just three. Whichever you like.'

The boy walked all round the table, reading the names. Choosing was easy. He had heard something of Gawain already and wanted to know more. So he chose him. The boy had a friend on Bryher called

Tristram, so he chose Tristram. And Bercelet was resting his head on Percivale's seat, and gazing up at him, waiting, it seemed, for his decision. Perhaps he was hinting. He chose Percivale for the third.

'Gawain, Tristram and Percivale,' Arthur said, nodding. 'You have chosen well – all fine men, three of the best. Come by the fire, and you shall hear their stories.' He felt the drying clothes. 'Won't be long now,' he said, and sat down opposite the boy. Bercelet lay with his nose in the embers.

'He likes his nose warm, doesn't he?' said the boy.

King Arthur laughed at that, and nudged him with his foot. 'He always has done,' he said. 'So I'll start with Gawain.'

# 7 GAWAIN AND THE GREEN KNIGHT

I REMEMBER IT WAS COLD AT CHRISTMAS THAT year, and colder still at New Year, the snow thick on the ground, the wind icy from the north. But neither the snow nor the wind could dampen our spirits. We were at Camelot and it was New Year's Eve once more. Everyone was gathered for the feasting, the knights all in their places at the Round Table; and my dear Guinevere sitting with all the ladies of the court beneath a great canopy. A blazing fire crackled in the hearth, the ale flowed freely and my harpist played as only he could play. Bercelet lay at my feet, waiting in high hopes for the feasting to begin. The boar's head, apple in his mouth, was carried into the hall, and we all of us pounded the table impatiently; for, as was the custom at Camelot, we knew we could not begin eating until we had heard of some new quest, of some stirring adventure. I waited. We all waited. The knights looked at each other, but no one rose to his feet. Nothing happened. Bercelet licked his lips.

At that moment, from outside in the courtyard, came the clatter of a horse's hooves on the cobbles. The doors of the hall flew open, and before I had time to call for them to be closed, a giant of a man rode in on a towering warhorse that pawed the ground, sides lathered up, tossed its fine head, snorting its fury. The man swept the hall with terrible eyes, wolfish eyes that froze the courage in a man's veins, eyes you could not hold with your own. But it was not the man's eyes that amazed us most, it was not his size either – and I tell you I'd never in my life set eyes on a bigger man – no, it was the colour of him. Green, the man was green from head to foot. Green jerkin, common enough; green cloak, again common enough, you might think – but his face was green, his hands as well. And I swear that his hair, which was as long as mine is now, was green too. The horse was green, and the saddle. He wore no armour, but carried a green axe in one hand and in the other a branch he'd ripped off some holly tree – a sign of peace, but he didn't look very peaceful to me.

He threw the branch to the ground as he spoke. 'And who might be the leader of this motley crew? I'll talk to no one else.' It was a moment or two before I could find my voice.

'Welcome, stranger,' I said. 'Why don't you come and join us?'

'I have not come here to waste my time in feasting. I can do that well enough at home. I have something else in mind. You are King Arthur?'

'I am.'

'Well, King Arthur,' he began, his thunderous voice heavy with sarcasm. 'I have heard all about the so-called bravery of you and your knights. The whole world is talking of little else. I have come all this way from my home in the North Country to find out just how brave you are. Looking about me, I see nothing but a bunch of beardless little boys. Are you quite sure I have come to the right place?'

At this there were howls of protest. 'You may bark loud enough,' he went on, 'but I doubt very much if there's anyone here man enough to accept my challenge. We shall see. We shall see.' And he held out his axe in both hands. 'You see this axe? I will submit myself right now to one blow from this axe, just one blow – but only if, in twelve months and a day from now, I can repay the blow in kind, just one blow. Tit for tat, how's that? There, is that simple enough for you dunderheads?'

I looked about the hall. No one moved a muscle. No one said a word.

'Well, I can see I was wrong,' he laughed. 'I said I saw boys about me. I see only chickens.'

Now my blood was up. I had had enough. 'You've asked for it,' I shouted. 'I'll do it, and with pleasure too. Down off your horse.' It wasn't so brave as it sounds. After all, a man without his head could hardly do you much harm, could he?

Then suddenly Gawain was on his feet beside me. 'No, my lord,' he said. 'Let me. I'll see to him. I'll shut his big mouth for you, once and for all. I've rested on my laurels long enough. It is time I proved myself fit again to sit round this table.'

'Very well, Gawain,' I replied, more than a little relieved. 'But be careful. Things are not always as they seem.'

With a great laugh, the Green Knight jumped down from his horse. 'So, Arthur, at least you have one man amongst all these boys,' he quipped.

'Enough!' cried Gawain, striding across the hall to meet him. Dwarfed, but not cowed, he squared up to the Green Knight. 'It will be a promise, a bargain between us,' he said. 'I promise, by my honour as a knight, that I will strike you just once, as you've said; and that in a year's time you can do the same to me – if you're still able to, which I doubt.'

'We shall see,' said the Green Knight, and he handed Gawain his axe. 'You do know which end to hold, don't you?'

'Kneel, you overgrown leek!' Gawain cried, gripping the axe tightly. The Green Knight knelt down and pulled aside his hair, so that his neck was bare. Gawain seemed to be hesitating for a moment.

'Come on then, Gawain, what are you waiting for? Are you frightened of the sight of a little blood? Strike man, strike!' Gawain hesitated no longer. He severed the Green Knight's head clean from his shoulders and sent it rolling across the floor. But there was not a drop of blood, green or red, not a single drop – and no time to wonder at it either, for the Green Knight sprang at once to his feet, picked up his head and vaulted headless on to his horse. It was the severed head under his arm that spoke.

'You have a year and a day, Gawain. I am the Green Knight of the Green Chapel in the Forest of Wirral. You'll find me easily enough. If you do not, then the whole world will know that the great Sir Gawain is a coward and all King Arthur's court with him.' With

that, he galloped away out into the snow, leaving the hall silent and aghast behind him. It was some time, I can tell you, before any of us felt at all festive.

The seasons passed as they always do, slowly enough for the young, but ever faster for the old. And for poor Gawain too, though still young in body and spirit, the year raced by. The following Michaelmas, I held my court at Caerleon and we had a great feast for Gawain to send him on his way. Lancelot was there, Bors, Gareth and Gaheris, Gawain's brothers, Bedevere and all the others. Even the Archbishop was there to bless him. In hushed silence, Gawain put on his fine gold-inlaid armour. We embraced without a word. Then he turned away from me, mounted Gringolet, his black warhorse and rode off. Few of us thought we would ever see him again.

What happened after this, Gawain himself later told us. Impetuous he may have been, but he was never one given to exaggeration or wild imaginings. He rode away from us with a heavy heart that day. He travelled up over the windswept hills of North Wales and down into the forests beyond. It was bitterly cold. The forests were a haven for robbers, savage men who could be hiding anywhere, ready to spring out and ambush any luckless stranger. Some, seeing the star of

Logres on Gawain's shield and knowing who he was, let him pass by. Others did not. Time and again, Gawain had to fight them off. Many a cold night he slept out in the open, and many a day passed with no food either for himself or his horse, so that they were both much weakened by the time they came at long last into the Forest of Wirral.

He asked anyone and everyone he met where he might find the Green Chapel, but no one seemed to have even heard of it. He began to despair of ever finding the place in time. On and on he rode, ever deeper into the forest, wading through marsh and mud; until, on Christmas Eve, he found himself fording a stream and riding through open parkland towards a fine castle. The drawbridge over the moat was down, so he rode across and knocked at the door.

A porter greeted him with a welcoming smile and invited him to come in. Gringolet was led away for a rub-down, then to a warm, dry stable where there was all the sweet hay and all the clean water he could want. Gawain was brought into the hall to meet his host, the lord of the castle. The moment Gawain set eyes on him, he knew he was in good hands, for everything about the man was courteous and kind, from his honest eyes to his open smile. Gawain told him at once who he was and where he had come from.

'No matter who you are,' said the lord of the castle, clasping his hand, 'you are more than welcome to my home. You need rest, and here you shall have all you need. My castle is your castle. Everything I have is yours for as long as you want to stay.' Gawain could hardly believe his good luck.

Then there began three days of Christmas celebrations. People flocked to the castle from miles around to meet Gawain, and he was feted royally. Nothing was too much trouble. The lady of the castle, his host's wife, saw to his every need – and she was as beautiful a woman as Gawain had ever met. Never had he enjoyed a Christmas as much as this; but from time to time a shadow came over him as he thought of the dreaded appointment with the Green Knight, now only a few short days away. The happier he was, the less he wanted to die.

'You are sad, Gawain,' said the lady of the castle, as they sat talking together late one evening.

'After all you have done for me, my lady, I have no right to be,' Gawain replied. He had tried so hard to drive away his black and fearful thoughts, to hide from them his growing anxiety. 'But I am afraid that tomorrow I shall have to leave and be on my way. I have promised to be at the Green Chapel on New Year's Day, and as yet I don't even know where the place is. I must not be late, I cannot be.'

'Nor shall you be,' laughed the lord of the castle, 'because the Green Chapel you speak of is no more than a two-hour ride from here, on a good horse. And Gringolet is a fine warhorse. So why don't you stay here for three more days, until the morning of New Year's Day itself? I shall have someone show you the way, just to be sure. How would that be?'

'That,' said Gawain, greatly relieved, 'that would make me the happiest man alive. You've been so good to me, so kind. I won't get in the way, I promise. I'll do anything you say, everything you say.'

'Well then,' said the lord of the castle, 'I shall be out hunting every morning. The distance you've travelled, I should imagine you've seen quite enough of a horse's neck – so why don't you just stay in bed and rest? My wife will look after you.'

'I can think of nothing better,' said Gawain. But he noticed then that the lady was smiling at him rather too knowingly.

'Now,' said his host, 'since it's still the festive season, why don't we play a little game? Let's you and I make a bargain.'

'Why not?' Gawain said.

'What if I promise that I will give you whatever I bring back from the hunt?' the lord of the castle went on. 'And you promise me, in return, that you will give me anything and everything that you manage to come by back here in the castle? Well?'

'It's a bargain,' Gawain laughed. 'Anything at all I come by, you shall have, I promise – though I can't for the life of me think what it might be.'

So Gawain slept in the next morning whilst the lord of the castle went out hunting. And as he dozed, the door of his room opened silently. Gawain opened his eyes to find the lady of the castle sitting on his bed smiling down at him, her eyes full of love. Gawain didn't know which way to look, nor what to talk about – and it was very obvious that she had more in mind than just talk. But talking was all Gawain would allow himself to do. After all, this was the wife of his kind host, his good friend. But how he was tempted! The woman was wonderfully beautiful, so beautiful he had to force himself to look away if he was to resist her. The trouble was, he didn't want to resist her, even though he knew he should.

'I am disappointed in you, Gawain,' she wheedled. 'You talk and talk, but you do not ask me to kiss you.'

'Well, if you're offering, my lady,' said Gawain, 'then who am I to turn you down?' And the lady leant over, took his face in her hands and kissed him gently.

When she had gone, Gawain got up, washed and

dressed, thinking all the while of the kiss. All that day, he lazed about the castle talking happily to the lady. She made him forget all his troubles, even his encounter with the Green Knight in the Green Chapel.

At dusk the lord of the castle returned, mud-splattered from the chase. He strode into the hall and threw down a roe deer at Gawain's feet. 'Yours,' he said. 'As we agreed. What have you got for me, then?'

'This,' said Gawain, and he took his host's face in his hands and kissed him. 'That's all. I promise.'

'I believe you,' laughed the lord of the castle, 'but what I'd like to know is how you came by this kiss.'

'Oh no,' said Gawain, shamefaced. 'That wasn't part of the bargain.' And they said no more about it. That night the three of them feasted together on capons and mead, and talked and laughed into the early hours.

In the morning Gawain woke to the sound of baying hounds and hunting horns. From his bed he could see the lord of the castle riding out across the parkland. As he expected, and as he hoped too, it wasn't long before the lady came into his room. She sat on his bed, closer this time, stroked his hair and talked again of love. Gawain laughed it all off as best he could, but it was not easy. When she offered him two kisses he did not find it at all difficult to accept; and this time the kisses were sweeter and longer than before, kisses he could not forget even if he had wanted to – and he did not want to.

That evening the lord of the castle returned from the hunt, a boar slung across his shoulders. 'Here we are,' he said. 'Not a bad day's work, eh? What about you?'

'Just this,' said Gawain. And at that he kissed him twice, though not, I imagine, as long nor as sweetly as he had kissed that morning. But he had kept his part of the bargain. Dinner went on again into the small hours and through it all the lady tried to seduce him with her eyes – and with her husband there at the same table. Although Gawain tried to look the other way, he found he did not want to.

Gawain scarcely slept at all that night. Haunted by thoughts of the Green Knight, he tossed and turned. It wasn't until dawn that he sank into a troubled sleep. When he woke, the lady of the castle was gazing down at him. She had never looked more lovely, but there were tears in her eyes. 'What is it?' she cried. 'Don't you like me? Am I that ugly to you? There's someone else, isn't there? You love someone else back at Camelot.'

'No, my lady,' said Gawain, taking her hand in his.

'There's no one else. It's not that. But you have a husband, a fine man, a noble knight. He's been a good friend to me. It wouldn't be right to love you. Do you think I don't want to? As a man I want to, but as a knight I must not, I cannot. Can't you understand?'

'But why not just this once?' The lady persisted, as she stroked his hair and traced his mouth with her finger. 'No one would know. I would tell no one. You would tell no one. Where's the harm in it? Please sweet Gawain, be nice to me.'

But Gawain would have none of it. He clenched his jaw and turned away from her. 'You should go, my lady,' he said stonily. The lady bowed her head and wept.

'Like it or not, Gawain,' she said, 'you cannot stop me from loving you. I shall always keep you in my heart. I shall never forget you, never.'

'Nor I you, my lady,' Gawain said, and he meant it too.

'Will you at least do one thing for me?' she pleaded. 'Just to remind you of me from time to time, will you take this?' And she handed him the belt she wore round her waist, a belt of green ribbon interwoven with gold thread. 'Wear it always Gawain, and I promise you will never come to any harm, for there is within it an all-powerful magic. Wear it and you will be safe, wear it and think of me. I know you are not my knight and should not wear my favour, but no one need see it. One day it may save your life. Make me happy, Gawain. Do just this one little thing for me. But promise me that, whatever you do, you will never tell my husband.'

Gawain needed no persuading about that. He had no intention of telling her husband, nor of handing over the belt either. Tomorrow he had to face the Green Knight, and this belt could be the saving of him. Now he would at least stand some chance of survival. Now he had some hope of living beyond tomorrow.

'Dear, sweet Gawain,' she whispered, and she kissed him three times, and so passionately this time that she left Gawain quite breathless, his heart pounding.

At sundown Gawain was waiting in the hall when the lord of the castle came in from the hunt, swinging a fox by its brush. Gawain went right up to him, took him by the shoulders and kissed him loudly three times. 'Three!' cried the lord of the castle, wiping his cheeks. 'And all I have to offer you in return is this poxy fox. Here, I wish you joy of it.'

Try as he might, Gawain could not enjoy the New Year's feast that night. There was wine, there was music, there was dancing. But hidden round his waist he could feel the lady's magic belt. He had not kept his promise to the lord of the castle; and worse, he knew it was out of cowardice that he had broken the bargain. The belt might save his life the next day, but it would not save his honour. All night long he lay in a turmoil of guilt, but he could not bring himself to hand over the belt and give up his only chance of life.

Gawain was up early on New Year's Day. He tied the belt round his waist, put on his warmest clothes and his fine gold-inlaid armour. Down in the courtyard he embraced his host for the last time, quite unable to look him in the eye. He looked for the lady of the castle but she was nowhere to be seen. He mounted Gringolet and waved his farewells. They let down the drawbridge and, with a squire ahead to guide him, Gawain rode out into the biting January cold.

For nearly two hours they rode on, following a winding, tumbling stream along a mist-filled valley. Suddenly the squire reined in his horse and pointed. 'Over there,' he said, his voice hushed. 'Beyond those trees, you can't miss it, the Green Chapel. Sir Gawain, I know it's not my place, but if I were you I wouldn't go any closer. The Green Knight who lives there fights anyone who goes near. And I'm telling you, he never loses. Plenty have tried, but not one of them has ever lived to see another dawn. Listen, you can hear the crows gathering. Turn back Gawain, before it's too late. I won't say a word, I promise.'

'What must be done must be done,' Gawain replied. 'I am a knight of King Arthur's court. We may feel afraid, but we do not flinch and we do not run.'

'On your head be it then,' said the squire, and he rode away and left Gawain alone in the swirling mist.

Gringolet pawed the ground, eager to be going. 'Don't be in such a hurry,' said Gawain aloud. 'I just hope and pray the lady was telling the truth about this magic belt. If not . . .' And as he spoke, he heard from somewhere ahead of him a grating, grinding sound. He listened again. It was just as he feared, metal on stone. The Green Knight was sharpening his axe. Gawain shivered in spite of himself. 'What must be must be,' he sighed, and he put his spurs to Gringolet's sides, urging him onwards.

He rode through the dripping trees, crossed a stream and came to a grassy mound. Near the mound stood a small chapel, the roof and walls all as green as the surrounding grass. From somewhere inside the mound itself, Gawain could hear the axe still being sharpened. It set his teeth on edge, and a shiver of fear ran down his spine. He thought of galloping off and,

but for the green belt, he would undoubtedly have done so. Instead he dismounted. 'Who's there?' he shouted. 'I am Sir Gawain from King Arthur's court, and I have come as I promised I would. Come on out.'

'When I am ready,' came the reply. 'When my axe is sharp enough. I won't be long.' And the gruesome grinding ground on. He waited, pacing up and down, until at long last out came the Green Knight, feeling the blade of his axe with his thumb. He was every bit as huge and as terrifying as Gawain had remembered him. 'That will do nicely,' he said, and he looked mercilessly down at Gawain out of his grey-green, wolfish eyes. 'Welcome, Gawain,' he said.

'Let's not waste time on pleasantries,' said Gawain, longing now to have it done with. He felt his courage ebbing away with every passing moment.

'As you wish,' said the Green Knight. 'Take off your helmet, then. This won't take long.' Gawain removed his helmet, knelt down on the wet grass and bent his head. He closed his eyes and waited, but nothing happened.

'Go on then.' He could speak in no more than a whisper. 'Go on. I won't move.'

The Green Knight whirled his great axe round his head, round and round so that it whistled through the air. In spite of himself, Gawain could not stop himself from flinching.

'What's the matter with you, Gawain?' the Green Knight scoffed, leaning nonchalantly on his axe. 'We aren't frightened, are we? I thought the knights of King Arthur's court were supposed to be so brave, and I heard Sir Gawain was the bravest of all. So, the great Sir Gawain is afraid of a little whistle, is he?'

'Get on with it, damn you,' Gawain cried. 'All right, I winced; but I won't do it again.'

'We shall see,' laughed the Green Knight. Once again he heaved up his axe. This time he held back the blow just a hair's breadth from the skin of Gawain's neck. Gawain felt the wind of it, but never moved a muscle.

'Well done, Gawain,' he said. 'That was just to see how brave you really are. This time though there'll be no holding back. Prepare yourself.'

'Can you do nothing but talk?' Gawain was more angry than frightened now. 'Strike man, strike. Or maybe you're a bit squeamish at the idea of killing a defenceless man, is that it?'

A third time now, the Green Knight swung up his axe. This time, the blade came close enough to nick the skin on Gawain's neck. Gawain felt the pain of it and the warm blood trickling down. He was on his feet in an instant, springing back and drawing his sword.

'That's it!' he cried. 'You've had your chance. One stroke, just one stroke. That was the bargain. Now I can defend myself, and by God I will.'

But strangely, the Green Knight just smiled and threw aside his axe. 'No, Gawain,' he spoke gently now, a different voice, a voice Gawain thought he knew from elsewhere. 'No, we shall not fight, you and I. We are friends. Do you not recognize me?' And as he spoke, the green of him vanished, his form changed, and he became the lord of the castle. Gawain was speechless. 'If I had wanted to, Gawain, I could easily have cut your head off, just as you did to me a year ago.'

'I don't understand any of this,' said Gawain, lowering his sword.

'You will,' said the lord of the castle. 'You will. Twice I held back my axe and drew no blood. That was because you twice kept your promise to me back in the castle, first with the one kiss my wife gave you, and then with the two kisses also. I see you remember it well. But Gawain, the third time, you deceived me. Yes, I had the three kisses she gave you, but she gave you something else as well, didn't she? She gave you a favour to wear, a green belt, a magic belt with power to save your skin, so she said. You never gave it to me. You never said a word about it. And for that I cut you

– though not too deep, I hope. You see, she told me everything. I knew every word that passed between you, every look. If you had once weakened, and dishonoured your knighthood, then I can tell you, your head would be lying there at my feet, your life's blood pouring out on the grass.'

'I feel sick with shame,' said Gawain, taking off the green belt and offering it to him.

'No need, Gawain. The belt was a little thing, a little sin. No one is perfect, but you, my friend, are as close to perfect as I have ever met, or ever shall meet come to that. Keep the belt so that you do not forget us, nor what has happened here – but I'm afraid it's just an ordinary belt, it has no all-powerful magic.'

'After what I did, I do not deserve such kindness,' said Gawain. 'I did you wrong. I broke my word. I dishonoured my knighthood.'

'Nonsense.' The lord of the castle took him warmly by the shoulders. 'You wished only to live. What man faced with death does not wish to live, tell me that? Come, Gawain, I've had my fill of this dank and dismal place. Let's go back to the castle and feast some more. I'm glad it's over. I tell you, I'm sick to death of green. We'll roast the boar.'

'I'm tempted,' said Gawain. 'And as you now know only too well, I've never found temptation easy to resist. But I will resist this time. I'd better be on my way home to Camelot. If I don't get back soon, they'll think I'm dead – as by rights I ought to be. But, before I go, tell me something. How were you able to turn yourself green as you did? How could you ride off with your head under your arm? And how was it that there wasn't a single drop of blood when I cut it off?'

'You deserve to know everything, and you shall,' said the lord of the castle. 'Mine is a strange story, but a true one nonetheless. My name is Sir Bernlak, Knight of the Lake. It was the Lady Nemue, the Lady of the Lake, who sent me to Camelot to test the courage of King Arthur and his knights, to find out if all the good things we had heard were true. I will tell her that there is at least one knight who is as noble as they say, and as brave and gentle too.' The two friends embraced, blessed each other and parted.

Some weeks later, Gawain came home to Camelot. And how we feasted! After he had told us his story, he showed us the scar on his neck; and as final proof, he gave me the green belt interwoven with gold thread. He need not have done so, for, knowing Gawain as we all did, none of us seated at the Round Table ever doubted a word of his story.

# 8 TRISTRAM AND ISEULT

OF ALL THE GUESTS WHO CAME TO CAMELOT, none were ever more welcome than the harpists, who wandered through the land telling their tales. Some were old faces telling old stories, old favourites we knew and loved, but they would tell them differently, each in their own way. There were tales of marsh monsters from the North Lands, of battling giants from Ireland, of the Lord Jesus walking on water and making blind people see, and we would sing to the harp and live the old stories again and again. But more often now, the stories were of the knights of the Round Table, of our own exploits and adventures. Camelot was fast becoming a legend in our own lifetime. It was often through these harpists, these bards, these storytellers – call them what you will – that we would find out what had happened to one of the knights, long ago gone and not heard of since.

Once, I remember, we were told a story of Gareth – he was Gawain's brother. A vivid, dramatic account it was, of Gareth's brave death at the hands of some hideous fire-spitting dragon. Gareth, who was sitting right there beside me, listened quietly until the harpist had finished. Then he stood up and said, 'You had it mostly right, my friend – a little colourful here and a little flamboyant there. I should tell you though, it was the dragon that died, not I. I am Gareth, and I should think I should know.' The hall fell to laughter, and in the end, the poor harpist had to laugh with us. So their stories may sometimes have been just stories; but, like most stories, they always had a seed of truth deep within them. The skill was in the telling, and in the playing, and in the singing. The best you believed, and with a story, belief is everything.

Late one evening, there came into the hall a tall young man with dark, sad eyes. He carried a harp under his arm, so we knew him for what he was. He hesitated at the door.

'Come in, come in,' I said.

'I have a song to sing,' he said, 'and a tale to tell, but I am weak with hunger.'

'Then eat first, and tell your story after,' said Gawain. 'We can wait.' All of us watched him eat, eager for his story, for there was something grave and honest about this young man. You would believe every word he said – he would tell a good story. We did not know then just how good.

'Do you know the story of Tristram and Iseult?' he asked, at last.

'We know of Tristram,' said Lancelot. 'All the world knows of Tristram, a fine knight, even if he is not of King Arthur's court.'

'But you do not know about the fair Iseult?' the harpist said, looking about him. 'Then I shall tell you.'

'For as long as anyone can remember, there have been bitter wars between Ireland and Cornwall. King Marc, whom you all know I am sure, had done all he could to make a peace with the Irish, but they would not have it. They came over the seas and attacked him as they had so often done before. They burnt, they pillaged, they plundered. There was only one man Marc could count on for help – and that was his cousin, King Rivalin. He alone had enough ships and enough men to drive off the Irish. Rivalin himself was no friend of the Irish for his own father had been killed by them. So he needed little enough persuading. The Irish came, and Rivalin and his men were lying in wait for them. They rose out of the heather, surrounded them and cut them down. As a reward for saving Cornwall, King Marc gave his sister to be Rivalin's wife, and the couple were as happy as it is possible to be. A year later, she had a son by him, but she died giving birth. King Rivalin, full of grief, could not even look at his baby son without hating him. He named him Tristram, which means sorrow, and sent him off to be brought up out of his sight.

'Tristram was brought up well-tutored in the arts of kingship, thanks mostly to Gorneval, a young knight who became like an elder brother and friend to the young Tristram. As he grew up, Tristram often wondered about his mother, for all he knew of her was her grave. And he wondered too about his father, whom he was never allowed even to see. He felt orphaned and alone. He longed to see the only other kinsman he knew of, King Marc of Cornwall.

'So he set off with Gorneval for Cornwall and came at last one evening to Tintagel, King Marc's clifftop castle in Cornwall. And there in the great hall Tristram met King Marc for the first time, and they became almost at once so close that they thought of each other thereafter as father and son.

'Tristram and Gorneval and their friends stayed at Tintagel with King Marc for some years, and Marc taught Tristram all he could, all that Gorneval had not yet taught him. No man could outmatch Tristram with sword and spear, no man could wrestle better, and certainly no man knew horses better nor could ride them faster. And, it has to be said, every lady in the court had her eye on the young man. So, for a time, life was good and sweet for Tristram.

'But a shadow hung over the peace of King Marc's granite kingdom. The Irish would not leave them alone. Time and again they had come back across the sea in their warships, and each time King Marc had been helpless to resist without his old ally. Rivalin was still so wrapped up in his grief that he would not leave even his castle, let alone his country. King Marc found himself alone. Forced by the Irish into an unjust treaty, he had to pay vast amounts in gold, in corn and in cattle each year, just to keep them at bay. Now the country was so poor that he could not pay any more. Every year, he had made some new excuse, but the Irish were becoming impatient.

'Tristram was there in the hall one day, when the Irish emissary arrived. He showed none of the proper courtesies to King Marc, but stood before him, hands on his hips, his chin high with arrogance, saying he had had enough of lame excuses. "These," he declared haughtily, "these are the terms my queen generously offers you. Either you repay your debts in full – and if you have no gold as you claim, then you can pay in slaves. My queen demands one child in every two born in Cornwall from this day on. But, you do have another choice. See how generous my queen is? She will allow you to choose a champion to defend your kingdom against our champion. If our champion loses – and he will not – then your debt is paid in full. If your champion loses – and he will – then Cornwall becomes just a little piece of Ireland until the end of time. So there you are. Pay in slaves or choose a champion. Take it or leave it. Leave it, and an army will come against you and raze Cornwall to the ground, leaving nothing but black rocks and burning corpses. Well?"

'"Who is your champion?" King Marc asked after a while.

'"I am," said the emissary. "My name is Marhault. I am the son of the Queen of Ireland." Every knight in the hall blanched, for all of them knew that before them stood the most cruel and savage knight on earth.

'King Marc sighed. "Murder or slavery – murder by fire, murder by your own sword or slavery for our people. Some choice you give me. You know I have no army to speak of, and no champion strong enough to stand against you. So you shall have your slaves. Better than half my people live in slavery than that all of us should die."

'At this, Tristram sprang to his feet. "Never," he cried. "I will fight him. I will be your champion." But it was only when Tristram stood before Marhault that he realized what he had taken on. The man was a Goliath, built like a tree trunk, forearms as thick as thighs.

'"And who is this little Cornish fighting cock?" laughed Marhault.

'"I am Tristram; and I shall be the death of you, Irishman." Tristram's voice trembled in spite of himself.

'King Marc did all he could to dissuade the boy – and boy is all that Tristram was. But Tristram had gone too far now to back down.

'"I shall meet you, one week from now," said Marhault, "on Mount St Michael, in the sea off Marazion. Come at dawn, and come alone. By that time, all the Irish warships will be there. When I have cut you into little pieces and fed you to the fish, they will sail in and take Cornwall for the Irish."

'"God will decide between us," said Tristram quietly.

\*     \*     \*

'And so they met at dawn on Mount St Michael, Marhault landing from the Irish fleet, anchored in the bay, and Tristram walking out alone across the tide-ribbed sand, leaving King Marc and the Cornish knights behind on the shore, where they climbed to the top of the dunes to watch the battle.

'Tristram knew from the moment the first blow was struck that he had only one chance, to keep moving, to tire the Irish champion out. He dodged, he ducked, he weaved, he backed away, and always Marhault came after him, his great axe swinging.

'"Stand and fight, coward," roared Marhault.

'"I will, when I am ready," said Tristram, and he skipped away over the rocks. When Marhault did get in close enough, his blows rained down on Tristram's shield, but never pierced it. Throwing aside his war axe, Marhault took up his great sword in both hands. As he did so, Tristram slipped on a patch of slimy seaweed and fell. Marhault saw his chance and thrust under Tristram's shield, piercing his thigh and pinning him to the rock. With a yell of pain that sent the gulls screaming into the air all over the island, Tristram felt the sword blade twist in him and withdraw. He saw his own blood soaking into the sand beside him. Now he threw caution to the wind and went after Marhault like a man demented, yet he knew what he did. He went for the head straight away, for the deathblow. There was a new and terrible strength in him, born of such pain and such anger that his blade cut clean through Marhault's helmet and into the skull bone beneath. It went in so deep that he could scarcely pull it out, so deep that a piece of the swordblade was left embedded in Marhault's head. Marhault dropped his sword and staggered back, clutching his head in agony. Then he turned away and ran. When the Irish saw what had happened, they came across from their warships, helped Marhault into a boat and rowed him away.

'Meanwhile, the Cornish knights came running across from the shore, and found Tristram lying half in the water, bleeding out his life-blood into the sea. They staunched his gaping wound as best they could and brought him back to Tintagel. King Marc sent for the best doctors he could find, and though for weeks Tristram hovered between life and death, at last the wound began to heal.

'Marhault was still alive when he reached Dublin, but only just. There, the queen's daughter, the Princess Iseult, did all she could for her brother; but in spite of all her herbs and potions and healing powers, he faded and died. Weeping bitter tears, she took out the splinter from his head and kept it safe in a silver casket. When they buried Marhault that evening, Iseult swore over his grave that, if she ever found the sword with a piece missing that matched the splinter she had taken from Marhault's head, then she would avenge herself on her brother's killer.

'Meanwhile, at Tintagel, the king held a gathering of all his knights, Tristram by his side. "I have thought long and hard about this," he said. "We cannot always be fighting wars with the Irish, else this quarrel will go on for ever. This time, we were lucky, we had Tristram to save us. But they will be back. They always come back, and the next time their hearts will be full of hatred. There is only one way I can think of to end this feud. We must hold out the hand of friendship – that is what the Lord Jesus Christ would want us to do. 'Love your enemies,' he said. So that is what I shall do. I shall ask to marry the Queen of Ireland's daughter, Princess Iseult. That way, our two kingdoms may at last live in peace, the one with the other. I have asked my dear kinsman, Tristram, to sail for Ireland as soon as he can and bring her home to be Queen of Cornwall, and he has agreed."

'A ship was at once made ready; and Tristram, Gorneval and their friends armed themselves to the teeth, for they knew well enough that no Cornishman would be welcomed on the soil of Ireland. They might have to fight their way back to the ship. So they went prepared for the worst, prepared for anything, every one of them knowing that the Queen of Ireland might have them put to death on sight, before Tristram could even explain why he had come. Within a week, the ship sailed out from Tintagel, west into the setting sun. There were many who watched them go who thought they would never be seen again.

'They were halfway across the Irish Sea when a great storm blew up. Night after day, day after night, the storm lashed and battered them; but the ship, although leaking badly, somehow held together. Sails torn, masts down, they at last sighted land. Huge seas hurled the ship up on to the rocks, and somehow every one of them managed to climb out alive. But the Irish villagers had seen them and came running along the beach towards them. Maybe it was to find out who they were, or maybe it was to slit their throats – Tristram and his friends could not be sure which. They drew their swords and made ready to defend themselves. But as they did so, the villagers began to point into the sky behind them. A pall of dark smoke was rolling down towards them over the cliffs, like a hellish black fog.

'"What is it?" Tristram asked.

'"The dragon-man," one of them cried, and they all began to back away. "The dragon-man. Run, run for your lives. He burns everything in his path. No one can stand against him, no one."

'"What is he?" said Tristram.

'"He's half-giant, half-dragon," said another. "A giant with a dragon's head, with eyes that burn you just by looking at you, with foul and fiery breath that will poison you. He has the heart of the very devil himself. Kill him, and you have the queen's daughter, Iseult, for a bride – the queen herself has promised it. Many have tried, but every one of them has perished in the dragon-man's fire." And they ran away down the beach and hid themselves amongst the rocks.

'Tristram turned to Gorneval. "Maybe chance has been good to us," he said. "I will fight this dragon-man."

'Gorneval tried to hold him back but Tristram broke free.

'"No, I shall do it. I shall kill the dragon-man, and so prove to the Queen of Ireland that we have come in peace. After I have saved them from the dragon-man, they will not be able to hate us, even if we are Cornish."

'Gorneval and his friends wanted to go with him, but he would not let them. He left them, and went off on his own, covering his face against the acrid smoke.

'Everywhere about him there was terrible destruction, great swathes of black through the yellow gorse, the dismembered remains of men and cattle littered about and stinking. Tristram walked on a little further, cautiously now; and then he saw a loose horse galloping towards him, with other riders following on behind. He caught at the reins of the horse and held on, but by the time he had the horse under control, the riders had passed him by, their eyes wide with terror. Tristram spoke softly, soothingly into the horse's ear and calmed him. Then he mounted and rode on, until he came up on to a rocky outcrop. From there, he looked down across a ravaged valley and saw the dragon-man sitting with his back against a tall tower, tearing a man limb from limb and eating him. Tristram knew that to stand looking any longer at this terrible sight would only sap his courage and with it his strength too. So, at once, he set his spear under his arm and rode at full tilt down towards him. But as he came closer, the dragon-man seemed to grow ever bigger and bigger. When he stood up, he was half the height of the tower itself. He laughed and cast aside the arm he was gnawing at. Tristram put up his shield and shouted his battle cry. Five times his size, the dragon-man simply reached out and wrenched Tristram's spear from his grasp. He would

have knocked Tristram from his horse too, but Tristram clung on with his knees and galloped on past him. He rode round the tower, looking for the door; but there was no door, only a window and that was high above his head. He jumped on to his horse's back, reached up, grabbed the window-ledge and hauled himself up through the window, and into the tower. Once inside, he ran up the winding stairway and came to a second window, which was just the right height for what he had in mind. He put his head out of the window. The dragon-man saw him and came for him, as Tristram had hoped he might. The head and the neck were close enough now. With all his force, Tristram thrust his sword out of the window and deep into the dragon-man's throat. For a moment, the dragon-man looked at Tristram in disbelief. In his death rattle, he belched out his last poison and the poison filled the tower, sending Tristram reeling down the stairs. He found his horse still waiting below the window, and let himself down on to his back, gasping all the time for clean air.

'There lay the dragon-man, eyes and mouth wide open in death. Tristram, his head swimming, dismounted, pulled his sword from the dragon-man's throat and cut out his forked tongue, so he could prove what he had done. With the poison spreading rapidly through his body, with his last strength ebbing fast, Tristram climbed up again on to his horse and the horse wandered off to graze, Tristram senseless now in the saddle.

'It wasn't long afterwards that the queen's steward – one of the riders Tristram had seen earlier – ventured back and there he found the dragon-man dead under the tower. For years, this steward had loved the Princess Iseult, and for years she had rejected him. Now at last he saw his opportunity, and he took it. He drew his sword and hacked and hacked until the dragon-man's head fell off. Now he had the evidence needed to show that it was he who had killed the dragon-man, and no one else. He strapped the severed head over his horse's withers and then galloped as fast as he could for the queen's castle in Dublin. There he was greeted as the saviour of all Ireland, although some found it difficult to believe, because they knew the man to be a liar and a cheat. But the evidence was before their eyes, and they could not argue with it. He had the head of the dragon-man. The dragon-man must therefore be dead, and the steward must have killed him. He came before the queen, threw the dragon-man's head down at her feet and claimed Iseult as his reward.

'Watching all this from a gallery above, Iseult ran to

her room and locked her door. When her nurse came to bring her down into the hall for her betrothal to the steward, she said she was sick, for she had always loathed and detested him; and besides, she just could not believe that he had had the courage to kill the dragon-man. Something was wrong – she was sure of it – and she needed to play for time so that she could find out what it was.

'That night, with her nurse, she stole away into the hills to discover what she could. Just before dawn, they came across a solitary horse browsing in amongst the gorse, and a man slumped in the saddle as if he was asleep. When they came closer, they saw his face was blackened and his hair singed.

'Half in his dreams, Tristram lifted his head. "I killed the dragon-man." He could barely speak. "Look." He reached inside his tunic and pulled out the dragon-man's forked tongue.

'So, with Iseult walking beside him, steadying him on his horse, they made their way back to the castle as the first grey light of day came over the hills. They took him in secret to Iseult's room, where they bathed him; and then Iseult gave him a healing potion of camomile and rosemary to draw the poison from his blood. When he was a little stronger, she brought in her mother, the queen, to see him.

'Tristram was sitting up in bed by now and feeling better with every moment.

'"Who are you?" asked the queen. Tristram was too tired to lie. Besides, he thought it would be safe enough now to tell her the truth, or most of it anyway. So he told them how King Marc of Cornwall had sent him to ask the Princess Iseult to be his queen, so that Ireland and Cornwall would be at peace for ever, as the Lord Jesus Christ would wish it to be; how his ship had been wrecked, and how he had fought and killed the dragon-man. All Tristram hid from them was his name.

'The queen smiled knowingly. "I thought all along it could not be the steward that killed the dragon-man," she said. "You shall have your peace, Cornishman. And we Irish will have our peace too. King Marc shall have Iseult for a wife too, but only if Iseult wants it."

'"I do," said Iseult. "I don't know King Marc; but if it means peace, then I will marry him."

'The queen left them and went down into the great hall where the steward was still waiting to be betrothed to Iseult, boasting all the time his courage and telling and re-telling the tale of his make-believe battle with the dragon-man. The queen listened for some time and then sent for Tristram who came down into the hall, with Iseult by his side.

'"Steward, you are a liar and a cheat," said the queen. "You see this man? He is the one who killed the dragon-man, not you."

'The steward tried to laugh it off. He pointed at the dragon-man's head, now hanging on the wall above the fireplace. "And that?" he cried. "Where do you suppose I got that? It was I who killed the dragon-man, I tell you. I and I alone."

'"Very well," said the queen. "Why don't you take a look into the dragon-man's mouth. Go on, open it, it won't bite." And when the steward reached up and opened it, he saw the tongue was missing. At that moment, Tristram held up the forked tongue for all to see.

'"The dragon-man's tongue," said Tristram quietly. "I cut it out, after I had killed him."

'At that, the steward went up to Tristram and slapped him across the face, calling him a liar and a coward, and challenging him there and then. Tristram accepted willingly. The day for the trial of strength was set by the queen – it would be in three days' time, she said, so that Tristram had time to recover from the dragon-man's poison.

'Tristram rested long in bed each morning and did all he could to regain his strength; but the Princess

Iseult was worried for him, for she knew he was still not strong enough to fight. One afternoon, while Tristram was out riding, she happened to notice his armour lying battered and rusty in the corner of the room. She began to clean it for him. Then she saw his sword belt, all chafed and charred. Only the sword itself looked fit to use. She drew it out of the scabbard to make sure, and found the blade was chipped. Her heart sank, for she realized at once what this might mean. She rushed to the silver casket where she still kept the fragment she had taken from her brother's head after he had died. As she feared, the piece fitted perfectly. She was sad, she was angry, she was confused. She went to the queen at once. When Tristram came back from his riding that evening, they were waiting for him in his room.

'"Who are you?" the queen demanded. "And this time be honest with us or you will never see Cornwall again. Are you the one who killed my son? Are you the one they call Tristram? Is this your sword?"

'Iseult held up the jagged chip. "I took this from my brother's skull," she said. "It fits your sword." Tristram saw then that there was no point in denying it.

'"I am Tristram," he said.

'Iseult, her heart full of vengeance, demanded he be put to death at once. But the queen shook her head. "What?" she said. "So you can marry the steward, so that that man becomes King of Ireland? Is that what you want? No, I think not. If Tristram can beat him, weakened as he is, then you can marry King Marc and we will still have our peace. It's the better way. And besides, we know the fight between Marhault and Tristram was a fair fight. Everyone who saw it said as much."

'"But he was my brother," cried Iseult. "He was your son." She threw down the sword and ran from the room.

'Tristram went after her and found her crying in the garden. He said nothing for some time, but sat silent beside her. "Just tell me what I must do, Iseult," said Tristram. "Shall I win and bring you back to King Marc? Or shall I lose and die and leave you for the steward? Tell me." She looked at him, suddenly tender.

'"Win," she whispered.

'The battle was held on the bank of the River Liffey and watched by thousands. Gorneval and all Tristram's friends from Cornwall were there too, and all of them knew that if Tristram were to lose, it would be the death of them too. The steward, filled with wine to give him courage, came flailing at Tristram, who stepped aside deftly time and again until the steward stood, legs apart, panting like a dog and knowing his death was coming. Tristram waited until he charged again and cut him down as he passed, so that the steward's head was struck clean from his body, rolled down into the Liffey and sank, the last of his breath bubbling to the surface.

'So Tristram won the Princess Iseult for King Marc and set sail for Cornwall in a ship given by the queen and crewed by Gorneval and his friends. The princess stayed long on the deck that evening gazing at the coastline, until she could no longer tell which were clouds and which was the coast of Ireland. Tristram watched her from a distance. She went down to her cabin with her old nurse and Tristram did not follow her. He sensed the sadness in her heart at leaving home, and also the grudge and hate she still held against him for the death of her brother. For the first few days at sea, he came nowhere near her. He longed to make his peace with her, to console her. Whenever she caught sight of him on deck, she would always look away at once; and when he did try to speak to her, she would not even answer him. Day by day, she was becoming colder and colder towards him.

'At last Tristram turned to Gorneval. "What is the matter with her?" he asked. "I saved her country from the dragon-man, didn't I? I saved her from marrying the steward, didn't I? And still she hates me."

'"There's none so blind as them that won't see," said Gorneval. "Even if you don't know it, everyone else on the ship does. She loves you, you fool."

'"But she can't," Tristram replied. "She's marrying the king. She can't love me, she mustn't."

'"That is why she won't look at you," said Gorneval. "That is why she won't speak to you. Now do you understand?" And, as he spoke, Tristram's heart slowly stirred. He thought of Iseult's sweet face and he knew then that he loved her too, and every time he saw her now, he knew it again. Still she shunned him, but now he knew why. She would not tempt him, for to tempt him would be to ruin him for ever.

'The last night at sea, Tristram could not sleep for thinking of her. For hours he paced the deck feverishly until he found himself leaning over the stern of the ship, looking down into the ever-widening wake. He felt someone coming, looked up and saw it was Iseult. She had not yet seen him. He stayed still, hoping she would not. She walked purposefully to the side of the ship, and stood there for a moment looking out to sea. Then she took a deep breath and began to climb over. When Tristram realized what she was doing, he ran across to her and held her back so that she could not jump.

'"Let me go!" she cried. "It's the only way. Can't you see? It's the only way." She struggled against him; but he held her fast, and carried her below, weeping in his arms. They said nothing, for each knew how the other felt. Each would have their one night of love, and each knew that was all the time they would ever have together. They thought no one could ever know of it, not the old nurse and not Gorneval. But they forgot the sailor on watch who had seen them go below. Before morning came, they vowed they would never speak of it again, never love each other again. To make and keep the peace they both wanted, Iseult would become King Marc's queen, and Tristram would stay loyal and true to his kinsman, the king. That is what they faithfully promised each other.

'The next day the ship docked at Tintagel. King Marc was there to greet his lovely bride. Tristram rode behind them up to the castle, the gorse on fire in the sun all around him, but for both Iseult and Tristram the world was grey and sad. Tristram made his excuses, and was not there for the wedding; and much to everyone's surprise, he was not there during the celebrations that followed either. For some time after this, he often seemed to be away on some adventure or other; and when he was home, it began to be noticed that if ever he rode out from the castle, the young Queen Iseult seemed to disappear as well, and was nowhere to be found. There were rumours, there were whisperings, and there was sailors' talk of a night of love on the ship that had brought them back from Ireland.

'No man is without enemies, even a man who has saved his country. Tristram's enemies, jealous and bitter against him, began to talk and the whispering became louder and louder until King Marc heard them. He thought at first it could not be true, that Tristram and Iseult would never do such a thing. But doubt and suspicion began to fester inside him until the very thought of them together grew in his head like a tumour. He had to find out one way or another whether it was true. So, one day, King Marc followed Iseult out of the castle, at a safe distance. She rode for a while into the countryside. Then, leaving her horse at the top of a rutty track, she beat her way through the head-high bracken, stopping every now and then to look around her. King Marc, treading softly, followed at a distance and came upon Tristram and Iseult lying together in the bracken. In an agony of jealous rage he leapt out and drew his sword. He would have killed Tristram on the spot, but

Iseult stood between them and he could not strike her down.

'"Only spare him," she cried. "And I promise never to see him again, I promise." And she pleaded on her knees for Tristram's life.

'Marc still loved her. He could deny her nothing. He lowered his sword and turned to Tristram. "Until now, Tristram, you have been like a son to me," he said. "For that, and for what you have done for Cornwall, I will spare your life. But from this moment on, I never wish to set eyes on you again. You are banished from my sight and from all my lands. If I see you again in Cornwall, I will have you hunted down like a dog, and torn limb from limb. If I capture you alive, I will have you burnt at the stake." And he took Iseult by the hand and dragged her away.

'That was the last Tristram ever saw of Iseult.'

The harpist put down his harp, and I passed him a drink to wet his throat. 'You tell a sad story,' I said to him, 'and you tell it well, so well I might almost think you yourself were there.'

The young man smiled at me ruefully. 'You have guessed it, my Lord Arthur,' he said. 'I am Tristram. I have been wandering like a lost soul these ten years or more; and everywhere I have been, I hear of Camelot, of Arthur, High King of Britain, who seeks to bring peace and new hope to this land. I have come to help, to join you, if you will let me.'

So Tristram stayed and became a knight of the Round Table. But he was different from the rest of us, for he was never one for feasting or jousting. He was a thinker and a philosopher. He kept himself to himself, and whenever he rode out on adventures – and he was often gone – he rode alone.

Whenever I think of Tristram, I think of horses. He had a way with horses like no other man I've ever met. Just by breathing into the nostrils of a wild, unbroken stallion, he could calm him and gentle him. He would talk secretly into their ears and they would listen and obey. No man in the world ever sat a horse better than Tristram. There was never any wrenching of reins and he wore no spurs – he had no need to. It was just horse and man in perfect harmony, a wonder to watch. But like so many of my knights, he went away on a quest and never came back.

It was from his good friend, Gorneval, that we learnt what had happened to him. It seems that on one of his adventures Tristram found himself a wife – another Iseult, strangely enough. She was the daughter of Javolin, of Arundel. He tried to love her all he could and to forget the first Iseult, his great love; but he could not and soon enough his wife knew it. A terrible jealousy began to gnaw at her and would not leave her alone.

Tristram was out riding one day with Gorneval, when a hare darted out across his path. All Tristram's skill as a horseman could not save him. The horse took fright and went over, rolling on Tristram and crushing his legs beneath him. Gorneval brought him back home to his wife, who nursed him as well as she could; but the bones would not heal as they should, and there was a bleeding inside him that would not stop. Tristram called Gorneval to him.

'I am dying,' he whispered. 'I know it, just as you will know it too, when your turn comes. I have only one wish. I want to see my sweet Iseult, just once more. Go now, go back to Tintagel and bring her to me, if she will come.'

Gorneval turned to go at once for he knew time was short, but Tristram called him back. 'One last thing. I will be here, watching for your ship from this window. If she is with you, then have white sails set; but if not, then let them be black. That way, I will know at once either the best or the worst.'

So Gorneval left him and went away to Cornwall, where he found Iseult and told her that Tristram was dying. She came away with him secretly, not telling King Marc; and bringing with her all the herbs and potions she might need to save Tristram's life, if she could only come in time. But on the voyage home, the ship was becalmed for weeks. Waiting in his castle, Tristram began to fret. Too weak now to go himself to the window, he asked his wife almost every hour whether she could see a ship coming into the bay. And of course she guessed – as any woman might – that it was more than a ship that he was waiting for. She asked Gorneval's servant. She loosened his tongue with gold and jewels, and he told her that Tristram had sent for Iseult from Cornwall. Now she knew for sure.

One morning, with the swifts screeching around the castle outside his window, Tristram asked her yet again. 'Gorneval's ship? Can you see it yet? Can you see it?'

His wife looked, and this time she did see Gorneval's ship. 'Yes,' she replied.

'And are the sails white?' Tristram asked, his face already drawn in death, 'or are they black? Only tell me they are white and I will die a happy man.'

She looked down at him and smiled with thin lips.

'They are black,' she said. 'Black as charcoal.'

At that Tristram turned his face to the wall and stopped breathing. When she saw what she had done, she tried to shake him alive.

'White!' she cried. 'They are white. She has come. Your love has come to you.' But it was too late.

When Iseult landed, Gorneval brought her at once to Tristram's room, and there she saw that Tristram was already dead. She knelt and kissed him on the forehead; and as she did so, her heart cracked within her and she died, breathing her last on his cheek.

Meanwhile, King Marc had discovered where his wife had gone and had come after her. He found Iseult and Tristram laid out on a bier together in the chapel, watched over by the faithful Gorneval. King Marc took their bodies back with him to Cornwall, and Gorneval went with them. There, they were buried in full honour, side by side in the chapel at Tintagel. Every day for the rest of his life, King Marc prayed at their graveside, and asked forgiveness. He told Gorneval once that he was never sure which of the two he loved most. Gorneval went to see the grave one last time before he left for Camelot. He said that a hazel tree had sprouted at the spot where Tristram lay and a honeysuckle had sprung up beside Iseult, and they were almost touching each other above the two graves.

# 9 PERCIVALE AND THE BEGINNING
# OF THE END

PERCIVALE CAME LATE TO CAMELOT. BOTH
Galahad and Mordred were young men by now, and
neither had lost the habits of their youth. Mordred
would forever be taunting Galahad because he did not
often go riding out on quests as the other knights did.
Instead, Galahad would spend much of his time with
the monks in the chapel, talking with them, studying
with them, and praying with them. It was the monks
who made for him a great white shield with a red
cross emblazoned on it. Galahad would never explain
himself to Mordred, nor to anyone else, except to say
that he was waiting for his one great quest and
preparing for it as he waited. Mordred knew,

however, not to go too far with Galahad, for he understood, as did every other knight at Camelot, that Galahad was now the strongest of us all. He had taken Lancelot's place in the tournaments, as the great champion everyone wanted to beat, but could not. I fought him just once, and once was enough. It was a brief encounter and painful even now for me to think of. I excused my defeat as best I could, by telling myself and Guinevere that I was getting too old for this sort of thing. Trained in combat by his own father, Lancelot, and now stronger even than he, he was the joy of his father's life, the pride of his eye.

Mordred too had become a fine warrior, but try as I did – and I did try – I could never bring myself to like him. Just to look on him would often make me shudder with shame, and not only because of my guilty secret, but because I had to acknowledge that this excuse of a man was indeed my own flesh and blood. Had he not been my son I would have long since banished him from Camelot altogether, for he had none of the knightly virtues. As a child he had always been mean and vindictive, the kind of boy that pulls wings off butterflies while they are still alive. Now he had become so cruel and so merciless that even Guinevere, who had doted on him so much as a child, could hardly find a good word to say about him.

In spite of all her motherly love and attention, of Lancelot's warnings and reprimands, in spite of all my urging and pleading, Mordred was turning into a monster in front of our eyes, and there was little we could do to stop it. All Camelot was happier when he was away on some adventure; but he would always return, boastful and as proud as ever, with his erstwhile opponent slung over his saddle. I was not the only one who noticed that Mordred never took prisoners, and that his victims were often very old or very young.

Yet, in spite of Mordred, these were the best years, the great years of Camelot. There were still a few Saxon incursions on the south coast or Irish invasions from the west, but our spies always warned us they were coming and we would be waiting for them in enough numbers to drive them back into the sea. Our island kingdom was now secure on all sides. And we had rid ourselves too of most of the rebellious warlords and petty tyrants in the land. In Britain now there was one God, one king and one law for everyone. Everywhere I rode, I saw about me contented people with a good fire always burning in their hearths, with shelter from the cold of winter and with enough food to sustain them. They cared for their young and their sick. They looked after their old.

The light of hope shone from their eyes. The Kingdom of Logres had been established in Britain as Merlin had hoped it would be. We had achieved God's promised land – or so we thought.

Into this still-happy Camelot came the young Percivale. I was a part of his story, but only a part – the rest he told me himself, about how he first came to Camelot and about the quest for the Holy Grail that should have been its crowning glory.

Percivale was the son of King Pelinore – you may remember that I once fought with him, and that afterwards he became my trusted friend and a true knight of the Round Table. He fought alongside me in those early days when my kingdom was threatened from all sides. It was he who had gone out after King Lot of Orkney, a rebel and a traitor. Pelinore ambushed him and killed him. Some of the very best knights of the Round Table were changed men, converts who had seen the error of their ways and afterwards fought the good fight with a fierce and fiery passion. Such a one was Pelinore. He was later killed in a private quarrel with Agravaine, the son of King Lot, who had come over to our cause and had himself become a knight of the Round Table, though never one I liked as it turned out, and with good reason. Foul play was suspected at the time, but nothing could ever be proved. Agravaine always claimed he killed him in a fair fight, but I never believed him. Pelinore's widow, overcome with grief, never wanted to see armour or sword again. Guinevere did all she could to comfort her, but one night she left Camelot with her baby son, Percivale, and we never saw her again.

She found a place far away from the world of men and built a hut deep in a great forest beside a river, brimming with brown trout. She had all she needed – food, water and quiet. There in the forest Percivale grew up. In all that time, he never met or talked to anyone except his mother. Dressed only in wolf skins, he became a creature of the forest, gathering berries and mushrooms and fruit. With a sharpened stick for a spear, he taught himself to hunt the boar, and the stag and the wolf.

One day, he was tracking a wolf through the forest when he trod on something sharp and cold, and altogether harder than wood. Crouching down, he discovered a spear amongst the leaves. The shaft was rotten and crumbled at his first touch; but the spearhead, although rusty, still had its edge. From the shape of it he knew at once what he could use it for. This was the first iron he had ever seen in his life. He ground away most of the rust with a stone, and what he could not grind off he burnt off in the fire. Then he burnished it and burnished it, until it shone so brightly in the sun that he could see his face in it. Marvelling at that, he ran home and showed it to his mother, who sighed as she shook her head and turned away. She had kept him from such things for so long. Percivale left her and went to the same ashgrove from which he always cut his spears, and he cut himself out the very best he could find for his new shining spearhead. He soon found that it balanced perfectly in his hand, that it flew straight through the air and that it could pierce a wild boar's hide at fifty paces. Every evening he sharpened it by the fire and his poor mother looked on, sorrowful; for she knew only too well what such weapons were used for in the world beyond the forest. Percivale did not even know there was a world beyond the forest.

As the years passed, Percivale strayed further and further from his mother's hut, exploring ever deeper in to the forest, though she had warned him often against it. One day, he had gone as far as he had ever gone from home and he was crouching in the forest, readying his spear for a browsing stag now within easy range. He whipped his arm over and sent the spear quivering through the air. But at that same moment, the stag lifted his head in alarm and leapt away into the trees and vanished. The spear fell to the ground and Percivale went after it. He was angry at himself. For half a day he had been stalking the stag. He was still trying to understand what had so alarmed his quarry, when he heard someone coming. He looked up. Three horses were coming through the trees towards him. Their riders were all in shining armour and helmets, great swords hanging at their sides and they carried shields of dazzling colours. Percivale had never in his life set eyes on such wonders. He stood gaping at them. He thought he might have dreamed about such people; yet here they were in the flesh, and now they were speaking to him.

'You stare at us as if we were ghosts,' said one of them.

'What are you?' Percivale whispered, backing away, his spear in his hands, ready to defend himself. They laughed at that.

'We won't harm you,' said the same knight. 'My name is Lancelot, and these are my brothers, Hector and Lionel. We are knights from the court of King Arthur, High King of Britain, your king and mine. We are on our way back to Camelot for the feast of Pentecost. Now, fair's fair, I've told you who we are. Tell us who you are and where you are from.' So Percivale told them and they could scarcely believe him.

'So we are the first people you have ever seen?' asked Lancelot.

'Besides my mother, yes,' Percivale answered.

'Well,' Lancelot went on. 'Beyond this forest, there is a whole kingdom surrounded by the sea. Thanks to our king, we are an island at peace now and a happy people.'

'Is it like heaven?' Percivale asked, lowering his spear. 'Mother has told me of God and of heaven and of the angels. I thought maybe you were angels.'

'No,' laughed Lancelot. 'It's not heaven, and we're no angels, I can assure you of that. But why don't you come out of your forest and see for yourself? Camelot is due west of here. Walk always towards the setting sun, and in a month or so, you will find us. If you get lost, just ask and they will tell you where Camelot is. When you come, and from the look of you I think maybe you will, ask for King Arthur or for me. You may be young, but you throw a spear as well as anyone I have ever seen. Such men as you are always welcome at King Arthur's court.'

Lancelot set his spurs to his horse and raised his hand in farewell. The horses began to walk away.

'I will come,' said Percivale. 'Thank you, thank you.'

'Think nothing of it,' Lancelot replied, 'I owed you

a favour. It was my horse tossing his silly head that frightened off your stag. You would have killed him else. You hunt well. I did not see you, nor did any of us, until we saw the spear fall.' And then they were gone again into the trees, saddles squeaking, harnesses jingling.

Percivale was tempted to follow them there and then to Camelot, but he remembered his mother and knew he could not leave without telling her. He ran all the way home with the long, springing lope of a born hunter. He found her cleaning a fish outside the hut, the ashes ready for cooking.

He waited until they had eaten before he told her what had happened in the forest. 'It's as if they came from another world, Mother,' he said excitedly. 'But they don't. They come from King Arthur's court at Camelot, and they want me to join them. They said I could. I'm going to be a knight at King Arthur's court, Mother. I will make you proud of me, you'll see.'

At this, his mother cried out and her face paled. 'No, you cannot!' she said. 'You must not. I know every son must go – every mother knows that. But not to Camelot, I beg you, not to Camelot.'

'Why not, Mother?' Percivale asked.

So she told him then what she had always promised herself she would never tell him, how his father had been King Pelinore, a great knight of the Round Table, and how Agravaine had deliberately tricked him into a quarrel and then killed him to avenge his own father's death. 'That is why I have kept you from the world outside,' she cried, 'to protect you. I did not want to lose you, too. You may be a king's son, but I have brought you up here in the ways of peace. And now you will go and learn the ways of war like your father did, and I shall lose you too.'

'You will not lose me, Mother,' said Percivale tenderly, though his heart was full of a sudden anger. 'But now more than ever, I am determined to go. I shall go to King Arthur's court and avenge my father's death.'

'No!' cried his mother. 'It is for the Lord God to avenge, not us. Have I not told you what Jesus said? We must love our enemies, not hate them. You may go to Camelot with my blessing, Percivale, only if you promise me faithfully never even to try to avenge your father. He would not have wanted it. What is done is done. You must promise me.'

And Percivale bowed his head and promised; but even as he made his promise, he was thinking of breaking it. He would go to Camelot, train himself as a great warrior, and become a knight. Then, when the time was right, he would seek out Agravaine and have his revenge.

The next morning, as the first birds sang in the trees and the sky was grey with dawn, his mother blessed him and kissed him. He promised he would come for her as soon as he could, and left without turning back. He went west, away from the rising sun. He went barefoot as he always did, and dressed only in wolf skins. For days, for weeks, he ran. Percivale could run all day without ever breathing hard. At last he came out of the forest and saw below him a great marsh that stretched as far as the eye could see. In the middle of it stood a hill with a great castle built around it, and over the castle arched a triple rainbow, the first Percivale had ever seen.

'Camelot,' he said. 'It must be Camelot.'

He found the causeway over the marsh and loped along it, spear in hand. Heads turned as he ran through the narrow streets and up towards the castle. When they laughed at him, he just laughed back and waved. When he reached the castle gate, he asked to see Lancelot or King Arthur. 'I don't mind which,' he said. 'I want to be a knight of the Round Table.' So, hiding their laughter as well as they could, the guards brought him to the great hall to see me. Bercelet went up to sniff at him.

The first time I saw Percivale, I remember thinking; is this a boy or a man? He has the body of a strong and powerful man, yet he has the face of a little child, wondering at everything and everyone around him. He was gawping, his eyes big with innocence. Kay was the first to speak to him.

'Will you look what Bercelet's brought in,' he sniggered, and then waved Percivale away. 'Go on, off with you. You stink like a polecat.'

Percivale ignored him. Bercelet came and sat down beside me, and I beckoned Percivale closer. He was still looking all about him.

'I am Percivale, and I am looking for King Arthur,' he said, 'or Lancelot – he's a friend of mine.'

Kay had not finished with his mockery. He took Percivale by the shoulder and wheeled him round to face him. 'I am the king,' he said. 'I am King Arthur. Address yourself to me, but kneel before you do so.'

Percivale looked at him for a moment, and then he said, 'No, you're not. You have the face of a weasel and the eyes of a pig. You cackle like a jay, you crow like a cockerel. A cockerel may be the king of a dungheap, but you are not King Arthur, High King of Britain.'

Everyone roared with laughter at that and banged the table. Kay lifted his hand to strike him, and he would have too, had Lancelot not held back his arm.

'Enough of your nonsense, Kay,' said Lancelot, and

Percivale turned and recognized him at once. He fell on his knee. Lancelot helped him up. 'No,' he said, turning Percivale towards me. 'You don't kneel to me. You kneel to your king. This is King Arthur, High King of Britain.' Percivale knelt before me.

'Why have you come, Percivale?' I asked.

'I want to be your knight, if you'll let me,' he replied quietly, 'as Lancelot is. He said I throw a spear well. He said I could come.'

Kay scoffed again, his mocking haw-haw laughter ringing through the hall. The echo of it had scarcely died away when it came back again, an echo of an echo; but this time it came from the door, and it was different, louder and more strident. We looked. In the doorway stood a huge knight, his armour the colour of flaming fire, his beard a burning gold. Hands on his hips, his eyes raked the hall as he laughed.

'So this is the great court of King Arthur is it? You're nothing but a bunch of lily-livered, wine-swilling drunkards.' At that he strode forward, snatched up the goblet I held in my hand and emptied it down his throat. 'I'll keep this, if you don't mind,' he taunted. 'And I don't much mind if you do mind.' He turned on his heel and walked out, leaving his mocking laughter echoing behind him through the hall.

At once every knight was on his feet and champing

to go after him. Bercelet rose with a growl, his hackles up, his lip curled, but I held him back. 'No, Bercelet,' I said. 'I cannot send a dog when there are a hundred and fifty knights baying to bring back the goblet.'

'Let me go, please,' said Percivale, his face so eager. 'I will go and bring back the goblet for you, and may be then you will knight me and I can become one of your knights.'

'You will need armour,' I said, 'and a sword.'

Percivale shook his head. 'I need only this,' he said, holding up his spear.

'A horse,' said Lancelot. 'You must have my horse.'

'Thank you, Lancelot,' Percivale answered, 'but I have my legs. Perhaps they will not go as fast as a horse, but they will keep going longer.'

'Well, at least have some food before you go,' I insisted.

'I eat as I go,' he replied, and he patted the pouch at his waist. 'Blueberries and sloes. I have all I need. I'll be back, my king, and with your goblet too, you'll see.' And he bowed low and ran out, leaving us all speechless.

I lay awake that night, the moonlight filling my room, wondering if I had done the right thing in allowing Percivale to go after the Golden Knight. The more I thought about it, the more I knew I had given in to him too quickly, too easily altogether. He was only a boy. I should have sent someone else. I should have gone myself. I had to go after him before he came to any harm, before it was too late. I got up, dressed in my armour, left Bercelet sleeping where he was at the end of the bed, and made my way along the ramparts to the tower where Guinevere had her room. She hated me going off without telling her. I remember a vixen cried and I looked up, feeling the cold of the wind about my neck, and I saw someone leaning against the ramparts at the foot of the tower.

'So you could not sleep either, my lord?' It was Lancelot's voice. He went on, 'It must be the moon.'

'It isn't the moon. It's Percivale,' I said. 'I'm going out after him, before he gets himself into trouble. I shouldn't have let him go. Are you coming?'

Lancelot did not hesitate. He never did. We found Gawain and Galahad still talking by the fire in the hall as we passed through. When they heard where we were going, they came along without even being asked. The four of us rode out into the cold of the night, Lancelot alongside me. I smiled across at him, happy to be going out again with him on a quest; but he caught my eye and looked away from me quickly, and I wondered why.

Meanwhile, Percivale had still not caught up with

the Golden Knight. On and on he ran, through the darkness. Dawn came, and everyone he asked said the Golden Knight had passed by only a short time before. Now he had tracks to follow, hoof prints in the mud. Stopping only to check them, and to drink from the streams, he followed the trail of the Golden Knight, not loping any more, but bounding along, like a wolf closing on his quarry. At last, at noon that day, he saw the Golden Knight ahead of him. He was crouching down at the foot of a tree, turning a rabbit over a small fire; and beside him on the ground lay the stolen goblet.

Percivale strode into the clearing and confronted him. 'You stole that goblet from King Arthur,' he said. 'Give it to me now or I will fight you for it; and if I fight you, I shall kill you, and you will have died for nothing but a goblet.'

'What!' roared the Golden Knight, standing up tall and drawing his sword. 'Do you dare to threaten me, wolf-boy? With this sword I shall split you down the middle, so there'll be two of you running around, on one leg each.' He guffawed, and came at Percivale, whirling his sword – he hadn't even troubled to put on his helmet. Nimble on his feet, Percivale let him come and stepped aside at the last moment. He hid behind tree trunks. He shinned up one tree,

climbed into the next and shinned down again. He darted this way, he dodged that way, all the while waiting his moment. Tiring in the noon-day heat, the Golden Knight came lumbering on, not thinking for one moment that this boy could or would ever use his spear.

'Your rabbit is almost ready to eat,' said Percivale. 'Just give me the goblet back and we shall eat it together in friendship. If you do not, then I shall have to eat it alone, when you are dead.' At that, the Golden Knight uttered a bloodcurdling war cry and charged at him. Percivale swayed to one side and thrust his spear upwards under his shield and into his neck. The Golden Knight fell to the ground, his last roar stuck for ever in his throat.

When, some time later, we came upon the scene, Percivale was bending over the Golden Knight trying to pull his armour off. He had little success, for he did not seem to know he had to unbuckle it first. 'You can't do it like that – you can't pull him out of it,' laughed Gawain, and he jumped down to help him. We buried the Golden Knight where he had fallen.

'I have never before killed a man,' Percivale whispered; and when he turned to me, I saw his eyes full of tears. 'It's not like killing an animal, is it, my lord? But it was just as easy. And all for a goblet.'

'You were not to blame,' said Gawain, putting a comforting arm round him, 'you did nothing wrong. He chose his own death; and, besides, there is nothing terrible about dying. Death is a part of life. The minute we are born we are dying. It's what we do while we are alive that matters.'

'To take a life is always wrong, always evil,' said Galahad. 'Sometimes, like today, it may be the lesser of two evils. But to rejoice at another man's death – whatever he has done – is always ungodly, and there is often too much such rejoicing at Camelot. For Mordred, and for some others too, a dead man is nothing but a trophy. He gloats over every corpse he brings home. It is shameful. It is wicked.'

Percivale thought for some moments, and said, 'Would it be right or wrong then, good or evil, for a son to kill a man who has killed his father?' None of us seemed to want to answer.

Then Lancelot spoke up: 'Well, Galahad? You are my son. Would it be wrong for you to avenge my death?'

'Yes, Father, it would be wrong,' Galahad replied, without a moment's hesitation. 'Revenge is not for us to take, but for God. We must leave it to Him. If the monks have taught me anything, it is that love will conquer all, all hate, all revenge.'

'That is what my mother told me,' cried Percivale,

and he fell to his knees suddenly before me. 'My king,' he said, 'I must tell you who I am and why I came to Camelot. I am the son of King Pelinore, cruelly done to death by Agravaine, a knight of your Round Table. It is true I came here to be your knight, but in my heart I came more for revenge, to kill Agravaine. Once knighted and trained in battle, I meant to seek him out and destroy him.' He looked up at me. 'I promised my mother I would not do it, yet I was going to do it.'

'We have all broken promises in our time,' I said. 'Promises are always easy to make, and they are easy to break too.' I drew out Excalibur and knighted young Percivale as he knelt there. Never before had I been so moved to knight anyone. It was his honesty that touched me.

'Right,' said Gawain, hauling him to his feet when it was over. 'That's that then. Now he has his armour. You can take the Golden Knight's horse too – I don't think he'll be needing it now. That'll make you half a knight. The rest I shall teach you myself.' And he put his arms round Percivale and held him close for a moment. Then he held him at arm's length and looked him up and down. 'Dear God,' he said, shaking his head ruefully. 'Look at him, will you? All bright-eyed, with his whole life ahead of him. How I wish I was young again.' Lancelot and I looked at each other and wished the same thing.

So we all came home to Camelot and there was a great feasting that night. Percivale sat down in his seat, his name miraculously written on it by an unknown, unseen hand, as it always was when a new knight first sat down at the Round Table. With the feasting over, I called Agravaine before me and, in front of Percivale and the whole company, he asked forgiveness for what he had done to King Pelinore all those years before. When the two of them embraced in reconciliation, the great hall erupted with clapping and whistling and cheering. They stamped their feet, they pounded the Round Table till the plates and goblets shook. Moved almost to tears, I glanced up at Guinevere, to her place under her canopy, to share the joy of the moment with her. But she was not there; and then I noticed that Lancelot's seat, next to Gawain's, was empty too. The cold hand of suspicion crept over my heart, and I thought back to my meeting with Lancelot on the ramparts below Guinevere's tower, and I knew now why he had been there. I closed my eyes so that my tears would not be seen. I cried inside for the friend I had lost, for the wife I had lost. When at last I opened my eyes and looked around me, I could see from their faces that they had known already what I now knew. An uncomfortable silence fell on the hall.

'Well?' I said. 'What are you staring at? Have you lost the cheer of the feast. Wine will bring it back, it always does. Drink, my friends, drink.'

How we drank that night, but I knew already the spirit of Camelot was gone for ever, that no amount of wine or ale could ever bring it back, that a long and bitter road lay ahead of us. In my drunken stupor, I went up to my bed and knelt down to pray as I had as a child. I prayed to Merlin, to the Lady Nemue, to Jesus, to anyone for help. No voice came back. I was quite alone.

By the morning I had decided what I should do. I was up early and sent for Lancelot to come hawking with me. Guinevere came running out into the courtyard as we left.

'Can't I come with you?' she asked. I could scarcely look at her.

'No,' I replied, stonily, 'we will go alone.'

'But we always go together,' Guinevere pleaded, her hand on my stirrup.

'We used to,' I said, and rode away from her, Lancelot at my side, his favourite peregrine, hooded, on his wrist. We rode on down the causeway in silence until we reached the edge of the forest where

I knew we would be hidden from sight.

'We will stop here,' I said. 'Set the peregrine on a perch, Lancelot. I want to talk.' He obeyed at once and came before me, his face ashen. He knew that I knew. I drew Excalibur and pressed the point of it into his neck.

'Will you kill me, my lord?' he said, and lifted his chin. 'I will not beg for mercy, even though I know I have wronged you. I have no defence, but to say that she is not to blame. She was true to you, and in her heart she still is and still wants to be. The blame is mine and mine alone. We have tried to keep away from each other – oh, how we have tried, my lord. We cannot.' I pushed Excalibur deeper into his neck so that the blood trickled out and ran back down the blade towards the hilt. I felt the red mist of anger rising inside me, as it had done so often on the battlefield years before. But, as we stood there, Lancelot on the point of death, a gang of crows came cawing over and flew down to harry the peregrine off his perch. Still hooded, the peregrine took fright and lifted off, flapping wildly in his blindness. He flew straight into the trunk of a tree and fell like a stone to the earth where he lay still, only the wind moving his feathers. We ran to where he was and crouched over him.

'He was my best,' said Lancelot, picking him up

gently and removing the hood. The head hung limp.

'And you were my best,' I said. 'It is a sign. This is what will happen to me. Like the crows, my enemies will gather again to finish me and it will be the end of the Kingdom of Logres.'

Lancelot stood up, his eyes burning deep into mine. 'Only forgive me, my lord,' he pleaded, 'and I will not let it happen again. I promise you. I promise you faithfully.'

'And will you leave Guinevere for ever?' I asked. 'Will you do that? Will you promise never to see her again?'

For a moment he did not reply. Then he lowered his eyes and shook his head sadly. 'That I cannot promise,' he said.

My temper had cooled. I sheathed Excalibur. 'I cannot kill you, Lancelot, but I can no longer count you as my friend, and whoever is not my friend must be my enemy. Galahad is right. Let God then dispose of you and me as He will. I shall not kill you, and I cannot banish you, for you have friends enough at Camelot who would stand by you, and then we should soon be locked against each other in civil war. But I shall be rid of you. One way or the other, I shall be rid of you. We shall never again speak as friends.' I left him and rode back to Camelot.

*　　*　　*

Pentecost came, but the feast was subdued as never before at Camelot. Guinevere had not left her room for days. I had not seen her. People talked in dark corners now, in whispering cliques, Lancelot's friends and my friends. Even my friends would not look me in the eye any more. I saw it for what it was, the beginning of the end. The light of Camelot was going out all around me.

That night at the feasting, Lancelot sat at his place at the Round Table. He was courteous, but cold, as I was; the whole world knew what lay between us. The Round Table was full, every seat occupied except the one where no one ever dared to sit, the one marked 'Perilous'. We were saying grace, our heads still bowed, our hands together, when the door opened. In the flickering torchlight I did not at first recognize who it was. The cloaked figure pushed back her hood as she came on slowly across the hall, and I saw it was the Lady Nemue. But then I noticed that no one else in the room had moved. No one else had seen her. They still sat, heads bowed, hands together and still as statues.

'My Lord Arthur,' she said. 'The time has come to fill the "Perilous" seat. The chosen knight will be the Grail Knight, the only one of this company pure enough to find the Holy Grail and drink from it. Only one knight in this hall has no sin in him.'

At that moment Galahad rose from his seat as if in a sleep and came towards the seat marked 'Perilous'. He sat in it, his head still bowed, his hands still together in prayer.

The Lady Nemue looked at me, and I saw nothing but pity in her eyes, 'I can do no more for you,' she said. 'What has been done, has been done. What has to be, has to be. I shall see you again at Camlan.'

And she was gone into the air and the knights were finishing their grace. Suddenly Lancelot started up, pointing at Galahad. 'Get up, my son! Get up!' he cried. 'It is death to sit there.'

'Not for me, Father,' said Galahad, 'for I am the Grail Knight, and I wait now for the quest of the Holy Grail for which I have prepared myself all these years.'

As he spoke, the hall filled with a sudden wind, and thunder rolled about the sky and crashed right above us so that the castle shook. The doors blew open and a fireball, or so I thought it was at first, rolled in, filling the hall with its light, a light brighter even than the sun itself, so bright that everyone covered their eyes and cried out in pain. Daring to squint through my fingers, I saw the light hover over the Round Table; and in the very core of the light was a cup, a cup of

olive wood seemingly untouched by the fire around it. It floated down on the flames and came to rest on the table itself, the burning light now only a shimmering glow around the wooden cup.

Lancelot was still on his feet. 'I saw it once before,' he gasped. 'At Corbenic, with King Pelles, when I had killed the dragon. It is the Holy Grail, the cup from which our Lord Jesus drank at his last supper on this earth, the cup that was brought to this country by Joseph of Arimathaea himself.'

Again the castle shook and a great wind gusted. Smoke and sparks from the fire billowed into the hall, and the cup rose in the air as we watched and seemed to be carried away in a fire so dazzling, so hot, we had to hide our faces again. Bercelet howled at my feet and hid his head against my leg. Then the doors closed, the wind ceased and the smoke settled. When I looked up, the cup was gone.

In the stunned silence that followed, Galahad came and knelt before me. 'I do not want to leave you, my lord,' he said, 'for I fear you will soon be in dire need of all your most loyal knights. But I have to go. I must seek out the Holy Grail; for, as my father says, it is indeed the cup our Lord Jesus drank from at the Last Supper. Nothing is more sacred. I shall never see you again, my lord. I shall never see Camelot again, for the quest will not be achieved until I have found the Grail and gone with it to my Father in heaven. May I leave with your blessing?'

'If you must go, Galahad,' I replied sadly, 'then you must, and you have my blessing. I am only your king on this earth. We all have a higher king, and it is Him you are obeying.'

Lancelot was suddenly there at his side, begging me to think again. 'Do not let him go, my lord. He is my only son. I have no one else to lose.' As I looked at Lancelot, I hated him for the first time. And then, in an instant, it came to me, a solution, a terrible solution, a way to rid myself of Lancelot. At worst it would mean that he and Guinevere would not see one another for a long, long time; and at best – I confess it now freely – at best, I might even be rid of him for ever.

'Then go with him, Lancelot,' I said. 'I cannot stop Galahad. In all the history of Camelot, there never was a more important mission than this. You know where Corbenic is, where you claim you saw the Holy Grail. Well, Galahad is your son. Why don't you ride with him, to protect him, to guide him? You would not let him go alone, would you?'

'As you wish, my lord,' he said, his eyes reading my dark intentions. 'I will go then.'

And as he spoke, Gawain leapt to his feet. 'And me!' he cried.

'And me!' cried Bors.

'Let me go too, my lord!' Percivale now. 'I shall not fail you.'

Soon half the knights in the hall were clamouring at me to let them go. Lancelot spoke to me, his hand on my arm.

'Your wish to see me dead has lost you your kingdom, my lord. You will have no one left to defend it, and you may well need to defend it. You have brought this on yourself.'

I knew he spoke only the truth, but his was a truth I did not want to hear. His hand on my arm was more than I could abide. I shook myself free of him.

'Take with you whomever you like,' I said to him. 'I never want to see your face again at Camelot.' I held up my arms and spoke to all my knights of the Round Table. I knew it would be for the last time. 'If you want to go on this quest,' I said, when they had quietened, 'then go, and go with my blessings on you. A man must go where his heart will lead him, isn't that right, Lancelot?' And he did not reply.

That night as I lay in my bed, Guinevere came to my door as I had thought she might. I had locked it against her. She pleaded with me through the door.

'Please, Arthur, let me in.' I said nothing. 'If you will not, then I beg you at least to hear me out. Do not let Lancelot go tomorrow. If he goes, I shall die of grief. Let him stay, and I promise I will be yours, and only yours, as we were before. I will make everything just as it was, Arthur. I promise you. Arthur, please?' I lay stiff in my bed and listened. There were tears on my face, but they were tears of anger. When I heard her weeping, I did not even pity her.

Come the morning, I was on the ramparts as the knights rode out from the courtyard below – Galahad and Lancelot, side by side, with never a look back; Gawain, Gareth, Gaheris, Bors and Percivale, his great horse prancing wildly, his golden armour glinting in the cold morning sun. I counted seventy others with them. They rode out along the causeway, and vanished into the mist.

I felt Guinevere beside me. 'What have we done?' she asked. 'What have we done?'

'We have destroyed ourselves,' I replied. 'The Kingdom of Logres is broken. Camelot is split wide open, and by our own hands.'

'Maybe it was too much to ask,' said Guinevere softly. 'Maybe you can't have heaven on earth. Maybe we can't be perfect.' Guinevere's fingers rested near mine on the parapet, and I so wanted to touch them.

'Maybe not,' I said. 'But we can try. At least we tried, didn't we?' And I looked down into those eyes I still loved and saw that she still had love for me, but we both of us knew it had become a blighted love.

Every day she watched at her window. For weeks on end she never left her room. My nights were long, hate and remorse and regret battling inside me. What I had done was terrible enough, but what I felt was worse still. I longed, not for news of the quest of the Holy Grail, but for news of Lancelot's death. I longed for his death, I prayed for it; and then I would ask forgiveness for praying for it. We were both waiting and watching. No doubt she was praying too, but we were praying very different prayers.

Less than twenty of the knights who rode out after the Holy Grail that day returned to Camelot. The first of the survivors to come back was Percivale. One dark evening, some months later, he rode into the courtyard; and with him was his new bride, Blanchefleur, younger daughter of King Pelles of Corbenic. I brought them at once into the great hall where the three of us sat down by the fire. How they smiled into each other's eyes. How I envied them their young love. But I had darker things on my mind.

'Well,' I said, unable to contain myself any longer. 'What of Lancelot, what of the Holy Grail?'

Percivale, like many a warrior who has lived through the nightmare of battle, did not want to dwell on what had happened. The telling of it troubled him, and saddened him. He took Blanchefleur's hand in his, and held it as he spoke. Lancelot, it seemed, had wandered far and wide through the Wastelands with Galahad, trying to find his way back to Corbenic, but the more he looked the more confused he became. In the end, Galahad left him and went off to search on his own. Like so many other knights, Percivale and Bors scoured every corner of the land, but could find no trace of the grail. Together they survived all manners of dangers and deprivations – and these he brushed over as if it pained him even to think about them – before they at last came upon Corbenic by chance. 'But, then, nothing is quite by chance, is it, my lord?' he said, and he went on. 'Galahad was there already at Corbenic when we arrived, and so was Lancelot. It was given to only the four of us to see the grail again. I don't know why. We passed it to each other, but only Galahad was chosen to drink from it. I was there in the chapel at Corbenic when he did so. Afterwards, we found his body still kneeling at the altar rail, his soul gone to heaven, and the Holy Grail with it. But the story is not all sad, my lord. That day, after I had held the Holy Grail, after we had buried

Galahad, I went to say goodbye to King Pelles. As I took his hand in mine, his old wound healed and he stood up for the first time in thirty years. I can't explain it, I won't even try. The king kindly asked me to stay for a while, and so did Blanchefleur.' He smiled at her and squeezed her hand. 'You can see that I did.'

'And Lancelot?' I said. 'What of Lancelot?'

'He left,' Percivale replied. 'No one knows where he went, and I have heard nothing of him since.'

They stayed for a few days after that. When Guinevere heard there was no news of Lancelot, she would not even come down to meet them. I begged Percivale to stay, but he would not. King Pelles, although completely cured of his old wound, was an old man now and needed his new son-in-law by his side. Percivale soon returned to be Lord of Corbenic, and I was never to see him again.

Bors was the next to come back. He came in the middle of the night, and was brought up to my room. Always a reticent man, he would say little of what had happened to him, other than that he had been with Percivale at Corbenic and had held the Holy Grail in his hands. When I asked after Lancelot, he said simply, 'He lives.' And then he went on. 'He told me to tell you that he loves you still, my lord; but that he also still loves her. He promises you that he will never return to Camelot.'

'I've heard his promises before,' I said. 'If he does come, then there will be war between us.'

'I know, my lord,' said Bors. 'He knows it and everyone knows it. If he comes, then we will have to choose between you.'

'And how will you choose, Bors?' I asked, but there was no time for his answer. Guinevere stood in her bare feet at the door, a candle in her hand. She seemed half in her dreams, sleepwalking almost.

'He is not dead?' she whispered. 'Then he will come back to me. I know he will.'

# 10 THE LAST DAYS OF CAMELOT

ONE BY ONE, THE KNIGHTS CAME HOME FROM the quest of the Holy Grail – Gawain, Lionel, Hector, Gareth, Gaheris and Gryflet, too. None of them brought any news of Lancelot; and for me, no news was very good news. For Guinevere, each shake of the head was a stab in her heart. Her last hopes were fading fast. She began to refuse her food. All day and every day, she lay pining in her room, her harp silent, the life ebbing from her. The doctor plied her with potions, and bled her with leeches; but none of it seemed to help her. 'To live,' he said, 'she must want to live.'

There was only one way to save her, only one

person to save her. I knew it, and the whole of Camelot knew I knew it. I could either do nothing and watch her die in her tower, or I could find Lancelot for her. I had no choice. So one morning, I climbed the tower steps, and brought her her food myself.

'Eat,' I said. 'Eat, and I will send for Lancelot. We will find him, I promise you. Eat, and he will come.' At first she turned her head away and would not believe me. I picked her up and carried her to the window, so that she could see all the knights riding out. 'One of them will find him,' I said.

She looked up into my eyes. 'Can I believe you?' she whispered.

'Believe it and eat,' I replied.

And she did, a little more each day until the colour came back into her cheeks, and her hair shone again in the sunlight. She took up her harp, and Camelot echoed once more with her sweet music. Spring came, and she went out riding, just as she always had done. But as soon as she returned, she would ask me, 'Has he come? When is he coming?'

'Soon,' I said, hoping he would, hoping he wouldn't. 'Soon, I promise.' And she believed me. She had such blind faith in me now, that I could not disappoint her. But the knights were returning to Camelot, and still there was no word of Lancelot. I dared not tell her. I forbade them to tell her. Instead, I lied. Again and again I lied. I told her he had been seen here, heard of there, that it could not be long now before he was found and brought home. And her eyes would smile at me with such love and such gratitude; smiles that warmed my heart and melted away all the jealousy and hate I had harboured for so long – so much so that, in time, I was myself longing to see Lancelot again.

But after a while I saw less and less of Guinevere. Now that she was so much better, she would often be out hawking from dawn to dusk. I became worried at her going out alone, and offered to go with her, or send one of my knights as an escort – whatever she wanted. 'I'll be all right,' she said. 'I'll take one of my ladies, if you like.' And so each evening, with her lady at her side, she would come riding in under the gateway, and the courtyard would ring with their pealing laughter. I think I had never seen her so happy. Better still, she scarcely asked after Lancelot any more. I dared to begin to hope that she was at last forgetting him.

I was sitting in my room late one night, Bercelet stretched out by the fire beside me. He woke with a sudden growl, his lip curling, his hackles rising. There were whispers outside the door, and then a knock. I knew from the growl that it must be Mordred. But he was not alone. Agravaine came into the room with him. From the smile on Mordred's face, I knew it must be bad news he was bringing me.

'We thought you'd want to know, my lord,' he said. 'Lancelot has been found. We found him ourselves, didn't we, Agravaine?'

'Where?' I asked. 'Where is he?' I was filled with a deep and sickening foreboding.

'Not far,' Mordred replied. 'In fact, it's quite near really, isn't it, Agravaine?' Agravaine nodded sheepishly. Mordred went on. 'I'm afraid there's more, my lord. You see, when we found him, he wasn't alone, was he, Agravaine? He was with someone. Why don't you tell the king, Agravaine?' Go on, tell him. Tell the king who he was with.'

I knew already, I held the scream inside me, and closed my eyes.

'I think a man should know how his wife spends her days, don't you, my lord?' Mordred was enjoying his moment. 'Don't be frightened, Agravaine. The king wants to know. Tell him.'

'Guinevere,' Agravaine could barely whisper her name. I opened my eyes to see Mordred patting Agravaine on his back.

'There,' he said. 'That wasn't so bad, was it?' He

grinned at me triumphantly. 'We thought you ought to know, didn't we, Agravaine? I mean, everyone else does. It's been going on for weeks now. All this hawking! I'm sure she's been up to all sorts of sports, but I don't think hawking was one of them.'

I rose from my chair with a roar of anguish, and struck him across the face, so that he staggered back against the door. The grin was still there as he wiped the blood from his mouth. 'It's not me you want to kill, is it, my lord?' he asked.

'You know where he is?' I asked. He nodded. 'Then take a dozen men. You know what to do?'

Mordred shook his head and tutted. 'You're losing your touch, my lord. Do you want it to look like murder? It's justice you're after, isn't it? Catch them together, red-handed, and take them alive. Then you will have right on your side, and the law too. The law says that adulterers must burn at the stake, does it not? And we all must live by the law – you've said it so often, my lord. Not one law for the rich and another for the poor, remember? The queen must die, my lord; and so must Lancelot.'

I did not mind how they died. I just wanted to have it done, and quickly, before I weakened. 'Follow her then,' I said. 'Follow her when she goes out hawking tomorrow. If you find them together, then take them, and let the law take its course.' I lay awake all that night. I had forgotten how to cry.

The next day dawned bright and clear. From my room I watched Guinevere and her lady riding out from the courtyard, a peregrine on her wrist. Even then I longed to shout out of the window to warn her. Some time later, Mordred and his knights clattered out after her. Hour after hour I stayed brooding in my room. Shortly before sunset, I heard a commotion down below in the courtyard. I could not bring myself to look at them. All day I had been trying not to think of them together, and now I certainly did not want to see them together. Mordred burst into my room. The smile had gone. His face was covered in blood, and his sword arm hung limp at his side.

'He escaped, my lord,' he breathed. 'Lancelot escaped. He killed Agravaine! He killed seven of us, and then rode off into the forest. We lost him.'

'And Guinevere?'

'We have her,' he said. 'And she must burn, my lord. She must burn!'

'No!' Gawain stood in the doorway. He pushed past Mordred. 'Don't do it, my lord. Banish her. Imprison her, but not the stake.'

'You knew, Gawain,' I said. 'You knew what was

going on, and you did not tell me.'

'Because I knew it would come to this, my lord,' Gawain replied. 'Because once you knew, once it was said aloud, then the queen would have to be punished.' He turned angrily on Mordred. 'There are some things, Mordred, better left unsaid.'

'Perhaps you are right, Gawain,' I said, 'but what is spoken cannot be unspoken. The queen must die.'

'But you cannot do it, my lord,' Gawain begged, going down on his knees.

'Cannot!' I cried. 'I am still king here, am I not? Tomorrow at dawn she goes to the stake. The law is the law. And when we find Lancelot, he too will burn. They have deceived me for the last time.'

All evening long they came before me to beg for her life – Gareth, Gaheris, Bors, Kay, Gryflet, and many, many others. But my heart was hard as stone, and I was deaf to all their entreaties. Guinevere's lady came too and wept at my feet. 'Only see her, my lord, she knows she has wronged you. She just wants to make her peace with you before she dies.' Just to see Guinevere would be to lose my resolve. I sent her lady away without a word of comfort.

Dawn came after the longest night of my life. A silent, weeping crowd filled the courtyard below. The stake and the pyre stood ready near the gateway. I watched from my room, but standing back so that I could not be seen. Gaheris and Gareth, Gawain's brothers, escorted Guinevere across the courtyard. She was as pale as her white linen nightgown, but she needed no support. She walked steadily, her head held high. I had never loved her nor hated her more. Mordred himself tied her to the stake, and her lips moved in her last whispered prayer.

He had the torch lit in his hand, when Lancelot came galloping in at the gate, his brothers, Lionel and Hector beside him, their swords whirling and cutting and slashing through the screaming crowd. In their blind panic, the crowd trampled each other into the ground, or crushed each other against the walls. I stood stunned at the horrors of the bloodbath below me. I saw Lancelot cut down Gaheris and Gareth too. And then he was by the pyre itself and hacking at the ropes. Within moments he had swept Guinevere on to his horse, and was scything his way through the crowd towards the gateway, Lionel and Hector close on his heels. Behind them they left the courtyard strewn with the screaming wounded and the silent dead.

I found Gawain kneeling by his dead brothers, and rocking back and forth, his head in his hands. He looked up at me, bewilderment hardening to anger.

'They were not even armed, my lord.' He spoke through clenched teeth, his mouth full of tears. 'He had no need to do it. He had no right. They were his friends.' And Gawain bent his head and wept like a child.

Mordred was beside me. 'See what your queen has brought you,' he said. 'See what the great and noble Lancelot has done. Now you know who your true friends are, my lord.'

Gawain leapt to his feet. 'I'll weep no more tears for them,' he cried, 'not till I am revenged, not till Lancelot is a corpse lying at my feet.' He turned to me. 'Let's waste no time, my lord. Let's go after him.'

A thunderous cheer went up all around me. 'Death to Lancelot!' they cried. I held up my hand for quiet.

'All in good time,' I said. 'First we bury our dead, and we see to our wounded. Tomorrow will be soon enough to hunt down Lancelot.'

It was a mistake. By the time tomorrow came, nearly thirty of my knights had deserted and gone over to Lancelot. They had stolen away in the darkness, Bors amongst them, and Gryflet too. I had not expected it, not after what Lancelot had done. I could not understand it. But Bedevere could. 'It's the queen they love, my lord,' he said, 'not just Lancelot. And you were going to burn her. You made them choose.' He was right of course.

So the next day, with our dead blessed and buried, I rode away with the army from Camelot, Gawain on one side of me and Mordred on the other. As we went, two buzzards wheeled above us, their mewing cries echoing over the marshland. A third came to join them, and for a while they soared and swooped and floated together. Then one of them seemed to be left on its own. Abandoned, it searched the skies for its friends, its pitiful cry plaintive on the air.

Gawain interrupted my thoughts. 'Not so downhearted, my lord,' he said. 'We shall find them.'

Gawain was right. We found them sooner than we dared hope. Word came back to us that Lancelot had taken Guinevere to Joyous Garde, his castle in Wales. So, he did not yet feel strong enough to stand against us in battle. He was running for cover. We would follow. We would either smoke him out or starve him out.

For long months we besieged Joyous Garde. Never a soul went in, and never a soul came out. We set fires against the walls. We shot burning arrows into the castle night and day. We dragged carcasses into nearby streams to poison their water. Knowing how hungry they must now be, we roasted oxen near the walls so that the smell might tempt them out. Every day,

Mordred expected them to come out and surrender; but I knew, and Gawain knew, that Lancelot was made of sterner stuff. Then came the first sign of weakening, the first of the fainted-hearted escaping over the walls at night and coming over to our camp for food. From them we learnt of the sickness and the starvation – they were having to eat their horses – so we knew that, sooner rather than later, Lancelot would have to come out and fight. Either that or he could come out and make terms.

Then one morning we saw him standing on the ramparts. Guinevere was beside him. It was the first time I had set eyes on her. Gawain and I rode out to parley with him. 'You will never take Joyous Garde,' said Lancelot. 'No one ever has.'

'Why don't you come out and fight?' I said. 'Just you and I. It is our quarrel, yours and mine. You have taken my wife, and you have all but destroyed my kingdom. Let us settle this now between us.'

'No,' replied Lancelot. 'I would fight anyone in the world but you. You were the best friend I ever had, and you are my king.'

'Hypocrite!' cried Gawain, beside himself with fury. 'You are a knight of the Round Table, yet you killed my brothers when they were unarmed and defenceless. You murder your friends, you betray your king, you take another man's wife. Are there no depths to which you would not sink? Come out and fight, damn your eyes! Stop hiding in your burrow like a rabbit.'

Gawain's words must have struck home, for that same afternoon Lancelot came riding out of Joyous Garde, his whole army behind him. We were ready for him. Many of them were on foot, and I thought we should overwhelm them easily; but they fought like lions. No quarter was given, and none was asked. No war is ever more savage, nor more bitter, than a civil war. That day I fought and killed men I had lived my life with. I had dined with them, laughed with them, sung with them. They were my friends. One after the other, I hacked them down; and always there was another coming at me, his face twisted with hate and bloodlust.

Exhausted, and sick to my stomach with killing, I rested for a moment, leaning on Excalibur. When I saw Bors standing before me, his broadsword raised high above his head, I hadn't the will or the strength to fend off his blow. I moved, but not quickly enough. He felled me to the ground, knocking Excalibur out of my hand. He stood over me, his foot on my chest, his teeth gritted, his eyes on fire.

'Enough!' Lancelot's voice rang out over the field.

'Let me finish him now,' said Bors.

'I will finish you if you do,' Lancelot cried. 'He is my king and he is your king. Stand back, I tell you.'

He helped me to my feet. Eye to eye we stood; and for some moments, neither of us could speak. 'I have done you great harm, my lord,' he said. 'I cannot ever expect you to forgive me. But I could not let you burn her, you must know that. Say you will forgive her, and you can take her back. I will go over the seas to Castle Benwick, my castle in France, and you shall never hear of me again. Pardon her, my lord; and she is yours again.'

All around us the noise of the battle ceased, and soon we were encircled by all that was left of our armies. Lancelot's eyes burned into mine, beseeching me.

'It was never her fault, my lord, always mine. It was I who tempted her. Her only fault is that she loves two men, my lord, two men who used to love each other. Promise you will spare her, and I will go away for ever. You have my word as a knight.'

'Your word as a knight!' cried Gawain. 'Didn't you break your word as a knight when you cut down my brothers, unarmed, and in cold blood? Well to today, Lancelot, I have killed one of your brothers. I fought with Lionel and killed him, but it was you I was after.

I shall have my revenge, whether on this field or another, it does not matter. For you, Lancelot, there is no hiding place.'

'Then I grieve for Lionel,' Lancelot replied sadly, 'as I do for all the good men who fell today. I don't blame you for his death. As for Gareth and Gaheris, I struck blindly. I did not even know I had killed them. We were all friends once. In the name of that friendship, forgive me.'

'Never!' cried Gawain. 'Not while I breathe.' And he would have launched himself at Lancelot there and then, had I not held him back.

'There will be no more slaughter today,' I said. 'Bring out the queen, and let's make an end of this.'

So ended the battle of Joyous Garde; but as with all battles, the only true victors were the crows and the ravens. Lancelot went over the seas to France, and I took Guinevere back home to Camelot. The people lined the narrow, winding streets up to the castle as they always did when we came home; but now they did not cheer and they did not wave. This time we were man and wife in name only. It was a hollow thing, and they could see it for what it was. I was her captor, and she was my prisoner. But we did have peace, for a while at least.

*    *    *

There is an inevitability about a storm, the lull when the air is still and heavy, the greying of the light as the dark clouds gather, the ominous warm wind that heralds the thunder, and then the first great drops of rain. You cannot fight it, you cannot run from it. You simply wait for it and endure it. You long to have it over with. You know it will pass, that the air will be clear afterwards and all the world will be new and fresh. I knew this was the lull before the storm.

Between Guinevere and me there was no rancour. Trapped inside our own hurt, we lived our lives apart. It was best that way, for we could not talk together, nor even look at each other without pain. I remember Merlin once told me that love is like a rock. You can chip away at it only so much, but in the end, even the most solid granite will crack and crumble. Our rock was cracked, but not yet in pieces.

Day by day the numbers round the Round Table dwindled. I knew well enough where they were going, but I did not want to be told. Mordred told me anyway, and in public, so that everyone knew I knew.

'They gather to him from all over Britain,' he said. 'Did you really imagine that Lancelot would sit there in France and do nothing?' There was little deference in his tone these days, not even mock deference; and I could quite see why. Lancelot wasn't the only one who was gathering his friends around him. Mordred's own gang, his clique of whispering cronies, was growing by the day. He had power now, and he was using it. 'You have to go,' he urged me, 'before it's too late, before he becomes too strong. I will stay and look after your kingdom for you whilst you are gone. You're not frightened of him, are you, my lord?'

Gawain was never among Mordred's friends, but he too was pressing me to do the same thing. He had his own reasons, and he did not disguise them. 'The sooner he is dealt with the better, my lord,' he said. 'Every day the man lives is one day too long. Have you forgotten that he is a murderer and a traitor? What he has done once, he will do again. I tell you, my lord, the longer you delay, the longer you stay here at Camelot, the weaker you become and the stronger he becomes.'

I had no one to advise me, no one to turn to, only Bercelet. I would talk to him in the privacy of my room. 'Speak to me, Merlin,' I said, looking deep into his great, grey eyes. 'I need you. More than ever now. I need you. Tell me what I should do, tell me.' And Bercelet would groan and whine at me – in sympathy, I think – but from him there were no magic words of wisdom. I was on my own. I could trust no one, neither the shifty look in Mordred's eyes, nor

Gawain's vengeful machinations. But in one sense, both of them were right. I could no longer do nothing. Things were falling apart. The rot was setting in. It was being put about the court – and by my own son – that the king had lost his way, just as he had lost his wife, that he was too old, that he did not relish a fight with Lancelot. There was a smell of rebellion in the air. I had to go. I had to prove myself.

So, leaving Mordred behind in my place to guard the kingdom. I led the army out of Camelot. I turned in my saddle to see the last of the castle, and saw a white owl circling Guinevere's tower. To see a screecher-owl out flying by day was a bad omen. A shiver ran over me, and I turned away. I knew at that moment that I would never see Guinevere nor Camelot again.

Castle Benwick lies in Brittany, not far from the coast of France. We laid siege to it, just as we had done to Joyous Garde. But this time Lancelot came out to parley almost at once. 'Why have you come, my lord?' he asked. 'I have not threatened you. I have kept my word and stayed here in France. There is no need for us to fight. You and I have nothing more to fight about. So why can't you leave me in peace?'

'After what you have done!' cried Gawain. 'We

shall hound you to the ends of the earth, if need be. My brothers' spirits cry out for revenge, and they shall have it. Arm yourself and fight. Let us settle this man to man.'

Lancelot sighed and shook his head sadly. 'I do not want to have to kill you, Gawain; but if I must fight you, then I will. I will make myself ready.'

The two armies looked on in silence as the two of them charged, spears couched. To begin with Gawain had the better of Lancelot. Gringolet, his great black warhorse, thundered over the field and careered into Lancelot's horse, knocking horse and rider to the ground. Gawain, chivalrous even in his vengeful fury, waited until Lancelot was on his feet. Then they set upon each other with such terrible violence that many could not bear to look. Here were two of the finest, bravest knights that ever lived, two old friends, and neither would rest until one of them lay dead. Every cut, every thrust, was another nail in the coffin of the Kingdom of Logres. A side-swipe sent Gawain's shield spinning through the air to land at my feet, and the next blow stretched him out on the ground, his head split open. I rushed forward to stop it, but Lancelot had already thrown down his sword.

'Have your life, Gawain,' he said. 'It is of no use to me.' And he turned to me. 'Guinevere, my lord, is she well?'

'Well enough,' I replied.

'And you, my lord?'

'I am tired,' I said. 'Old and tired.'

Lancelot reached out and took me by the arm. 'Go back home, my lord,' he spoke urgently. 'They say you have left Mordred to rule in your place. How could you have done such a thing? Don't you remember how he was when he was a boy? In happier times, when you loved me, when you trusted me, you once told me your secret – about Mordred, you remember? I never told Guinevere, you know; though I was often tempted, I can tell you. You told me how it was Morgana Le Fey that sent Margawse to your bed that night. Can't you see what she's done? The boy was planted on you, to destroy you. Through him, she is winning the struggle for your kingdom. He provoked you into attacking me, didn't he? And if I'm right, then it was Mordred himself who suggested he should stay behind. He seeks your kingdom, my lord. It is Mordred you should be fighting, not me.'

I pulled my arm away. It was too uncomfortably close to the truth. I didn't want to hear any more. I called for help, and we carried Gawain back to my tent. The wound was deep and gaping. For days on end he lay delirious and on the brink of death. I sat beside him, hoping and praying it would be over quickly. But the spirit in him would not let his body die. I had fallen asleep in the chair. When I woke, I found him sitting up and looking at me. 'We're wasting time, my lord,' he said, the battle-fever still in his eyes. 'Where's my armour? Where's my sword?'

So the siege of Benwick dragged on, skirmishes, raids, ambushes, disease, all taking their terrible toll. Hector, Lancelot's surviving brother, was cut down by Gawain right under the walls of the castle, and his body dragged triumphantly by the heels back into our camp. Lancelot came riding out under a flag of truce to ask for his body.

'Are we even now, Gawain?' he said, closing Hector's eyes. 'Are you happy now?' And Gawain could not answer him.

It was whilst he was there, that the messenger arrived from Guinevere with the news I most dreaded. Mordred had pronounced himself king, and was telling the world that Arthur Pendragon was dead. Any who resisted, he butchered. Guinevere had fled to London with my brother, Kay; and Mordred was at the gates claiming her for his queen.

'Let me come back with you, my lord,' said Lancelot.

'I do not need you,' I replied, knowing full well I did, but quite unable to admit it. 'I can look after my wife without you, and my kingdom too.'

'Then may God bless you and save you, my lord,' he said sadly. 'I think we will never meet again, not on this earth.' And Lancelot rode back into his castle, his dead brother slung over the saddle in front of him.

Leaving our sick and wounded behind to be cared for by Lancelot, we lifted the siege and hurried back to our ships. It was a dejected army that landed at Dover. We had left nearly half our number buried in French soil, and we knew we had the greatest battle of all still to fight. We were scarcely on dry land before Mordred surprised us. With our backs to the sea, we fought a long and desperate fight. I stood shoulder to shoulder with Gawain, Excalibur wreaking terrible havoc amongst Mordred's men, until at last they had had enough of the slaughter, and they turned and ran.

I thought at first that Gawain was on his knees thanking God for our victory, but then as he was wrenching off his helmet, I saw the blood pouring from his old wound. As I caught him up in my arms, I knew he was dying. He clutched at me, fumbling at my face. 'I can see nothing but blackness,' he said, his eyes searching the sky. 'I won't see you again, will I, my lord?' I hadn't the voice to answer him. 'Then do something for me, my lord. Write to Lancelot. Say to him that as I die, my last wish is to make my peace with him. Ask him to forgive me, as I forgive him. And tell him to come, my lord, tell him we are lost without him. Write it, my lord. Do it now while I still breathe.'

Kneeling beside him on the shore, I wrote his letter to Lancelot, and then read it out to him. He had strength enough just to reach out and touch my arm in thanks, before he closed his eyes and died, the gulls shrieking above us. We stopped only to bury Gawain and the others in the chapel at Dover. I sent a trusted messenger back across the sea to France with Gawain's letter, and then we set off after Mordred, in hot pursuit. As we rode through the countryside, the people came running out to greet us, and some of them joined us too. It was so like the old days again, when we went off to fight the Saxons at Mount Bladon. Once again, I was their saviour, once again they loved me.

My son, Mordred – it hurts me still to call him so – the tyrant, Mordred, had burnt and pillaged his way across my kingdom. He was moving westwards, living off the land, and leaving a wake of destruction behind him. We followed his scorched path across Britain. I wanted to go first to London to see Guinevere. But it was far out of the way; and besides, he could not harm her now.

We were soon hard on the heels of Mordred, harrying his stragglers, and picking up his deserters. On we marched, on through Wessex, across the River Tamar, and up over the wild moors into Cornwall. There was nowhere else for him to run to, nowhere else to hide. From every hilltop, we expected to see his army drawn up in front of us. In every forest, we expected an ambush. By the campfires at night, we sharpened our weapons and steeled our hearts with songs and stories. Tired as we were after the long march, every one of us yearned now for battle, to avenge Gawain's death and to see the usurper dead. We did not care that his army might be stronger than ours. Every rebel in the country, it seemed, had flocked to his flag during his retreat across Britain. He had Irish with him, and even the hated Saxons. All had common cause against us. But our resolve strengthened with every day that passed.

Bedevere, riding ahead to scout as he always did, saw them first. He beckoned me forward to the ridge. I thought it was the sea itself glittering under the evening sun. But it was not. It was a sea of armour and swords and helmets, that stretched out over the valley as far as the eye could see.

'What is this place?' I asked.

'The valley of Camlan, my lord,' said Bedevere, and

the name stirred my memory, but I did not know why.

'We will camp here, and attack in the morning,' I said. 'At least we will have surprise on our side. We will come down on them out of the sun, and be on them before they know it.'

We lit no campfires that night. We talked in hushed whispers. We muffled our swords and spears, and led the horses away deep into the forest. Nothing must give us away. I never slept well the night before a battle – it was excitement as much as fear, I think. And Bercelet too seemed to be restless. All night long he sat beside me, his ears pricked, almost as if he was expecting someone.

I must have drifted into some kind of sleep, for, one moment I was alone in the tent with Bercelet, and the next there was someone else with us. I had neither heard nor seen him come in. He was standing at the foot of my bed. Only when he moved towards me, did I really believe the evidence of my own eyes.

'Who are you?' I said.

'Bercelet knows me,' he replied; and he reached out and scratched Bercelet's head where he liked it. He came closer, and I saw it was Gawain.

'But you're dead,' I whispered.

'I know, my lord,' he replied and his voice seemed to come from a long way off. 'More's the pity, for you need me now as you never needed me before. I have come to warn you, my lord. Fight Mordred tomorrow, and it will be the end of you, and the end of all hope for a thousand years and more. The Saxons will flood in again, and Britain will be plunged into ages of darkness.'

'I don't understand, Gawain,' I said. 'You always wanted to attack, attack.'

'All the more reason you should heed me now, my lord,' he replied. 'Lancelot has landed in Dover and is now only a week's march behind you. Wait for him. He will more than double your strength. With him at your side, you can drive Mordred into the sea. Without him, you are lost. Trust me, my lord; and wait for Lancelot.'

'How can I?' I asked. 'I can hide my army for a night maybe, but not for a week. Sooner or later Mordred will know we're here.'

'You must parley,' said Gawain. 'Promise him what you like; but at all costs you must avoid a battle tomorrow. I cannot stay, I cannot stay.' And as he was still speaking, he vanished into the darkness.

At first light, I sent a messenger into Mordred's camp, proposing we should meet in the middle under a white flag of truce, and with only one knight each as an escort. He agreed, but before I left with Bedevere,

I gathered my knights together and spoke to them. 'Have all the men lined out along the ridge, but several paces apart so that we seem to be more than we are. Have them hammer their shields as I ride down to meet Mordred. I want to put the fear of God into him. But do not let them charge, unless you see a sword raised near the white flag – I do not trust Mordred as far as I can spit him. If once you see the flash of a blade, then loosen the leash and let them come on like a pack of hungry wolves, and let no one sheath their sword until Mordred lies dead on the field.'

With my army drawn up on the ridge behind me, I rode down the hill, Bedevere at my side, a white flag fluttering from his spearhead. Bercelet came loping along between us. I tried to send him back, but he would not go. Around us now, the valley filled with the roar and thunder of ten thousand men drumming on their shields. Ahead of us lay Mordred's silent army, Mordred himself and his knight spurring towards us through the brush.

'Well, old man,' he scoffed, reining in his horse. 'Have you come to surrender?'

'Enough blood has already been spilt,' I replied. 'I have come to offer you half my kingdom in return for peace. The rest is yours at my death.'

For a moment or two he was taken aback. Then he smiled. 'But, if I kill you today, then I can have it all now.'

'If I die today,' I answered him, 'then you will die also, that much I promise you. Then you will have nothing. And as you can hear, as you can see, we are more than ready to fight, if that is what you want.' His eyes narrowed for a moment, as he gazed at the horizon behind me.

'Very well,' he said, 'but it is a pity. I was looking forward to killing you, you and that old dog of yours. Still, old dogs, like old men, die soon enough. I can wait.'

Bercelet was snuffling through the brush, his tail circling excitedly. He was after something. A snake slithered out of the long grass, and wriggled towards Mordred's horse. The horse took sudden fright, whinnying and rearing, his eyes flashing. With a cry of alarm, Mordred drew his sword and slashed at the snake, cutting it in half, so that both ends of it were left twitching on the ground.

The hammering had stopped. For a moment or two I wondered why. Then Mordred's naked swordblade flashed in the sun and I understood. A heavy silence lay over the valley. I turned to see my army moving down the hill, spears couched. I heard their battle cry, and the ground began to tremble at their charge. I galloped towards them to try to stop them, but even as I did so, I knew it was pointless. It was too late. They thundered past me, and I was soon swallowed up and lost in a mêlée of horses neighing and men yelling. I found Excalibur in my hand, and whirling about my head as if it had a life of its own. I heard my own war cry as if it were another man's voice. I carved and hacked my way through the enemy, searching everywhere for Mordred, for his black armour and his blood-red shield, knowing that only with his death could I stop the slaughter now. Then my horse was speared and died underneath me, and I was too busy defending myself to look for him any more.

We were driving them back and back. Now it was Mordred's army that had their backs to the sea. They fought like stags at bay. I stabbed, I parried, I cut, and at last they broke and ran. They had nowhere to run to but the sea. Like a madman I hurled myself after them, until there was no one left to fight, no one left to kill. I walked back over the battlefield. Hardly a man was left standing. Everywhere about me lay the dead, and the dying, their cries of agony filling my head. I could not bear to hear it. I dropped Excalibur, and put my hands over my ears. Only then did I realize I had been wounded. My helmet was split

open, and I could feel the chill of the wind on my open wound.

Some way off, I saw Bedevere rising to his feet, and Bercelet picking his way over the battlefield. Bedevere seemed to be waving to me, calling to me; but I could not hear what he was saying. Something made me turn around. Mordred was staggering towards me, his broadsword in his hands. His hair was matted with the mud and blood of battle, his breath rasping in his throat. I picked up Excalibur and ran at him, knocking his sword easily from his grasp. He stood before me, swaying and helpless. I had Excalibur at his throat. But then I looked into his eyes and saw the boy in him, the infant I had wanted to murder all those years before, and I heard again Merlin's words in my head. 'Have I not told you that evil can never destroy evil. Only good can do that.' I could not do it.

'No,' I said. 'A father cannot kill his son.' He gaped at me in disbelief. 'I speak the truth, Mordred. I am your father, and you are my son. So you see, you would have had the kingdom after me anyway, and without all this bloodletting. I would have told you before, but I could never trust you. Sooner or later, you would have told Guinevere, and I never wanted her to know. Only Lancelot knows, and now you. The secret will die with us.' I could not stand to look at him any more, I turned away. 'Go Mordred. Out of my sight. Never let me see you again.'

'As you wish, Father,' he said softly, too softly.

Bedevere was shouting at me now, and running. I felt a sudden blow between my shoulder blades, and I was falling forwards on to my face, my fingers unable to hold on to Excalibur and then unable to pick it up. I rolled over on to my back to see Mordred standing above me, his sword raised above his head. He was laughing out loud; but then I saw his eyes widen in sudden terror. I heard a roar like a bear behind me. Bercelet had him by the throat and was shaking him like a rabbit. For some moments they rolled together on the ground. Then Bercelet was astride him, his jaws tightening, throttling, until Mordred lay limp beneath him, his last struggles stilled.

Bedevere was trying to raise me up. His eyes told me what I already knew. The mists of death were closing in on me; and through the mists I saw a lake, and I saw an arm reaching up out of the water, the same arm in the white silk sleeve that had given me Excalibur thirty or more years before. 'Is there a lake nearby?' I asked.

'Yes, my lord,' he replied.

'Take Excalibur,' I said, 'take it and throw it in. Then come back and tell me you have done it. Go now, and quickly.' He was gone, and I was left alone.

As I lay there shivering in the cold of dusk, Bercelet came and lay down beside me, to warm me and to comfort me. My eyes closed, and I could see Bedevere walking down to the lake, Excalibur in his hands. He lifted his arms to throw, but then seemed to think better of it. He looked around him nervously, bent down and hid it in the reeds. It was my anger that kept the mists at bay until he came back.

'You have betrayed me,' I said. 'You didn't throw it in. You hid it.'

He did not try to deny it. 'Believe me, my lord, it was not to steal it that I hid it. Excalibur is not just a sword, it is the symbol of our hope, it is all that is left of Camelot. It is not something to be thrown away and lost for ever.'

'Do as I say, Bedevere,' I replied, gripping his arm. 'Obey me in this last thing.'

Agan he left me, and again I saw him go down to the lakeside; but still he could not bring himself to do it. When he returned this time, he was carrying Excalibur with him.

'My lord,' he said, falling to his knees. 'Do not make me do this, I beg you.'

'Do you love your king, Bedevere?' I could barely speak now.

'You know I do, my lord.'

'Then in God's name, do it.' And I fell back, a swirling blackness dragging me down.

When I woke, Bedevere was cradling me in his arms and weeping. 'I did it! I did it!'

'And what did you see?' I asked him.

'A hand, my lord, and an arm in a white silken sleeve. The hand reached up and caught Excalibur and drew it down into the lake. And the water never moved, my lord, not even a ripple.'

'Good,' I whispered. I looked up at the sky for the last time, and saw a white screecher-owl floating past on silent wings. I remember nothing more, until I heard the sound of waves lapping about me. I found myself lying on a boat, the Lady Nemue leaning over me. And around me stood five other ladies, all in black. Beyond them, Bercelet was standing on the bow of the boat and looking out over the sea. I could just make out Bedevere, alone on the shore. I wanted to wave, but was too weak now even to raise my hand.

'I said I would see you at Camlan,' said the Lady Nemue; and I remembered then where I had heard the name before. 'Oh Arthur, this is the saddest day there ever was. But you will live, and you will come back. The tree may have withered and died, but you

are the acorn and your time will come again.'

'Where are we going?' I asked her.

'To Lyonesse,' she said. 'To a place where we can look after you, a place you can rest, a place where no one will ever find you.'

# 11 THE ACORN

FROM SOMEWHERE FAR AWAY, A FOGHORN sounded, and brought the boy back to himself. Bercelet sat up suddenly, his nose covered in ash. Arthur Pendragon laughed. 'So, here we are and here we have stayed,' he said, 'for close on fourteen hundred years. And until today, the Lady Nemue was right – no one ever did find us. Then you came along, but I'm glad you did. We both are, aren't we, Bercelet? I've always wanted to tell my story, our story, as it was, as it really happened. I want people to know the truth, you see, the good and the bad; and to know I'll be back if ever they need me. You will tell them, won't you?' The boy nodded.

The foghorn sounded again. 'I think I'd better get home,' he said. 'They'll be out looking for me. They'll be worried sick.'

His clothes were stiff with salt, but dry now and warm. He shivered with pleasure as he put them on. He looked around for his rucksack, but then remembered he had left it behind on Great Ganilly. They were climbing the great stone stairway before the boy dared to say what had been on his mind.

'What about Lancelot?' he ventured. 'And Guinevere? What happened to them?'

Arthur Pendragon stopped and looked down at him from the step above. 'They grew old and died, like people do. The Lady Nemue tells me Guinevere died in a nunnery. He became a hermit; and when he died too, they buried him with her.' His eyes filled with tears. 'I miss them both. After all this time, I still miss them.' He turned away, but the boy had to know one more thing, and plucked at his coat.

'But how come, if you've been here for fourteen hundred years, how come you're not any older? I mean, how come you're still alive? How come Bercelet's still alive?'

Arthur Pendragon smiled and ruffled the boy's hair. 'A good question,' he said, 'deserves a good answer, and I shall do my best. In this half-world we live in down here, time passes for us much as it does for you. We have hours and days and years, as you do. We live in time, but we do not move with it. Here in this place, we are beyond the reach of time. So that is why we do not age with it. There, now are you any the wiser?'

'I'm not sure,' said the boy, and he was still trying to work it out when he was aware that the steps had led them into a long torchlit tunnel with a disc of daylight at the end. Bercelet bounded on ahead.

'See how he likes a run?' said Arthur Pendragon, and he put his arm round the boy as they walked together down the tunnel and out into the bright white of the fog. They were on a hillside of bracken and gorse. The light hurt his eyes, so the boy closed them for a moment. When he opened them, he could make out six dark figures in the fog, all standing still as stones.

'The boat is ready.' One of the stones spoke, came forward and became a lady in black.

'The Lady Nemue, my guardian and my keeper too,' said Arthur Pendragon. The Lady Nemue bowed her head, but said nothing. He turned to the boy. 'I don't even know your name, do I?' he asked. 'But no matter. I shan't forget you; and just so you don't forget me, here's a little something. Nothing much, but it may grow on you.' He laughed, and dug deep into his pocket. He brought out an acorn. 'From Merlin's tree in the courtyard at Camelot. Here.' And he handed it to the boy. 'Plant it,' said Arthur, 'and remember me.'

They walked down over the rocks and across the sand, Bercelet racing into the shallows. The prow of a boat loomed out of the fog and ground into the sand. 'In you get,' said Arthur Pendragon. 'Don't worry, it'll get you home.' Bercelet brought the boy a stick, but then wouldn't let go of it. The boy shook it as if he was shaking hands. He looked up at Arthur Pendragon, High King of Britain, and wondered if he should bow. He decided against it. He smiled instead.

The boy ran into the water and jumped on board. At once the boat began to move out to sea, and the fog closed in around him. The boy stumbled towards the tiller, but stopped when he saw that it was moving on its own, unaided. When he looked back towards the shore, he could see only a dark figure. He hoped it was Arthur Pendragon, and waved.

The Bishop's Rock foghorn gave him some idea where he might be, somewhere between St Martin's and Tresco, he thought. But the boat knew where it was going. Of that he had no doubts whatsoever. The boat seemed ordinary enough, long and low, with one white sail. It was wider than the racing gigs he knew so well, higher in the bulwarks, and about twice the length. What was strange, was that as it moved through the swell of open sea, there was no pitch and roll, none whatsoever. The boat seemed to be floating on air.

He sat down by the tiller, and his thoughts turned to home. He laughed out loud. He'd been missing for more than a day now. Everyone would have given him up for dead. Maybe they had found his rucksack on Great Ganilly. Morris Jenkins on St Martin's would certainly be bragging that he'd been the last person to see him alive. There'd be a lot of hugging and kissing and crying when he got back. He wasn't looking forward to that part of it much. And then there'd be the questions. What on earth was he going to tell them? He thought about that, and about little else now; but he still had not even begun to work out a believable story by the time the boat passed the beacon in the Tresco Channel. He was almost home.

The boat came alongside the quay at Bryher without so much as touching it. He looked around him. Thank God for the fog. There was no one about. No one had seen him. He jumped off and ran down the quay. Someone was playing the organ in the church and the light was on inside. The masts of invisible yachts clapped in Tresco Channel. He looked back along the quay. The boat had already vanished into the fog.

He ran all the way home. At the garden gate, he composed himself, decided he would just have to make his story up as he went along, and then burst through the front door and into the kitchen. 'It's me,' he cried. They were all eating their supper, and the television was on in the corner.

'Who else would it be?' said his mother with a smile.

'Any luck with the shrimps then?' his father asked, pushing his plate away. He must have told them that he'd be going shrimping. He couldn't remember. It seemed such a long, long time since he last saw them.

'No,' he said.

'Sshh!' his sister hissed at him, barely looking away from the television.

The boy went out without saying a word. He

walked slowly up the stairs, his mind spinning. He sat on his bed. The acorn in his hand told him he could not have dreamt it all. He had lost his rucksack. His watch was misted over. He had met Arthur Pendragon. It had all happened. Yet the digital clock on his bedside table was telling him he'd only been gone a few hours, that it was still the same day as yesterday. Arthur Pendragon's words sounded in his head: 'Here in this place, we are beyond the reach of time.'

He planted the acorn that evening in the shelter of the escalonia hedge at the bottom of the garden. When he looked out of the window the next morning, he almost expected to see a fully grown oak tree. It wasn't there. He was disappointed, but at the same time he was relieved. That was one more thing he wouldn't have to explain away. A robin flew into the bay tree below his window, eyed him for a moment and then sang his heart out; and the boy remembered another robin, in another place and in another time.

# The
# Sleeping Sword

## MICHAEL MORPURGO

*Illustrated by* **Michael Foreman**

EGMONT

*To the people of Bryher,*
*for all the warmth and kindness*
*over the years*
MM

# CONTENTS

# BEFORE I WROTE MY STORY

Before it happened, before the world went black about me, I used to read a lot. I've tried Braille, and I am getting better at it all the time, but reading is so slow that way. So now I listen to my audio tapes instead. I've got dozens of them on my shelf. The trouble is I can't tell which is which, so I've put my three favourite ones side by side on my bedside table. That way I can find them more easily.

Left to right, it's *The Sword in the Stone*, *Sir Gawain and the Green Knight*, and *Arthur, High King of Britain*. I've listened to those three so often I can say bits of them by heart. But it's *Arthur, High King of Britain* I've listened to most often, not because it's the best – *The Sword in the Stone* is probably the best – but because *Arthur, High King of Britain* begins and ends on Bryher, on the Scilly Isles, where I live. I can picture all the places so well inside my head and that helps me to feel part of the story, free to roam inside it somehow, to be whoever I want to be, do whatever I want to do.

And that's my trouble at the moment. There's so

much I can't do now that I used to do without even thinking about it – you know, ordinary things like going down to the shop, hurdling over mooring ropes, playing football on the green, watching telly, seeing my friends whenever I felt like it, messing about in boats, diving off the quay with them in the summertime. I can still go swimming, but someone always has to be with me. That's the worst of it, really. I can never go free like I used to.

It's not so bad at home. I've got a sort of memory-and-touch map of the house inside my head, every room, every doorway, every chair. And, provided my father doesn't leave his slippers in the middle of the kitchen floor – which he often does – and provided no one shifts the furniture or moves my toothbrush, I can manage just about all right. I really hate it if I trip or fumble about or fall over. No one laughs, of course they don't. In a kind of way I wish they would. Instead they go all silent and feel sorry for me, and that just makes me angry again inside.

And there's so much I miss – all the colours of the sky and the sea, the blue and the green and the grey, the black and white of the oystercatchers. I can't picture colours in my head any more, and I can't picture people's faces either, not like I could. So, like the oystercatchers, everyone's a voice now, just a voice. I'm getting used to it, or that's what I keep telling myself, anyway. I should be after two years. But it still makes me angry when I think about it, the bad luck of it, I mean. I try not to think about it, but that's a lot easier said than done.

That's what's so good about 'reading' stories, and 'writing' them, too. I've made up lots and lots of short stories. I love doing it because I can be whoever I like inside my stories. I can make my dreams really happen. I'm the maker of new worlds. Inside my dreams, inside my stories I can run free again. I can see again. I can be me again.

I don't actually write my stories, not like other people do. I find the Braille machine slows me down, like it does with my reading. Instead, I tell them out loud into a recorder. That's how I'm doing this now, and it's brilliant, because it lets the story flow. I get things wrong of course, and often too, but I just record over my mistakes and on I go. Easy.

A few days ago, I finished my very first long story and this is it. It took me the whole of the summer to write it. It's dedicated to Anna – you'll see why soon enough – and I've called it. . .

# THE SLEEPING SWORD
## BY BUN BENDLE
### *For Anna*

## CHAPTER 1

## THE DIVE OF MY LIFE

IT WAS NO ONE'S FAULT EXCEPT MINE. I WAS showing off. True, I didn't exactly want to go in the first place, but then I shouldn't have allowed Liam and Dan to persuade me. On the way back on the school boat from Tresco it had been cold and blustery. All I wanted to do was to get back home and finish reading my book about King Arthur.

Mum was out somewhere on the farm when I got in. We grow organic vegetables (onions, courgettes, tomatoes, lettuces - all sorts) to sell to the visitors - we get a lot of tourists on Bryher, especially in the summer. As usual, she had left my tea on the table. Dad was out checking his lobster pots. I was deep in my book, munching away at my peanut butter sandwich, when Liam and Dan banged on the window. They were in their wetsuits and breathless with running.

'Bun, we're going down the quay,' Liam shouted. 'You coming?' It wasn't really a question at all.

'I'm reading,' I replied, 'and, anyway, it's cold.' Liam ignored me.

'See you down there,' he said, and they were gone.

On Bryher we were the only boys of about the same age (there's only eighty people living here on the island anyway; one shop, one church, no school). We grew up together, went over to Tresco school every day together, we went fishing together, did just about everything together. 'The Three Musketeers' they call us. If we had a leader it was Liam, most of the time, anyway. He was the smallest of the three of us, and was by far and away the cleverest, too. He had a real gift of the gab, and was a fantastic mimic, as well. Anyone from Mrs Gee ('BF' Gee we called her) in the shop - 'Get your mucky hands off my ice-creams' - to 'Barking' Barker our head teacher - 'Look at my voice, Liam, I'm speaking to you!'

Dan was like a big friendly puppy, full of energy and bouncy. He always made us laugh a lot. Of the three of us I was the quietest, happy enough usually to go along with whatever the other two dreamed up. I just liked being with them. But I had my own very private reason, too, for going along with them. Anna.

Anna was Dan's big sister, and I loved her. Simple as that. I loved her. I couldn't tell her of course, because I was ten and she was fourteen. I didn't love her just because she was beautiful, which she was (just the opposite in every way to big, lumpy Dan), but also because we talked - and I mean *really* talked - about things that really mattered, like books, like feelings, like oystercatchers. Liam and Dan were my mates, best mates, but Anna was my best friend and had been as long as I could remember.

I was finding it difficult to concentrate on my book. I kept regretting I hadn't gone with them down to the quay. It was the sudden thought that it was Friday and that Anna might possibly be there, back for the weekend from secondary school on St Mary's, that finally decided me. I would finish the book later.

I pulled on my wetsuit and ran down the sandy track through the farm to the quay. As I rounded the corner by the shed, I saw them all larking about on the quay. Anna *was* there. She'd already been in swimming, I could see that, but the other two hadn't. They were standing on the edge, looking down into the water and hesitating.

The sea was murky and choppy and uninviting. I didn't want to go in, not one bit, but Anna had seen me. I saw an opportunity to impress her, and just went for it. I charged down the quay going full pelt, screaming like a mad thing. Anna tried to wave me down but I ignored her.

I dodged past Dan, who was shouting at me to stop, sprang off and launched myself into the most spectacular swallow dive I could, the best dive of my life, just for her. I remember thinking that it seemed to be taking longer than it should to reach the water. After that I remember nothing.

# CHAPTER 2

## 'NOT A MUMMY MUMMY'

WHEN I CAME TO, I KNEW AT ONCE I WAS IN hospital. Nowhere else sounds or smells like a hospital. At first I thought that I was back visiting Gran in hospital in Truro, but then I realised that it was me lying there on a bed, not Gran. I couldn't see where I was because there was a bandage round my eyes. I could feel it. In fact, most of my head seemed to be swathed in bandages. Someone was holding my hand and telling me not to worry, not to move. It was my mother. I wasn't worried, but I was hurting. My whole head was heavy with pain.

'What happened?' I asked.

'You're fine, Bundle. You're in hospital. You had an accident.'

'What happened?' I asked again.

'You went in off the quay. But the water was too low. Your head hit a stone. You were lucky, Bundle. It could have been a lot worse.' It felt bad enough to me.

'You need water to dive into, Bun, you silly chump. Didn't you know that?' My father was there too, and his voice sounded strange, as if he'd been crying. Now I *was* worried. 'Created quite a stir, you did,' he went on. 'Anna dragged you out of the sea, and gave you mouth-to-mouth. You'd have drowned else, and the boys went for help. We had the air ambulance in and they flew us straight here to Truro.'

'You've broken your arm, and you've had a bit of an operation on your head,' my mother was saying, 'so you'll have to stay in here for a few days. You sleep now.'

She didn't have to tell me. I was already drifting away. I was in and out of sleep for days and nights, nearly a week they told me afterwards. My mother always seemed to be there when I woke up. Doctors and nurses came, to ask questions mostly and occasionally to examine my head. These were the only times the bandage came off – not that it made any difference, because my whole face was still so swollen that I couldn't even open my eyes to see.

The doctors always seemed very pleased with me. I

was making a good recovery. I wasn't to worry they said. The swelling would go down in time and I'd be going home soon. I had visitors every day and my mother would always tell them the same thing, that I had had a very lucky escape, that I'd be fine.

I woke up one afternoon and heard my mother saying much the same thing, again. 'He'll be fine. But if it hadn't been for you, Anna, there'd have been no lucky escape at all, and that's the truth of it.' Anna was there! In the room! She'd come to visit me. Oh God, how I wished I could see her.

'And you two boys,' my mother went on, sounding a bit weepy – it could only be Liam and Dan – 'going for help like you did. You were wonderful, all of you, truly wonderful.'

I didn't know what to say to any of them. I was overjoyed they were there, but somehow I couldn't say it. Why is it that the most important things are so difficult to say? As it was I just pretended I was asleep under my bandages, and listened.

'He's sleeping now,' my mother was saying. 'But the doctors are sure he'll be fine. Like I said, he's lucky to be alive. You stay with him for a while, will you? I need to see the staff nurse. I shan't be a moment.' And I heard her go out.

For some moments no one spoke. Then Dan whispered, 'With all those bandages, he looks like a mummy or something. Not a mummy mummy – an Egyptian tomb mummy, the haunting kind. You know what I mean.' At that, I curled my hands into claws and then rose up, howling horribly. The giggling that followed was infectious. In the end all four of us were quite helpless with it. It made my head hurt, but I didn't mind. I was just so happy, so relieved to be back with them.

'I'll come and see you again, Bun,' Anna said as she left. 'As often as I can.'

I cried behind my bandages when they left, but out of joy, not sadness. Anna had come to see me, and she'd be back. I'd be out of hospital and home in just a week, a couple at the most, that's what they'd told me. Everything would be back to normal.

# CHAPTER 3

## INSIDE MY BLACK HOLE

THE NEXT DAY THE BANDAGES CAME OFF SO that the doctor could examine the wound on the side of my head. 'Good, Bun, very good,' said the doctor. 'The swelling's gone right down. You can open your eyes now.'

It took some doing – they felt a bit gummed up. But I did it. I opened them. The trouble was that I couldn't see anything. I blinked and tried again. Blackness. Only blackness. I squeezed them tight shut, and opened them again. I felt I was deep inside a black hole, that there was no way out. I was drowning in blackness, unable to breathe, my heart pounding with sudden terror.

'That looks a lot better, Bun,' the doctor went on, turning my head with his cold hands, 'a lot better.'

'I can't see,' I told him. 'I can't see.' There was a long silence. Then I could feel his breath on me, his face close to mine. He was lifting my eyelids.

'What about now?' he asked me. 'Can you see a light? Can you see anything?'

'No,' I said.

'What's the matter with him, Doctor?' My mother was asking just the question I wanted to ask, and she was frightened, really frightened. I could hear it in her voice.

'Well, it's a little difficult to say at this stage,' the doctor said. 'I expect it's just a side effect of the trauma. He's had a nasty crack on his head. It'll correct itself in time, I'm sure. But we'll do some tests. It's nothing to worry about, Bun.' His hand squeezed my shoulder. 'You'll be fine.'

If I had a pound for every time doctors told me that in the next few months, I'd be rich, extremely rich. But you can't blame them. What else could they say? They had to try to reassure me. Everyone was trying to reassure me. When they discharged me and I got back home, it was the same old refrain: 'Don't worry, Bun. It'll be fine.'

To begin with I believed them, because I wanted to believe them, needed to believe them. All the tests – and there were dozens and dozens of them, in Truro, in Bristol, in London – showed that I should be able to see. But the fact was that I couldn't.

Every morning I opened my eyes hoping and praying, but no longer believing, that this time I'd be able to see something. I never could. Everything else had healed up long ago by now. The plaster was off my broken arm, and the stitches out of my head.

Dan said cheerily, that he preferred me when I'd looked like a mummy. Liam, I could feel, didn't know what to say, so he said very little. He didn't know how to include me, so he didn't.

Only Anna didn't pretend with me, didn't feel awkward. She was just herself. She'd sit and talk, talk about anything and everything. She seemed to understand, without my having to tell her, what no one else did: that I felt lost, bewildered and frightened in a strange black world where I was entirely alone. She knew that I just wanted everyone to be normal, as they had been, so that I could still be part of the real world I remembered, their world.

My father was endlessly encouraging, taking me out on the fishing boat as he used to, trying to pretend my blindness didn't exist. From time to time I'd hear my mother crying quietly downstairs, and I knew only too well why. But when she was with me she was always positive, always concerned and comforting and cuddly, more so than she ever had been, too much so.

No one ever spoke the word 'blind', not in my hearing anyway, either at home or in the various hospitals. So in the end I mentioned it myself, to Anna, because I knew she'd be honest with me. 'I'm blind, aren't I?' I said to her, interrupting a story she was reading to me.

'Yes,' she replied quietly. 'But because you're blind now, it doesn't mean you will be for ever, does it? I mean, your arm got better, so did your head. Why not your eyes?'

'What if I stay blind?' I asked her. 'What if I don't get better?'

'It won't change anything, not really. You'll still be the same person. I'll still be your friend. I always will be.' I cried then as I'd never cried before, and Anna put her arm round me. It wasn't exactly worth going blind to have her do that, but it comforted me as nothing else had; calmed my fears, made me feel less alone inside my black hole of despair.

# CHAPTER 4

## ONLY ONE WAY OUT

AFTER THAT, RESIGNATION GREW IN ME SLOWLY, imperceptibly. I would never see again. Never. There was to be no going back. I was going to have to live with myself as I was, sightless and alone, in permanent unending darkness. For a while I could think of nothing else and sank into a deep sadness, a bottomless pit of bitterness and self-pity. Anna tried to get me out of it, not by pitying me but by arguing with me.

'It's like a living death,' I told her once.

'You can't say that,' she said. 'You know nothing about death. You haven't been there and neither have I. We're alive. All right, so you can't see. But you can live. We've got to think about living.'

Anna came over to see me whenever she could, whenever she was home from school. More than anyone else she lightened my darkness. We'd talk of all the good times we'd had together and laugh about them. She brought me some of her CDs - Robbie Williams, Britney Spears, the Corrs - and some audio tapes as well - *The Sword in the Stone, Sir Gawain and the Green Knight*, and *Arthur, High King of Britain*. With their help I managed to banish the hateful silence of my room and to fill my life with sound. This seemed to help, to distract me, to take myself out of myself - at least, for a while. But as time went on I found I also had something else to worry about. I had tried to ignore it, to pretend it wasn't so. But I couldn't, not any longer.

At first I hoped it might be temporary, just a phase that would pass. But it didn't pass. If anything it became worse. It was something I had to hide, something I'd told no one about, not even Anna. Ever since the accident I had been unable to remember things, little things that might not have mattered so much on their own. But there were also, I discovered, important parts of my life that had just gone missing. For instance, apparently we'd all been on holiday to Canada when I was five, to see my uncle Bill, my father's brother, who lived in Toronto. People still talked about it. I remember I'd seen the photographs. It was the only time I'd been up in a jumbo jet. But I couldn't remember any of it.

Nor could I recall anything of a trip up to London only a year or so ago, when we'd been to the zoo, and to the Science Museum, to the Tower of London, and to Stamford Bridge to see my favourite team Chelsea playing Tottenham Hotspur. All these events were a complete mystery to me. In fact, I had no memories of even *being* a Chelsea fan.

My mind, I was discovering, was full of blank spaces, gaps in my memory that were completely unpredictable, so that I was never prepared for them.

The vicar came to see me one day – 'just to cheer you up,' as he put it – and started going on about a production of *Joseph and the Amazing Technicolor Dreamcoat* he'd put on the year before in the church, apparently.

'You've a fine singing voice, Bun,' he said. 'Everyone said so. You were a wonderful Pharaoh, just wonderful.'

I didn't have a clue what he was talking about. I had no memory of it whatsoever. I covered up as best I could, but how well I had covered up I could never really be sure, because of course I couldn't see people's faces to see how they reacted.

As each new memory gap became evident I became more and more terrified, because it made me fear I might now be losing my mind as well as my sight. It was my darkest, deepest secret and I kept it to myself.

There was even worse to come. It was becoming obvious that I couldn't go back to school with the others on Tresco, that sooner or later I'd have to go to a 'special' school for the blind. There was no school for the blind on Scilly. I'd have to go to the mainland. I'd have to leave home.

When the time came my mother tried to break it to me as gently as she could. 'All the kids have to go to school on the mainland at sixteen anyway, for their sixth form. You know that, Bundle. You'd just be doing the same thing, only a few years earlier, that's all. And it's just the right place for you. Dad and I have been to see it. They've got all the right equipment, all the specialist teachers you need. Lovely grounds, too. It's only up at Exeter. Not far. We can come and see you, and you can come back home often. I promise.'

It was the final confirmation that I was indeed different from everyone around me and that, therefore, I was to be treated differently.

'It won't be until the end of the summer, Bun,' said my father, laying a hand on my arm. 'And it won't be so bad, honest it won't. You'll see. I went away to school at your age, and I loved it. Lots to do, lots of new friends.'

I was to be separated from home, from everyone I knew and loved, my mother, my father, from Liam and Dan, and from Anna, too. It was more than I could bear. I lay there all night thinking it through. By the time I heard the dawn chorus of gulls and oystercatchers, I had made up my mind.

There was only one way out, and I would have to take it.

# CHAPTER 5

## HELL BAY

NOW THAT I'D MADE UP MY MIND I DIDN'T think twice about it. Still in my pyjamas, I picked up the boathook from the porch and walked out of the house, down the path to the front gate, and out on to the track. I hadn't been further than this on my own since the accident, and I knew that even with my boathook feeling the way for me, I'd be bound to stumble. The track up to Hell Bay was uneven and stony, difficult enough to climb *with eyes*, let alone without them. But I'd done it a thousand times before and I knew the lie of the land almost instinctively. I could do it.

I felt the hill rising under my feet as I came up to

Hillside Farm, where Anna lived, where she would be sleeping. I stopped for a few moments outside her house. 'Goodbye, Anna,' I whispered. 'Thanks for trying. Thanks for everything. I'm sorry.' I felt the tears coming, felt myself weakening.

I turned away and walked on, out around Bryher Pool and Popplestones Bay. Here I tripped and fell badly, barking my knee on the ground. I sat there for a while rocking back and forth, waiting for the pain to subside.

I heard a flock of turnstones peeping along the shore, and listened to the surge of the sea as each wave fell and washed up the beach. I knew that it was a beautiful world I was leaving, but it was a world I could no longer see, a world I no longer felt I belonged in.

As I got to my feet I thought I heard someone close behind me. I stood and listened for a while and decided I must have been imagining things. It must have been the wind sighing through the dunes. It was far too early for anyone to be about.

From now on the track was both steep and dangerous, easy enough to follow but narrow and tortuous, in places soft with springy thrift, then suddenly treacherous with loose stones underfoot and slippery wet rock. In places I had to go down on my

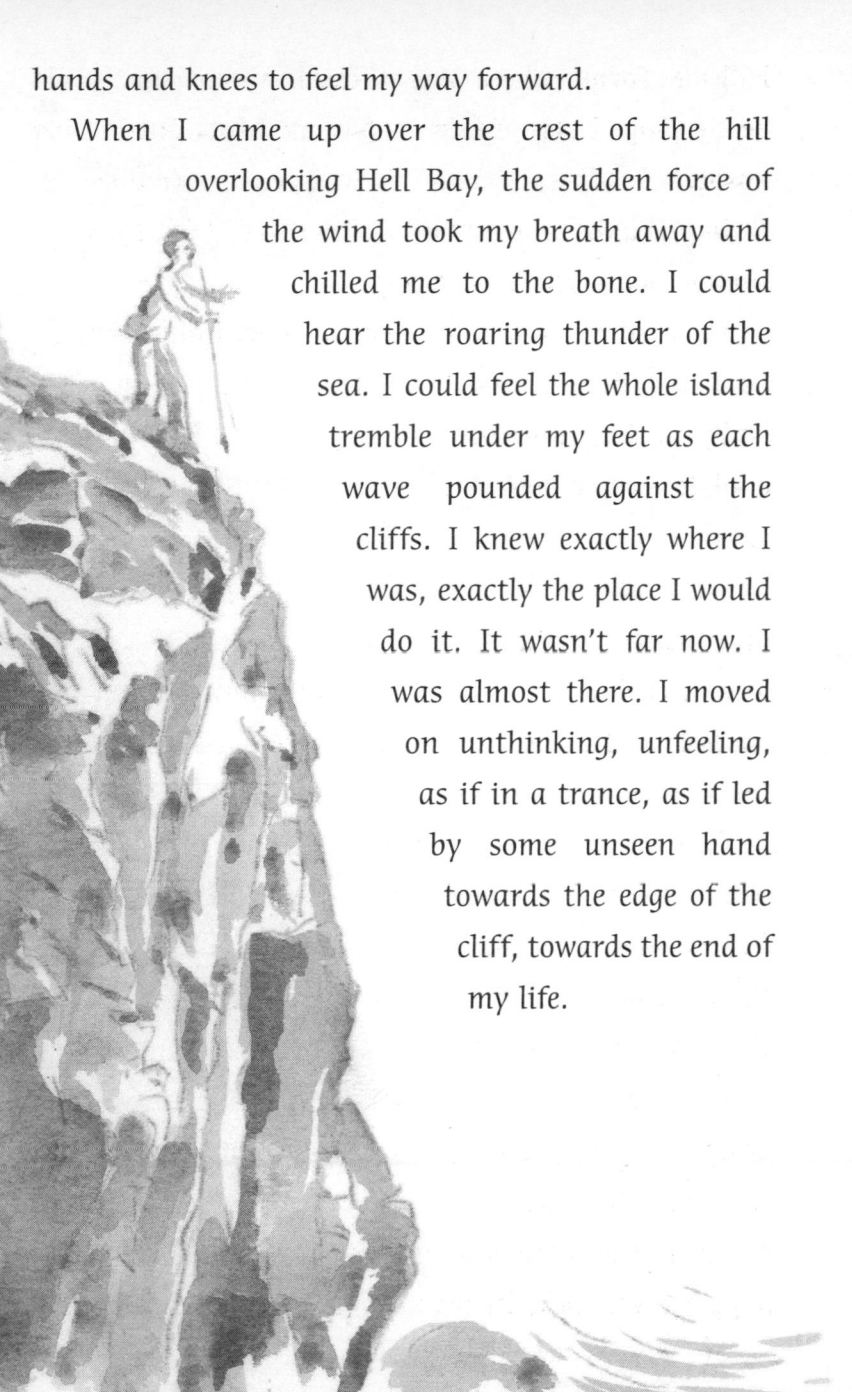

hands and knees to feel my way forward.

When I came up over the crest of the hill overlooking Hell Bay, the sudden force of the wind took my breath away and chilled me to the bone. I could hear the roaring thunder of the sea. I could feel the whole island tremble under my feet as each wave pounded against the cliffs. I knew exactly where I was, exactly the place I would do it. It wasn't far now. I was almost there. I moved on unthinking, unfeeling, as if in a trance, as if led by some unseen hand towards the edge of the cliff, towards the end of my life.

A voice spoke from behind me, gentle, ethereal. 'Don't, Bun. Don't.' Then a hand, a real hand, grasped me firmly by the arm. It was Anna. 'Come away,' she said. 'Come away. You're too close to the edge.'

I did not resist as she led me away, her arm round me. She helped me down on to a carpet of soft thrift and sat down beside me, letting me cry until I had no more tears left to cry. She did not talk and she did not touch me, but I could feel her willing me to explain why I had tried to do it. She wanted to understand, she needed to.

So I told her why. I poured it all out about the 'special' school for the blind on the mainland, how they were banishing me to another world, forcing me away, driving me out. I had nothing to live for any more.

'Didn't you tell them? Didn't you tell them how you feel about it?' Anna asked me.

'Yes. Well, no. Not exactly. I tried, but I can't talk to them like I can to you. And maybe they're right, in a way. I am different now. Maybe there is no choice. Maybe I have to go. You won't tell them, will you? About this, I mean.'

'Course not, Bun. But if you won't tell them what you feel, then I will. We all will: Liam, Dan and me. We'll tell them we don't want you to go, that there's got to be another way. But you've got to promise me something. You've got to promise me, Bun, that you'll never give up, that you'll never think of killing yourself again. Promise?'

I promised, and I meant it. A promise to Anna was one I would always keep.

We started off back home, her hand holding mine tight all the way.

# CHAPTER 6

## ONE OF US

SOMETHING HAD BEEN PUZZLING ME BUT IT WAS only as we passed Anna's house that it came to me what it was.

'How did you know?' I asked her, 'I mean, how did you find me?'

'It was strange, really strange. I don't normally wake up this early. Something woke me. Like a voice in my head, part of a dream, maybe. I don't know. I was just about to go back to sleep when I heard footsteps outside. I opened the window and there you were walking away up the track in your pyjamas. I thought you were sleepwalking. I didn't know what else you could be doing. What I did know is that you're not supposed to wake up sleepwalkers, so I just followed you. But by the time you got to Hell Bay I knew you couldn't be sleepwalking. You seemed to know exactly where you were going. I never thought you were going to . . . you know . . . until the very last moment when you went near the edge.'

'I'm glad you woke me up,' I said.

'Me too,' she said, and she squeezed my hand. 'I'll talk to the others. We'll sort something. Don't worry.'

She took me as far as my front door and then left me. I found my way in all right and managed to get myself back upstairs and into bed without waking anyone up. I was exhausted, and went to sleep almost at once. When my mother woke me later, it was as if the whole thing had been some half-forgotten night-long dream. But my bruised knee and my gritty feet were real enough to convince me that some of it, at least, had been no dream.

Only when Anna and Dan and Liam turned up at the house that evening, and Anna began talking, could I be quite sure that I had dreamed none of it, none of it at all. Now I knew for certain that last night, up on the cliffs at Hell Bay, Anna had indeed saved my life – again.

'We've been talking, all of us,' Anna began hesitantly, 'and we've been thinking, and . . . well, Bun says you want to send him off to a sort of special school on the mainland. And we . . .'

'No, Anna,' my mother interrupted. 'That's not right, and it's not fair. That's not how it is at all. We don't *want* to send Bun anywhere. Of course we don't, but we have to. He can't go back to school on Tresco. It wouldn't be fair on the teachers, or fair on Bun. They just couldn't cope. He needs to be taught by specialist teachers now, who can teach him to read and write in Braille, that sort of thing. He can't do it here on the islands. There just aren't the facilities.'

'But he can.' It was Liam's voice. 'We've been asking around. My dad says there's this lady, who's come to live on St Mary's, just retired. Dad's done some building work on her bungalow. Anyway, she's blind and she reads Braille, and she was a teacher, too, on the mainland. And so my dad rang her up and asked her if she would give Bun lessons, and she said she would. And she's very nice, he said.'

'And you know those people on St Agnes with about six children?' Dan was joining in now, 'The ones that grow all their own vegetables and have a café in the summer for the visitors, y'know, just by the lighthouse? Well, they teach their kids at home, and they're all right, aren't they? I mean, they can read and write and they can play football and stuff, just like we can.'

'And so we all thought,' Anna again, growing in confidence now, 'we thought, didn't we, that you could teach Bun here at home, and then he could go off to St Mary's for his Braille lessons with that lady, and that way he wouldn't have to leave us. So we've brought you a petition. Everyone's signed it, everyone we could find anyway, because we all want to keep Bun here on Bryher where he belongs.'

For some time no one spoke. I could hear my mother or my father leafing through what I supposed to be the petition. Then one of them got up suddenly and went out of the room. It sounded like my mother's footsteps.

'Well, Bun,' said my father, 'it seems your friends don't want you to go any more than we do. Your mum's a bit upset, Bun. Not *upset* upset, not cross, nothing like that. I think she's just touched by the nice things they wrote in this petition. I'll read it, shall I?

*We, the undersigned, want Bun to stay here on Bryher with us and not go away to school on the mainland. He's grown up here with us. He belongs here. He's one of us, one of the Bryher family, and we don't want to lose him.*

'And then everyone's signed it, and there's nice messages, too. Mrs Gee at the shop says, "Don't you dare send Bun away. I'd miss his mucky fingers." And here's another – old Percy at the Boathouse: "We'll be his eyes for him. Let him stay." And there's pictures, too, from some of the kids of dolphins, puffins – and an elephant. Don't know what that's doing there. He's got five feet!'

He paused for some moments. 'Of course I'll have to speak to Bun's mum,' he went on, 'and I can't promise anything. But I reckon if this lady on St Mary's is all you say she is and if she's willing to do it, then we'll give it a go. Lord knows what we'll be like as teachers. To be honest, it's not something we'd even thought of. We've got a lot of hard thinking to do, all three of us, and a lot of talking, too. We'll try to keep him with us, I promise. We'll do our best. You can be sure of that.'

# CHAPTER 7

## 'BE HAPPY. DON'T WORRY.'

SO THANKS TO ANNA'S PETITION, I STAYED HOME.
Three times a week, weather permitting, I went over to
St Mary's for my Braille lessons with Mrs Parsons. My
father did less of the fishing and was back to working
on the farm most of the time, so that my mother could
become my full-time teacher. I didn't learn my Braille
as quickly with Mrs Parsons as I should have done,
because I was reluctant to do my homework each day,
and because I found it so hard to concentrate on touch.

In time, Mrs Parsons taught me a great deal more
than just Braille. She taught me to be more positive,
to accept my blindness for what it was; not to embrace
it exactly, but to stop feeling so angry about it all the

time. She herself had been blind for most of her life, after some illness or other. She'd brought up two children, travelled half the world, and been an English teacher in a school in Manchester. All with no eyes.

'I look at it this way,' she'd say (and she'd say it often – Mrs Parsons did repeat herself a lot), 'everyone out there, except you and me, has got five senses. We've got four. But it's what you do with them that counts, Bun. I'm telling you, we can see a whole lot better than they can. With our ears, we can see sounds. They can't. We can see with our noses, with our tongues, with our fingers. They can't. We make up the pictures in our head as we go along, don't we? We don't *need eyes*.'

She had a favourite little ditty she'd warble at me all too frequently, just to remind me to cheer up. It began, 'Be happy. Don't worry.' And what's more, she made the best lemon drizzle cake I'd ever tasted.

Back at home, with the help of the teachers at school, my mother had worked out a whole programme of lessons based on tapes and radio. For project work she used the Internet, too, which she'd read off for me. And sometimes, for special occasions like sports days and plays and concerts, I'd go across in the boat with Liam and Dan and the others for a day at school on Tresco, and it would feel just like old times again.

My mother wasn't a natural teacher, but she was no worse than some I'd had. From time to time she'd get a bit snappy with me, particularly when we were doing maths. We'd have a go at each other, which would end in one or both of us having a good long sulk. But then we would be friends again, after a while.

When it came to writing, though, she was inspired. 'You used to love writing stories at school,' she told me one day. 'You could do it again. Use your memory to see. Use your mind's eye. Then when you write you'll be able to see as well as anybody. You can dictate and I'll write it down.' We'd do that together often. And she was right – I found I could see my stories in my mind's eye as I told them, and that was brilliant.

My father, on Mrs Parsons' advice, to build my confidence I think, took me out with him on the farm in the tractor whenever he could. So I'd spend about half a day at my lessons in the kitchen with my mother, and then after lunch I'd be off around the farm with my father. To start with I wasn't a lot of use, of course. But after a while I began to mix the pig food for him, clean out a shed, feed the hens, collect the eggs, take the vegetables to the stall outside the house, collect the money the visitors left in the kitty. The more I did, the more useful I could be, the better I began to feel about myself, about everything.

Weekends were best, because on Friday night Anna would come home from school on St Mary's. Together we'd go on long walks right round the island, from Samson Hill to Rushy Bay, past Gweal Hill and Popplestones, up around Hell Bay, and back over the heather, through the bracken past Hangman's Rock to Fraggle Rock Café, where we'd stop for a Coke, and then home along the beach to Green Bay. She'd be my eyes, giving me a running commentary on what she saw, the birds, the boats, the people. Sometimes I'd hear an oystercatcher or a kestrel or a plover before she saw it and I'd point it out to her. I liked that.

Often, at low tide, we'd visit the stone my head had hit (now known as 'Bun's Stone' by everyone on the island) and I'd jump up and down on it telling it just what I thought of it. And she'd laugh. How I loved to hear her laugh. For me these were the most magical hours of my week. We were often silent together, but it was a golden silence, a golden time.

But I hadn't dared tell her about my intermittent lapses of memory. The trouble was that I didn't know how much of my life was missing. Whenever I discovered something new, that I should have known about but had forgotten, I worried all the more. There were whole episodes I simply could not piece together. I'd lie awake at night wracking my brain to recall anything about the visit to London, or maybe the trip to Canada, but my memory remained obstinately unreliable, full of blind alleys that led me absolutely nowhere.

There was something else, too, that was keeping me awake at nights. We had money problems. Because my father couldn't go fishing as much as before, there was less money coming in from the lobsters and crabs. To make matters worse, the field of potatoes had failed - most of them had just rotted in the ground. I knew my lessons with Mrs Parsons were costing money, more money than they had. I'd hear them worrying over it and arguing about it downstairs, and of course I realised full well that I was the main cause of the trouble. They were cheery enough about everything in front of me, but all the same I could tell how tired and jaded they had become.

My father had always been a loud and laughing man, full of energy and high spirits, but he had changed noticeably in just a few months. He was having to work much longer hours than before, trying to do two jobs at once and he was exhausted. In the evenings he often fell asleep in his chair in front of the television, and he'd never done that before. When I was out working with him, he wasn't nearly as jokey and chatty as he had been. Sometimes I could feel he wanted to be alone, that I'd just be a nuisance to him out on the farm. Then I'd stay behind and listen to the audio tapes Anna had lent me and try to lose myself in a story.

*Arthur*, *High King of Britain* was my favourite. It was about a boy living on the Scilly Isles who finds King Arthur still alive and living with his dog in a cave under the Eastern Isles. The old king tells him all about his life, about the Knights of the Round Table. I listened to it over and over again, until I knew it by heart almost. Somehow, it all seemed so real to me, as if it had actually happened to me, as if I was the boy in the story, as if it was not a story at all.

# CHAPTER 8

## 'BE AN ANGEL, BUN'

ONE AFTERNOON I WAS LYING ON MY BED listening once again to the story of Sir Gawain and the Green Knight, when my mother came in. 'Bun, dear,' she said, 'could you be an angel and pop out and fetch your father in for his tea? He's ploughing down in the potato field, I think. Can you find your way?' I didn't want to go. I hated being an angel – I wished she wouldn't say that – and was happy doing what I was doing.

'Do I have to?' I grumbled.

She said, 'Bundle!' in the way that she does. So I went.

I needed my boathook, of course, but by now I could find my way easily enough round the farm. I knew every gate, every escallonia hedge, every rut in the farm tracks. I knew from their songs where the thrush nested, and the blackbird, too. I had the whole farm and its sounds and smells etched in minute detail in my mind. I needed the boathook only as hazard detector in case of any unexpected obstacles left lying around or blocking my path, like a bucket, or a fork, or even the tractor.

I'd walked into the tractor once before and given myself a nasty shock, and a nasty lump on my forehead, too. At least today I knew the tractor was out of the way; I could hear it chuntering up and down in the potato field under Samson Hill. So I walked on, confidently waving and tapping my boathook in front of me, and lifting my feet up to avoid tripping over the stones. There was a wind whispering in the escallonia hedges, and as I came closer I could smell the turned earth, metallic and new.

I remember I was finding the furrows of the ploughed field very unpredictable and difficult to negotiate as I staggered on towards the sound of the tractor. I kept waving the boathook and calling out to my father. Suddenly, I felt the ground open up beneath me. I dropped like a stone, feet first, grasping at something to save myself. There was nothing. I landed with a jolt and fell on to my hands and knees. Clearly I hadn't fallen all that far, because I was unhurt. I was shocked, and I was terrified, but that was all.

I felt all around me. On every side there were earth walls. In a panic, I got to my feet. There was an earth roof above me, too. I felt above my head for the hole I must have fallen through and was very relieved to find it. I had begun to imagine I might be completely entombed. I tried again and again to haul myself up through the hole, but the soil roof kept giving way and falling in on me. I must have been aware of the rumble of the tractor, but only now did I realise that it was close and coming closer, that it was heading straight towards me.

I thought my father must surely have seen me fall in, or perhaps he had spotted me struggling to get out, and was coming to help me. But then why was he not slowing down? Why was he not stopping? I screamed. I waved. But he kept coming on, the engine still at full throttle, roaring, thundering. Closer. Closer. Nearer. Nearer.

# CHAPTER 9

## DRY BONES

I YELLED. I WAVED. BUT IT WAS NO USE. I LEFT IT as long as I dared. At the very last moment, I ducked down into the hole and threw myself on the ground, curling up tight and screaming in my terror. The tractor was almost on top of me when the engine finally slowed and died. I heard my father calling me and scrambled to my feet. I reached for the hole above me, found it, and stuck my head out.

'Bun? Ruddy hell, Bun,' said my father. 'How the blazes did you get yourself in there?' He grasped my outstretched arms, hauled me out and dumped me unceremoniously on my knees in the dirt. Then, for some reason I couldn't understand, he began laughing, and went on laughing.

'What is it?' I asked.

'You,' he replied. 'You should see yourself. You look like a chimney sweep.' Still laughing, he wiped the dirt off my face; and then I was laughing too, out of relief, sheer relief, and because I could visualise now what I must look like. When he'd cleaned me up and we'd stopped laughing, my father turned his attention to the hole.

'An old field drain, I shouldn't wonder,' he said. 'Cracked, broken. It happens sometimes. The water leaks out and washes out its own little pool underground. A little pool becomes a big pool. Then the pool dries up and you've got a sort of underground cave. I'll have a look. You stay where you are.'

When he next spoke, his voice sounded far away and hollow. I guessed he must be peering down into the hole – I'd become good at that kind of guessing. 'Pitch black. Can't see a ruddy thing. I'll fetch a torch and have a look later. Come on.' He got me to my feet, helped me up on to the tractor beside him and we drove back home.

My mother wouldn't let me in the house. She stood me in the porch and peeled off my clothes there and then. After that it was straight upstairs and into a hot bath. 'It's everywhere,' she complained. 'In your hair, in your ears, in your nose, down your neck, everywhere.' She washed my hair for me and grumbled on and on – only half jokingly – about how accident prone I was.

'What is it with you, Bun? You dive onto rocks instead of into water. You dive down holes that were never there? What next? Haven't I got enough grey hairs? Dad says he only just saw you in time. A few more feet, he said, and he'd have driven right over you.'

Later, downstairs in the kitchen, she was rubbing my hair dry and still worrying on about what might have happened, when I heard my father come back up the path. He didn't pause outside the door to stamp his feet in the porch as he always did. Instead, he came bursting straight into the room.

'It's not a cracked drain. It's not a drain at all.' He was breathless with excitement. 'You know what it is? It's a tomb, some sort of grave. I shone the torch in. I'm telling you, it's a grave.'

I was suddenly sick to my stomach. I'd been in a *grave*! I'd laid down in a grave! Only now did I recall that it hadn't been soft underneath me, that it had felt like sticks and stones. But it hadn't been sticks and stones at all. It had been bones, dry bones! A cold shudder came over me.

'And what's more, there's other things down there, too,' my father went on.

'Don't,' my mother cried, echoing precisely my own thoughts. 'I don't want to know. I don't want to hear it.'

My father went on anyway. 'No, no, you don't understand. Not bodies, not bones. Not that sort of grave. It's a tomb, an ancient tomb, like those old tombs up on Samson Hill. You know, where they buried those ancient chieftains, fifteen, sixteen hundred years ago. So far as I know, they were always empty when they were discovered. Someone had been there before and robbed them. But this one isn't empty. There's stuff down there, all sorts of stuff.'

'What do you mean, stuff?' asked my mother.

'Well, I can't be sure, not till I've had a proper look, but there's a sword down there for a start, and what looks like a shield, too. Honestly, I'm not kidding.'

'No actual body?' I said, still horrified, yet fascinated, too, by the more gruesome side of the discovery.

'Not that I could see. Gone to dust, I shouldn't wonder. After all, whoever he is, he must have been down there a very long time. Dust to dust, and all that.'

I had been covered in that dust, I thought, and shuddered all over again.

'I mean, this could be important,' my father went on, 'this could be a really important archaeological find. And valuable, too.'

'Valuable?' my mother said. 'What do you mean, valuable?'

'Well, there could be gold down there, jewels, all sorts, you never know. You remember that Saxon bracelet a visitor found on the beach at St Martin's a while back? It fetched a small fortune up in London, didn't it? These things are valuable.'

'Not to us they're not,' my mother replied. 'If I remember our lease rightly, and I know I do, then anything that's found on the farm doesn't belong to us at all. It's not finders keepers on this place. It all belongs to the Duchy of Cornwall, to the landlord. It's in the lease.'

'Okay, so maybe you're right,' my father said. 'But it's still valuable, isn't it? And it's on our place, our farm, right? We found it. Well, it was Bun that found it, and me that did the ploughing that helped him find it – comes to the same thing. Anyway, it's ours, for the moment at least, and so we're going to get a first look at it.'

'Well if you ask me, I think you should leave it where it is,' my mother said, pouring the tea as if nothing at all had happened. 'I mean, you don't want to go digging around down there disturbing everything. It's like grave robbing. And, anyway, you're not supposed to. There's proper experts, archaeological people who know all about these things. You should leave well alone.'

By now I was beginning to worry less about the bones and the dust. I was thinking about what my father had said, that the grave was about fifteen or sixteen hundred years old. That would make it about 400 or 500 a.d. Wasn't that at about the same time as King Arthur had lived, the King Arthur on my tape?

'We wouldn't be disturbing things that much,' I said, 'not if we just took the sword and the shield. After all, like Dad said, we did find it, didn't we?'

'And besides,' my father went on, 'we can't just leave the hole like it is, can we? There's always visitors walking around. Someone could fall in and get hurt. We wouldn't want that, would we?'

My mother tried to interrupt, but he wasn't in the mood to listen to any arguments. 'Here's what I'll do. I'll take the tractor-trailer down to the field, fetch up the sword and the shield, unhitch the trailer, leave it over the hole and then come back home. It'll take a bit of a while. And in the morning, after we've had a good long look, we can put them back where they came from. Simple. No one'll ever know the difference.'

# CHAPTER 10

## 'ISN'T THAT MAGICAL?'

I WANTED TO GO WITH HIM BUT MY MOTHER wouldn't hear of it. She'd already lost one argument and she certainly wasn't going to lose another. 'You've got your Braille homework for Mrs Parsons,' she said firmly. 'You keep saying you're going to do it, and you still haven't done it. What's the point in paying good money for those lessons if . . .' And on, and on.

I gave in, because I knew from her tone it was a hopeless cause. I went up to my room, but I couldn't concentrate on my homework at all. I was far too wound up. All I could think about was that sword, a sword from the time of King Arthur and Lancelot and Gawain and Tristram and Percival. We had discovered it! And I would soon be holding it!

In the end I abandoned my homework altogether and put on my Arthur tape. It was the part where King Arthur is in a boat out on the lake, and a silken arm comes up out of the water offering him Excalibur, the magical sword that brought him his kingly power, the sword he would use all his life in his struggle for good against evil. I was still listening to the tape when I heard the tractor come rumbling back into the yard.

My father was already in the kitchen by the time I got downstairs, and I could hear my mother spreading newspaper out on the table, complaining bitterly.

'I'm telling you. We shouldn't be doing this,' she was saying. 'It's not right and, what's more, it's not hygienic, either.' Suddenly she stopped talking. I heard a sharp intake of breath. Then a silence. 'Oh my God! It's beautiful. Here, Bun, come and touch it.' She took my hand and guided it. 'Can you feel it?' she whispered. 'Can you feel it? It's incredible, incredible. Can you feel it? Isn't that magical?'

I ran my hands the length of the sword, from the hilt to the point. It was massive, stretching from one end of the table to the other. I had expected it to be encrusted with age, but it wasn't. It was smooth all along the length of the blade, except where it was engraved. I could feel the

patterns. I found the hilt and gripped it. The moment
I did so my darkness exploded into sudden light that
vanished at once and left millions of fiery sparks
whirling about inside my head. I tried to let go of
the sword, but I couldn't. It was as if my hand
was glued to the hilt, stuck fast.

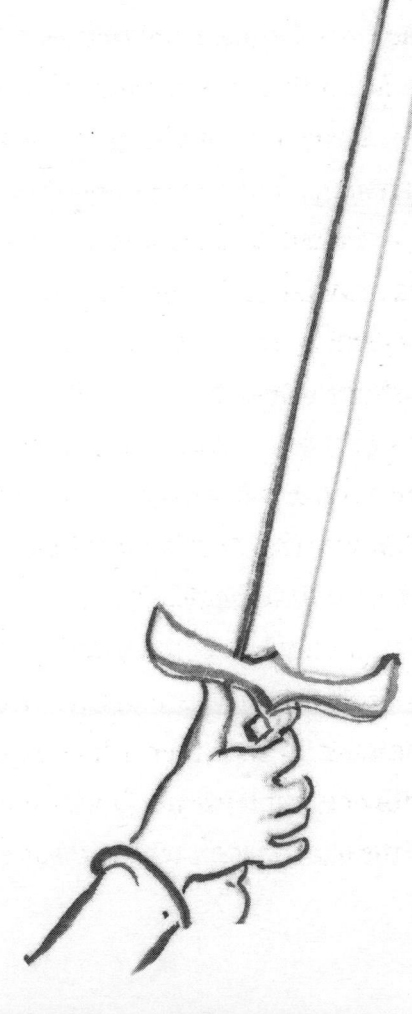

I could hear my mother's voice from far away saying, 'And to think that's been lying down there under our potatoes all these years, and it's still so well preserved. It's wonderful, just wonderful. Look at the blade. You can still see the engraving.'

My hand was suddenly released. I dropped the sword and staggered back clutching my hand. 'What's the matter, Bun? You've gone quite pale. Are you all right?' my mother asked. I couldn't answer. I felt stunned, breathless, unable to speak.

'And you just wait till you see the shield,' my father was saying. 'I'll have to unwrap it. I wrapped them both in corn sacks, Bun, so that no one could see. We don't want some nosey parker finding out about it, do we? Stand back a bit.' I heard the newspaper shifting as he laid the shield down on the table.

'Will you look at that!' said my mother. 'It's massive. How could they possibly hold a thing like that and fight at the same time? Looks like bronze if you ask me, bronze and leather. Amazing, just amazing. And there are marks on it, Bun. Cuts. Slashes. Battlescars I shouldn't wonder.'

'Here, Bun.' This time, it was my father who took my hand to guide it to the table. But I pulled my hand free of him.

'What's the matter?' he asked.

'I don't want to touch it,' I said, backing away. 'I just don't want to, that's all.'

Outside in the night the Bishop Rock lighthouse sounded its horn, as if it was both warning me and beckoning me at the same time. I felt shivery all over.

# CHAPTER 11

## 'NO SUCH THING AS LUCK'

ALL THAT EVENING I KEPT WONDERING WHAT great chieftain might have once owned the sword and the shield. What battles had he fought in? What knights had he killed? How had he died? They took photographs of the sword and the shield lying side by side on the kitchen table, then one with me in the picture standing over them, and another on the timer, all three of us together, arms round each other and laughing.

All the while I could still see sparks inside my head. I had felt an awesome power in that sword, and although it fascinated me, it frightened me more. Yet still I found myself tempted to try again, to reach out and touch it, but in the end I just couldn't do it.

'I'll put them back first thing in the morning, then I'll call the archaeology people at the Duchy offices,' my father was saying. 'I expect they'll send someone at once to take them away and investigate the site. So, we'd better make the best of them while we've got them.'

All through a supper of toasted cheese and mustard sandwiches - my favourite - we talked about how extraordinary it all was, about how lucky we had been, that it had happened on our farm, that we had found them. Then my mother said something very strange: 'There's no such thing as luck, Bun. Everything's meant.'

And I said, 'Even my diving off the quay that day and hitting my head?'

'Yes,' she replied, 'maybe even that.'

Afterwards, my mother drew sketches of the sword and the shield just in case the film didn't come out, she said. We stayed up half the night. None of us could bring ourselves to go to bed. It was as if the sword and the shield held us in some magical thrall from which we didn't want to escape.

When at last we all trooped upstairs, leaving the sword and the shield on the kitchen table, I could not resist one last look back. Of course, I could see nothing. But quite suddenly the sparks in my head had stopped whirling, and were replaced by a pulsating glow that suffused first my head, then my whole body with a wonderful warmth. I shuddered at the pleasure of it.

My mother must have felt it, for she put her arm round me to comfort me as we went upstairs. 'It's all right, Bun,' she said, 'there's nothing to be frightened of, you know.'

'I'm not frightened, Mum,' I told her. And it was true. All my fear of the sword had vanished and was replaced now by a deep longing, a need almost, to be near it again, and not just to touch it, but to take it, to hold it, to own it if only for a moment.

As I felt my way along the wall to my bedroom, running my knuckles over the familiar woodchip wallpaper, it came to me that I could, and I would, do exactly that. I would wait till they had gone to sleep, then go back downstairs and hold the sword in my hand.

'And remember, Bun,' my father went on after he'd said his goodnight, 'not a word to a soul. All we did was find them in the potato field. But we never had them in the house, right?'

I heard my mother still fretting as they went into their room. 'But I still say you shouldn't have brought them inside like that. What if anyone finds out?'

'They won't,' my father replied. 'No one saw me. Bun won't say anything, and neither will we. What do you think they are going to do? Look for fingerprints? What could possibly go wrong? Once I've put them back in the tomb in the morning, they'll just find them there, and that'll be that. The place is a mess anyway, full of stones and fallen soil. They'll never know anything different. You worry too much. Just enjoy it. Just think of it. Fifteen hundred years old maybe, and we're the very first people to see that sword after all that time.'

And sometime later I heard my mother say, 'Do you know what I wish? I wish Bun could have seen it.'

'Maybe he did,' said my father, 'in his own way, I mean. That boy's got a terrific imagination.'

'Don't know where he gets it from. Not his father's side, that's for sure,' quipped my mother.

'Thanks,' he replied, and then they were both laughing.

I lay there in bed, hearing but no longer listening to their muffled talk. The warming glow in my head was still there. Like the darkness I was so used to, I couldn't see through it, but it was so much better, so much easier to live with than that endless blackness. I knew, without a shadow of a doubt, that the glow in my head had come from the power of the sword, just as the sparks had before it.

They talked on much longer than they usually did. I knew I must wait until they were asleep, and fast asleep, too. But I was having trouble keeping awake. I kept drifting off, and then bringing myself back from the brink of sleep. I heard the Bishop Rock foghorn sounding again outside, and thought of the fog swirling in over Annet and St Agnes, rolling over the sea towards Bryher. I liked fog. It blinded everyone and put me on equal terms with the rest of the world.

That was why I liked my dreaming, too. In my dreams I was like everyone else. I could see. I could see again just as I had before. The whole world of my dreams was vivid and bright and coloured, full of the faces and places I knew and loved so well. I could see oystercatchers and gannets and turnstones, and watch the Bryher gig racing down the Tresco Channel. I could see the sun setting over the sea, watch the seals basking on the Eastern Isles.

But tonight I did not want to sleep, did not want to dream. I fought back the heaviness that was coming over me. I heard the foghorn sound once more and then there was silence. I couldn't help myself. I had to sleep. I would go. *I would go in my dreams.*

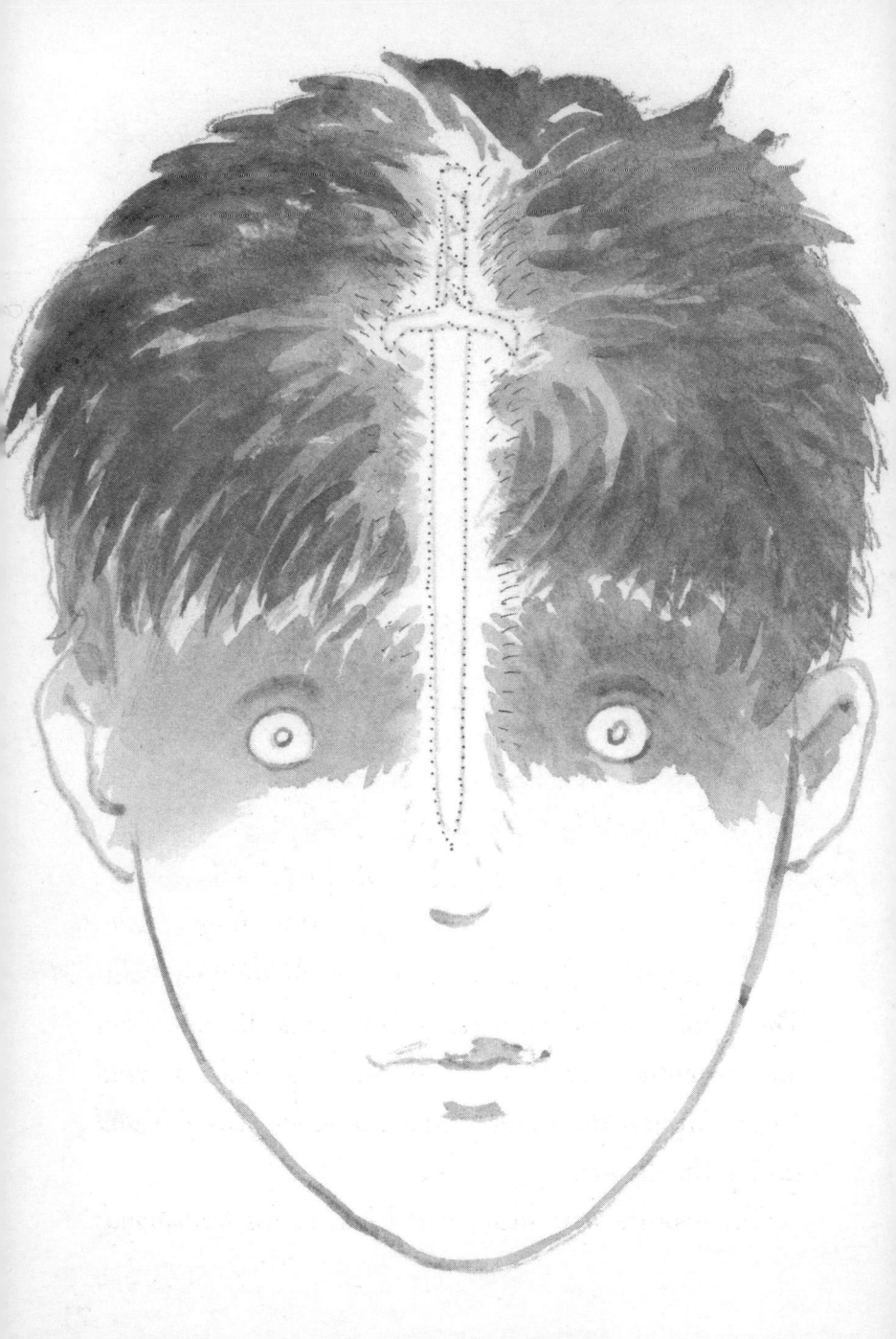

# CHAPTER 12

## IN MY DREAMS

THE CLOCK TICKED LOUDLY ON THE landing as I passed it by. All the way down I kept to the side of the stairs where I knew they creaked less. I lifted the latch carefully on the kitchen door and made for the table. I felt for the sword, found the hilt, took a deep breath and grasped it firmly. The glow in my head burnt bright, brighter still, then burst again, as I had half-expected it would, into dazzling light. The whole kitchen seemed to be dimly lit now, but intermittently, and I wondered how this could be until I saw through the window that the moon was full and surfing the clouds.

The sword was so heavy that I had to use both hands

just to lift it off the table. Once I was accustomed to the weight, I summoned all my strength and whirled it round my head, savouring its savage power as it sliced through the air. But I couldn't do this more than a few times before I had to lower the point of the sword on to the table and rest. That was when I had a sudden feeling I was not alone in the room. I thought at first it must be my father standing there, that I had been discovered. Then the figure moved into the moonlight.

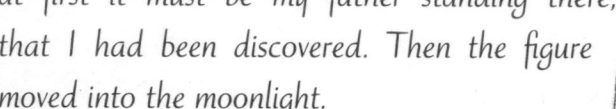

There stood before me an ancient man swathed in a dark and tattered fleece, his long hair and beard matted with filth, his face grey with grief and age. Holding the sword out in front of me, I backed away until I felt the sink behind me and could go no further. His eyes followed me all the way, but he made no move to come after me.

'I have not come to harm you,' he said, his voice little more than a hoarse whisper, 'but only to send you on your way. My name is Bedevere from the Court of King Arthur. I have been sent by Merlin who has raised me from my long sleep, to put right at last the unforgivable wrong I did all those years ago. The sword you now hold is Excalibur. After the last dread battle I took it from the hand of the wounded Arthur, my liege king and brother-in-arms, the most noble and most unfortunate king that ever lived.

'I took his great shield also, that had so long protected our beloved Camelot. It is Merlin's wish that both be now restored to their rightful owner, to Arthur, High King of Britain. And it is Merlin's wish that this quest should be yours. You have been chosen, because you alone of living people know where to find him, where to go, for you alone have been there. For this purpose you were sent to discover my tomb today and my poor dusty bones, and for this purpose also I have come here tonight.' His eyes filled with tears. For a moment or two he seemed unable to speak.

'I have a favour to ask of you. When you see good King Arthur, tell him that Bedevere loves him, and always did, and seeks his forgiveness. Tell him also that I did what I did, not out of greed, nor out of treachery. But I know now that in my pride I deceived my king, betrayed him, and denied his last wish. Instead of casting Excalibur into the lake, as he had demanded time and again that I should, I kept it and hid it.

'I told him only what I knew he wanted to hear, that I had cast it into the lake, that a silken arm had come up out of the water and taken the sword with it back down into the depths. And how did I know this? Because he had often foretold that at the end it would be so, that thus Excalibur had come to him and thus it would be taken from him. There wasn't a knight of the Round Table who did not know the story, how the end of Excalibur was to be.

'But I did not want to believe it was the end, that his wound was mortal, and for that reason I deceived him. I thought only to save Excalibur and his great shield, to save them for him, and so preserve the spirit of the Round Table and the holy kingdom of Camelot. All these years I have lain in my grave with my lie and longed to undo my guilt. Now at long last Merlin has done it for me and I can rest in peace. Go now. Arthur is waiting for you.'

He advanced towards me, and at once I lifted the sword

to protect myself. But I had mistaken his intentions, for he simply picked up the shield and gave it to me. Then with a nod of his head, as if in farewell, he faded before my eyes.

I did not doubt a single word he had told me, for even as I stood there in the kitchen, I knew in my heart that I could find my way to Arthur, and I knew more too. I knew that in another time, in another life perhaps, I had been there. I had met him. The great king himself had spoken to me, but what he had said and where and how I had found him I could not remember.

Merlin had chosen me for this quest. He had put his trust in me, but I knew I could not do it alone. There was only one person in this world I wanted to help me on this quest, only one person I could trust.

## CHAPTER 13

## THE QUEST BEGINS

THE PATH OUTSIDE WAS CLEAR AND BRIGHT in the moonlight. The Bishop Rock foghorn still sounded, but I could see no sign of fog about me. I could not run, though I very much wanted to; Excalibur was far too heavy for that. I carried it in both hands, holding it out in front of me all the way, the moon glinting on its blade.

Once outside Anna's house I laid Excalibur in the long grass and ran back to fetch the shield. It didn't take long. With both sword and shield now lying in the grass at my feet, I collected a handful of pebbles from the track and tossed them up at Anna's window. I had to do it three or four times before at last I saw her face appear at her window.

She opened it and looked out. 'Bun?' she whispered. 'What are you doing, Bun? What's up? What's going on?'

'I need you,' I said. I knew that was all I had to say. Moments later she came out, pulling a coat over her dressing-gown. Without a word I gave her the shield to carry.

'I'll tell you all about it on the way,' I said, picking up Excalibur. 'Come on.'

She waited only until we were out of sight of the houses before she stopped me. 'Bun, where are we going? What are we doing?' she said. 'The sword, the shield, where did you get them? This is mad, Bun. For God's sake, it's the middle of the night.'

I told her the whole story, exactly as it had happened. She listened to me without interrupting once. When I'd finished, she simply gaped at me and said nothing at all. 'It's true,' I told her. 'All of it, I swear.'

'Are we dreaming this?' she said, looking about her. 'I mean, am I here? Is that really Excalibur? Is this really King Arthur's shield?'

'It's no dream, Anna,' I said. 'It's all as real as we are. Touch it if you like.'

She laid the shield on the ground, and I offered her Excalibur to hold. The moment she touched it I could see her eyes suddenly widen with alarm as the power of

Excalibur surged through her.

'It's all right,' I said, holding it with her. 'It won't hurt you. I promise it won't.' I looked her in the eyes. 'Do you believe me now? Do you believe it's real? Do you believe it's Excalibur?'

'I believe it,' she whispered. 'I believe it.'

We walked in silence past the church and down towards the quay. 'That old man you met, the man in the kitchen, is it true what he said?' she asked.

'About what?' I said.

'Do you know where Arthur is? Do you know how to find him?'

'I only know that I will find him, and I know what will happen next. I know there'll be a galley waiting for us at the quay. It will take us wherever it will take us, wherever we need to go.'

'How can you be sure?' she said.

'All I know,' I replied, 'is that I know, but I don't know how I know.'

As we came past the graveyard the sea in Tresco Channel was moon-dappled and dancing, and there was the galley waiting for us at the quay. I put the sword in first, leaning it carefully up against the side of the boat. Then I stepped in. After a few moments hesitation, Anna gave me the shield to hold for her, and joined me in the

boat. At once the galley moved out over the sea, leaving the water quite undisturbed around us, and no trace of a wake behind us. There was no rudder, there were no oars. We were on board a ghost ship.

# CHAPTER 14

## GHOST SHIP

THERE ARE TIMES WHEN WHAT IS happening to you seems a distant echo of the past, nothing you could say you actually remember, but none the less you are quite sure you have been there and been through it before. As the ghostly galley glided out over the silver sea, I had exactly this sensation. I had been there before. I had done this before.

Anna and I sat silently side by side, Excalibur lying across us on our laps and the great shield lying at our feet. The Bishop Rock foghorn sounded again, and as it did so we found ourselves cocooned entirely in a sudden dense fog. We could see no rock, no island that might tell us where we were. Only the moonlight came with us, lighting the fog above us. Anna's hand crept into mine. 'I don't like this, Bun,' she whispered.

'It's all right,' I said. But even as I spoke I felt myself gripped by panic. Until that moment it was as if I had sleepwalked through all this. The truth was that I had no idea as to why it should be all right, nor any notion of where the galley might be taking us, nor what might happen to us, nor how we were going to get back. In my sudden terror I grasped the hilt of Excalibur tight, and all at once felt a great calm come over me. I knew without a shadow of doubt that we were in safe hands, that we could come to no harm.

Oystercatchers piped somewhere nearby, and I looked for them, but the fog was impenetrable. The galley sped over the sea, eastwards I thought, for the Bishop Rock foghorn sounded from behind us now, to the west, and fainter every time I heard it.

'It's not far now,' I told her, though how I knew this I did not know, and almost as I spoke we came out of the bank of fog and saw the Eastern Isles ahead of us in the shining sea. The Ganilly sandbar, lit by the moon, was a bright swathe in the ocean, a golden arrow pointing us where we were going.

Overhead I heard the sudden singing of wings and looked up. Six swans flew above us, their shadows moving over the water ahead of the galley as if they were guiding us in. The sea was shallow now, and translucent all around the ship, the seaweed reaching up towards us, tendrils wafting us in, waving us on, and there were silver fish flashing and flitting by, all swimming in the direction we were going. It was as if nature was taking us by the hand and leading us.

And then I knew. Then I remembered. I knew on which island we would find him. I remembered precisely where we had met before. 'Little Arthur,' I told Anna. 'He'll be waiting for us on Little Arthur.'

'How do you know?' she asked.

'I was there before,' I told her. 'I saw him there once before. I met him. I talked to him.'

The swans landed in perfect formation in the sea in front of us, drawing us in behind them towards the shore, towards Little Arthur. It was an island I knew well, that we both knew well, for it was to Little Arthur we often came for picnics in the summer. We'd lie on the top of the hill and see the seals below basking on the rocks, and watch the gannets diving into the ocean all round us.

Anna was pointing at the hilltop. 'Look!' she whispered. 'The rocks. Can't you see it? It's like a sculpture, a warrior's head. It's like he's lying there. You can see his helmet, his nose, his chin.' And it was true. The whole outline of the cliff face on the western side of the island did indeed resemble the head of a sleeping warrior, a sleeping king. The galley slowed as we neared the shore and then stopped.

## CHAPTER 15

## METAMORPHOSIS

'THERE WERE SIX BLACK QUEENS,' I SAID, suddenly remembering. 'When I came before there were six black queens.' And at that moment I felt Anna grasping my arm. I had no need to ask her why, for I had already seen what she had seen. A metamorphosis, a metamorphosis before our very eyes! On the shore the six swans were transformed into six black queens all in flowing black cloaks, their jewelled crowns glittering in the light of the moon, and one of them was beckoning us to come, to follow them. I climbed over the side of the galley and let myself down into the shallows. Anna leaned over and handed me down the sword and then the shield.

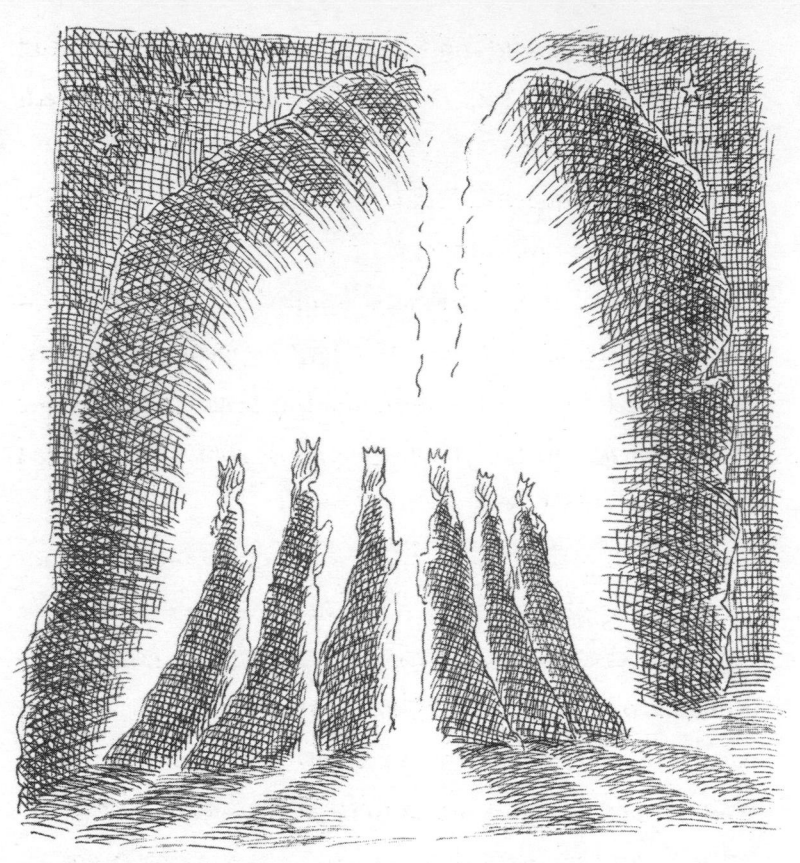

'Do I have to come any further?' she asked.

'I need you to,' I said. 'I want you to be there with me when I meet him. Please, Anna.' For a few moments she looked at the six black queens, and then up at the king's sleeping head against the sky.

'He's waiting for us,' I said. 'Please.' And then losing patience a little, I added, 'Look, I can't carry the sword and the shield on my own, can I?'

'All right,' she said, and she clambered over the side and joined me on the sand. 'I don't like them,' she whispered. 'They're like witches.'

'They're his queens,' I said. 'They look after him. They've looked after him for hundreds of years.'

It was coming back to me. I could see it all in my head now, every detail of it, just as it had happened before. As we followed the black queens up the beach towards the rocks, I turned to look back. The ghost ship had vanished altogether.

Ahead of us the rocks seemed to open up and we could see a golden glow of light. The black queens moved on in silent procession. We followed where they led into a long tunnel lit on either side by flaming torches. I was suddenly aware that Excalibur was no longer heavy to me, that it rested almost weightless in my hands, as if it was straining to leave me, longing to be back once again in the hands of the great king to whom it belonged. I gripped it tight and walked on up the tunnel, a long and winding tunnel where I now knew for sure that I had walked once before. And I knew too where it must lead us.

# CHAPTER 16

## ARTHUR, HIGH KING OF BRITAIN

WE CAME AT LAST OUT INTO THE VAST cavern I remembered, with its vaulted rock ceiling, and I saw the great Round Table set all about with chairs, and by the fire the dog, toasting himself with his nose in the ashes.

'Bercelet,' I whispered to Anna. 'That's his dog.' And even as I spoke the dog rose from his sleep, stretched himself awake, yawned, and came towards me wagging his tail in recognition.

From the chair by the fire came a voice. 'What is it, Bercelet? Has the boy returned as Merlin promised? Does he have it? Does he have Excalibur with him?'

The old man, who now rose slowly from the chair to stand by the fire waiting for us, was just as I remembered him, his hair and beard long and silver white, his face etched with age. The sight of him froze me to the spot, not with fear, but in awe. Before us stood the great Arthur himself, High King of Britain, the sleeping king, not dead, not a ghost, but alive, as alive as we were.

His whole life story seemed to pass before me as the king came towards us. How Merlin had called him, and trained him. How the young Arthur drew the sword from the stone in London, and became the chosen king of Britain. How he freed his people from fear and evil. How he drove out the Saxon invaders. How he loved Guinevere. How Mordred, his own son, had contrived to corrupt the kingdom and all it stood for — the protection of the weak, honour, chivalry and justice for all. How Guinevere had loved Sir Lancelot, and left Arthur alone to face Mordred at the last terrible battle at Camlan, where so many of the knights of the Round Table had perished. Where the wounded Arthur had killed Mordred, and been borne away from the beach by the six black queens in a galley, leaving Sir Bedevere on the shore.

As he came towards us, the great king was not looking at me, or at Anna. He had eyes only for Excalibur. I held it out to him, and as he took it from me, I saw his eyes close in rapture. He grasped it by the hilt, and lifted it high above his head.

'Oh, Excalibur!' he cried. 'I have you at last. With you in my hand I have the courage and the strength to be a king again, to do whatever it may be that I am called upon to do. How I have longed for this moment.' He brought the blade down and gazed into it. 'I see again reflected in this blade the king I once was and can be once more. And the next time, I shall not fail. I shall not fail myself. I shall not fail the people.'

He looked up at us and smiled. 'Merlin told me you would bring a friend with you on this quest. She has my shield, my trusty shield. Let me have it, girl, let me hold it.'

Arthur stood before us, a warrior once more, Excalibur in hand, his great shield held before him.

# CHAPTER 17

## THE SLEEPING SWORD

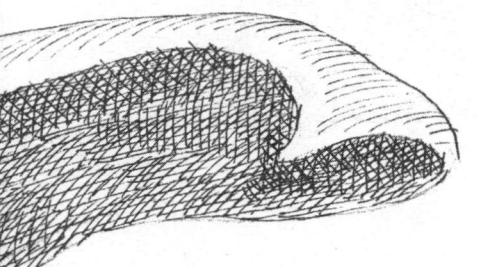

THE DOG APPROACHED THE SHIELD cautiously, sniffed at it once and stepped back nimbly. Arthur laughed at his timidity. 'Do you remember Bercelet, boy? Do you remember me?'

'Yes,' I replied, remembering it all now as if it were yesterday, but whether it was yesterday's truth or yesterday's dream I was not sure. 'When I was younger I was trying to walk across the seabed from island to island, and I was cut off by the tide. You saved me from drowning. You brought me back here and dried my clothes, and then you told me the story, your story.'

'So I did. So I did. And I always hoped and believed

that one day you might return,' said the great king, 'but I did not know when. And now you're here. I could not know that Merlin would choose you for this quest, that you would be the one who would at last bring me back Excalibur.'

'It was just luck, I suppose,' I told him. 'We discovered the sword and the shield at home, in our potato field. Lucky accident, that's all it was.' Arthur shook his head, turned and led us towards the fire. 'No boy. There is no such thing as luck. It was meant. All this was meant. All that happens is meant to happen. Merlin told me I should soon have my Excalibur again, that he had chosen a messenger who would bring it to me. Nothing happens unless Merlin means it to happen.'

He sat down heavily and laid Excalibur across his knees. For some moments he sat there running his hand up and down the blade, almost in disbelief it seemed.

Bercelet came to lie down between Anna and me, and looked up into her eyes. 'Bercelet trusts your friend. He loves her, and I see you do too, else you would not have brought her here. Ah, love, trust,' sighed the king, sitting back. 'To love or not to love. To trust or not to trust. This was ever the great dilemma of kings, of men and women everywhere. But I am old enough now and wise enough, I hope, to know better than I did, and I see in her eyes that she is a good friend to you and to me and can be trusted. Tell me, boy, tell me how it all happened. How did Merlin contrive to bring you to me?'

So I told him the whole story from the moment I fell down the hole in the potato field to the appearance of Sir Bedevere's ghost in our kitchen. 'He told me I had to bring Excalibur and the shield back to you, that Merlin had chosen me for the quest. And he told me other things too. He wants you to know that he loves you, and always did, and meant you no harm by disobeying you after Camlan, after the last battle. It was just that he could not bring himself to throw Excalibur into the lake as you told him. He did not want to believe you were dying, and he thought it would be the end of Camelot if he did. So he tricked you.'

Arthur laughed at this, and shook his head. 'Old men's tales,' he said. 'Old men believe what they want to believe. They invent their own myths. I should know, for I have been an old man for a very long time now. Bedevere did not trick me. My memory of that last battle is as clear as crystal. I killed Mordred. I killed my own son. No man, however old, would invent such a myth. I remember it all, every dreadful moment of it.

'After the battle, even as my queens bore me still bleeding from my wounds to the galley, I knew Bedevere might have betrayed me. He was a good man, but a weak man, too. I hoped he had done my bidding, but in truth I always doubted it. Of all my knights, Bedevere was the only one left alive. There was no one else to help me and, besides, I was too old, too tired to care, near death as I thought.'

As he talked on, as we listened, the six queens brought us each a beaker of soup and some bread, and fish laid out on a great platter. 'These I caught myself,' said the king, his eyes suddenly bright and mischievous. He leaned forward and spoke to us confidentially, almost conspiratorially.

'They let me out only from time to time, rule me with a rod of iron, and they're such silent companions. Never a word. Never a smile. No king ever had a smaller kingdom than this little isle. It is my penance. For centuries I have walked every rock of it, with none but Bercelet for company. Loyal friend though he is, he is not much of a one for conversation. But he loves a walk, to chase after the birds, and while he does so, I fish. These fish I caught early this morning. Eat my children, eat. They are fresh.'

I had not expected Anna to speak for she had done little until now but gaze at him wide-eyed. 'Excalibur, sir,' she began hesitantly, 'is it really a magical sword, as the story says?'

The great king thought for a while before he spoke. 'This sword,' he began, 'in the hands of a good king can be a force for good, for justice, for healing. But once corruption and despair have darkened and embittered the spirit, as it had mine in my later years, after Lancelot left, after my beloved Guinevere left with him, then Excalibur lost its power and became a sword like any other, an instrument of death, no more.

'And now Excalibur is but a sleeping sword, sleeping all these centuries, waiting for a new time, until his king was thought deserving of trust once again. That you have brought it back to me is a sign from Merlin that he believes I am fit once again to be king, should I ever be needed. And when that time comes, he will come himself and bid me once again draw the sword from the stone as I did before. Then, and only then, will this sleeping sword truly awaken. So Merlin has told me and so I must believe.

'In the meantime, boy,' he said, turning his gaze on me, 'when you have both eaten your fill there is one last task I have for you, that Merlin has for you, before your quest is finished. But do not hurry over your eating. It can wait. All these years I have longed to hold Excalibur again, and I do not want the moment to be over too soon.'

'How long?' Anna asked. 'I mean, how long have you been here on Little Arthur?'

He smiled at me. 'She is full of questions, your friend. And so she should be. How else do we learn wisdom? I have not counted the years, girl, but my keepers, my guardians, my six queens tell me I have been waiting here for nigh on fifteen centuries. Fifteen centuries I have waited to do this.' And the old king got to his feet, and readied himself, Excalibur held in both hands. 'And for all I know,' he said, 'I may have to wait another fifteen centuries before I can do this again. So I shall make the very best of it.'

And with that, he whirled Excalibur about his head, and cut and parried and slashed and thrust, until at last he was left leaning on the sword exhausted, his eyes bright with excitement, and laughing, laughing out loud.

# CHAPTER 18

## END OF THE QUEST

THE SOUP WAS HIGHLY SPICED AND warming to the roots of my hair, to my fingertips. Both Anna and I drank it eagerly and then ate our fish in our fingers, pulling the flesh from the bones. I had never liked mackerel until then, thinking it rather tasteless — like pollock, only fit to be used as bait to catch lobsters and crabs.

When we were done eating, Arthur led us out into the centre of the great torchlit cavern, and around the Round Table, Excalibur resting easily in the crook of his arm. And as we went, Arthur spoke of all the knights whose names were inscribed on the seats, of the quests they had followed, of the wonderful feats of courage and chivalry they had each performed, of Gawain and Percival and Tristram. Even as he spoke their names, I knew their stories word for word, the stories he had told me once before.

When he came to his own seat he stopped. 'And here I sat,' he said, 'with my beloved Guinevere on my right and Lancelot on my left, and around us a company of the dearest friends, the noblest friends. Such friends, such a time.' He sighed. 'And it was all so quickly over, a tiny flame that glowed brightly, brilliantly and then flickered and faded but, thank God, was never quite extinguished, not entirely.

'When Merlin came to me in my dreams and told me I must expect you, that Excalibur was to be restored to me, I had hoped my time had come. But sadly it is not to be so, not yet. Excalibur, he told me, was to be mine again, but I may not use it, may not wield its power until he comes to see me in person to tell me the time is right. Until then I have to bide my time, and be patient, he says. And for its safe keeping Excalibur will remain here with me.

'Do you remember the sword in the stone? Do you remember how all the knights and princes in the land tried to pull it free, and that only I had the power to do it? So it will be again. Excalibur, Merlin told me, is to be thrust into the rock you see behind you. Read what you see upon it.'

We went closer and bent down to read it. In the flickering of the torchlight it was not easy to pick out the words. I could read it only slowly.

When the right time comes, only Arthur,
the rightful High King of Britain, shall pull
this sword from the stone.

'And now,' said Arthur, handing me Excalibur, 'it is for you to thrust it into the stone.' I took the sword from him and looked at the rock face in front of me. It was solid, flawless, not a crack to be seen.

'But how?' I asked. 'How can I do it? It's impossible. It won't go in.'

'Do it. Believe it will happen and it will, I promise you,' said Arthur. 'Go on. Thrust, and thrust with all your strength. Anywhere you wish. It will go in. Have faith.'

I turned and looked at Anna, and saw no flicker of doubt in her eyes. If she believed I could do it, then I could do it. I grasped the sword, and ran full tilt at the rock face, and thrust it in. The blade sunk in almost up to the hilt, as easily as if the rock had been butter.

'That was well done,' said Arthur, his hand on my shoulder. He reached for the hilt and pulled at it. 'Stuck fast,' he said. 'And so it will stay now until the day I am needed once more. You have done me great service tonight. But the night is for sleeping, for me and for you, and you must go back home where you belong. Come.'

With Bercelet's nose touching the back of my leg as

I walked, we left the great cavern behind us and went down the winding torchlit tunnel following in Arthur's footsteps. He stopped as he came out into the night air and breathed in deep. 'The air of this place is good for the body, good for the soul, too. Go now, your galley is waiting to carry you home.'

And so it was. The six black queens stood like silent sentinels on the rocks watching us go, but no one except the king himself spoke a word as the galley moved away from the shore. He waved and called out after us, 'May your days be full of laughter and light. May all our dreams come true.'

We watched him as long as we could, his great shield resting on the ground in front of him, Bercelet beside him gazing after us. Above us we heard a sudden singing — the swans, the six swans flew above, drawing us into the fog, taking us home. When we looked again Arthur was gone and the island with him.

The fog lifted as we came into Tresco Sound. All this while we had sat silent in the galley, alone with our thoughts. As we passed below Samson Hill, I looked up and saw the moon riding through the clouds, coming with us all the way. That was when Anna spoke. 'If you weren't here with me,' she said, 'I wouldn't believe any of this. I'd think it was all a dream, a wonderful dream.

But I see you.' She put her hand on my arm. 'I feel you. I hear the oystercatchers. I smell the sea. It has all been real.'

The six swans flew across the moon and circled overhead as the galley came alongside the quay. We stepped off, and watched it glide away and vanish. We were back on Bryher, and we were suddenly cold. We parted by the church.

'You'll tell no one?' I said.

'No one,' she said. 'It's our secret.' She kissed me on the cheek, and she was gone.

The house was still dark when I got home. Only the moon lit the windows. No one stirred. The newspapers lay spread out on the kitchen table. No sword. No shield. It had happened. I had imagined none of it.

I climbed into bed, pulled up my duvet and shivered myself warm. I heard the Bishop Rock foghorn sounding and the cry of an early gull, and thought of Arthur, of Excalibur, of the six black queens, of Bercelet, and of Anna, with whom I had shared the greatest secret of my life. I felt my cheek, felt the kiss that was still there. I wondered if she was asleep yet, and then fell asleep myself.

# CHAPTER 19

## 'IS IT REALLY TRUE?'

I WOKE AND OPENED MY EYES. IT WAS LIGHT. It was *light*! IT WAS LIGHT? I closed my eyes and opened them again. Still light. I looked around. The Chelsea team poster I hadn't seen for two years was still on the wall, the collage of all my bird pictures was above my bed. My green dressing-gown was on the end of the bed, my audio tapes on my bedside table, and the radio too. I got up. I looked at myself in the mirror. Me. I was older, taller than I remembered, but it was me. I wasn't imagining it. I was seeing again! I could see! I could see! I could see!

I thundered down the stairs into the kitchen, shouting and screaming at the top of my voice. No one was home. The newspaper was gone from the kitchen table. I rushed out of the house, and saw them coming back up the farm track from the potato field, my father on the tractor, my mother sitting, legs dangling, on the trailer behind. I waited for them, wondering how to tell them, what to tell them.

Should I say that it was the power of Excalibur that had healed my eyes? Should I tell them everything? Should I tell them anything? As I stood there a robin sang at me from the apple tree. I remembered a robin singing at me at London Zoo, and the massive dinosaurs at the Natural History Museum. I remembered everything about the trip to Canada too, the Niagara Falls, the Toronto Tower, the black bear we had seen in the forest. I didn't just have my sight back, but my memory too.

They jumped down and came towards me. 'All done, Bun,' my father laughed, ruffling my hair. 'Buried them both, put the sword and the shield back where they belong. No one'll know a thing.'

They couldn't have! It was impossible, impossible.

'I was worried sick all night long,' my mother said. 'Never slept a wink.'

'You've put the sword back, and the shield?' I asked.

'Yes,' my father replied. 'No one'll ever know we had them out. I'll call the Duchy after breakfast.'

'But you couldn't have!' I cried. They were both looking at me in astonishment.

'Why not?' my mother asked. 'Is anything the matter, Bun?'

'No, Mum.' I was trying to work it all out, trying desperately to make some sense of it. Hadn't Anna and I taken Excalibur and the shield to King Arthur in the night? And if we had, then how could they have just buried them? But I knew it must have happened as I remembered it. Otherwise how could my eyes have been healed? How else could it have happened? I *was* seeing, wasn't I? Or was I imagining that too?

'Mum? Dad?' I said. I was bursting to tell them, but still uncomprehending, still unsure of the reality of anything.

'What, Bun?' My mother was clearly anxious about me. 'Are you feeling all right?'

'That's the thing,' I said. 'I'm feeling fine. In fact, I think I can see again. I mean, I can see you, both of you. I can see the sky! I can see the sea! I can see that robin over there on the hedge. I can see!'

They didn't take it in turns to hug me. There were four arms round me, and they were both crying, and then I was crying, and I didn't care any more about swords or shields, about what had happened or what I had dreamed. I could see and that was all that mattered.

The news was all over the island within the hour. Soon the entire house, and garden too, were full of people, laughing and crying. I'd never been so hugged in all my life. Liam didn't hug me, nor did Dan, thank goodness, but they did have tears in their eyes, and I was pleased about that.

In the end I escaped up to my room and sat on my bed, my head a whirl of incomprehensible contradictions. And that was where Anna later found me. She came over, crouched down and took my hands in hers.

'Is it true?' she said, looking up into my eyes. 'Is it really true?'

I just smiled at her.

'You can see again?' I nodded. She was the only person I really wanted to hug me, and when she did, my joy was complete.

'Anna,' I whispered, my head buried in her shoulder. 'Last night. Do you remember last night?'

'What about last night?' she replied. 'What do you mean?'

'You don't remember? You don't remember anything?' I said.

'I went to bed. I slept. That's all. What are you on about?'

'Nothing,' I said hurriedly. 'Nothing. I was just wondering that's all. I was dreaming a dream last night and you were in it, and I wondered . . . It's nothing, nothing at all.'

'You are funny,' she laughed. 'By some wonderful miracle you've got your eyesight back, and you go on about dreams. This isn't dreaming. This is real, Bun. You're seeing me, you're seeing again. It's all real.'

'I hope so,' I said. 'I hope so.'

THE END

# AFTER I WROTE MY STORY

That was my very first long story, the first one I ever made up that had a beginning, a middle and an end. I didn't tell anyone about it for a long time. The trouble was that almost everyone I wanted to tell was in the story, because truth had played such a big part in it. All my characters were real people, friends, family. I hadn't even changed their names. I wasn't sure how much they'd like me writing about them.

Then one day Anna was up in my room. It was Friday evening. She'd dropped in on her way home for the weekend from school over on St Mary's. She'd got a new computer, she said, and it was brilliant. It did everything, word-processing, games, the Internet, e-mail, the lot. I came out with it before I'd even thought it through.

'I've done this story,' I told her. 'It's all on tape. I just told it on tape. I was wondering, could you put it through your word-processor? Then if you think it's good enough, maybe I could send it off to a publisher or something.'

'Course,' she said. 'I need the practice.'

She didn't come to see me all weekend after that, so we had no walk around the island as we usually did, no sitting and chatting together on Rushy Bay. I really missed it. I really missed her. On Sunday evening I was sitting on my bed feeling very lonesome and very miserable, when I heard her voice down in the kitchen. Then I heard her come running up the stairs.

'Bun,' she said from outside the door. 'Are you there, Bun?'

'What do you want?' I was deliberately sullen, angry at her for ignoring me all weekend.

'I've done it. Your story, Bun. I've done it on disk. I've got a copy. I've read it. Can I come in?'

'I suppose so,' I said, my heart beating suddenly fast. She came and sat down beside me.

'It's lovely, Bun,' she said. 'I loved it, the whole thing. It's good, and I mean good. And I liked being in it, too, being a part of it. It felt true, really true. Shall I read it to you? Would you like that?'

She read the whole thing from beginning to end without stopping. I liked her reading it, I liked the story, but most of all I liked her liking it.

Before she left I made her promise to tell no one about it, about any of it. 'A secret,' she said, 'like our secret in *The Sleeping Sword.*' And she kissed me on the cheek. 'Like in the story,' she said, 'except this is for real.'

It was only the next day that I decided it was time I tried to venture out of the house more on my own. I was fed up with being cooped up. My mother went down to the shop after our morning lessons, and all I had to look forward to for the rest of the day was a trip to St Mary's to Mrs Parsons' Braille class that afternoon. I could hear my father's tractor rumbling away somewhere under Samson Hill. I'd go and see him, show him I could do it on my own, give him a surprise.

I went downstairs, picked up the boathook from the porch and went out into the yard, tapping from side to side. I felt my way along the escallonia hedge in the little field where we grow the daffodils, and then out over the ploughed field towards the sound of the tractor.

I was calling out, waving at my father when it happened. I felt the ground simply give beneath my feet. I went straight down landing in a crumpled heap. I was at the bottom of some kind of a hole, and the tractor was coming on towards me, closer and closer, nearer and nearer, the engine thundering, roaring, still at full throttle. I stood up, and felt for the opening above my head. I waved. I screamed. He had not seen me. The tractor was coming straight for me . . .

But suddenly I was not worried. Suddenly I knew the tractor would stop, that it had to stop. When it did, when I heard my father's voice calling me, I knew how it must be, that there would be a light at the end of my dark tunnel, and that I would reach it. It was *meant* to happen, and so it would happen, all of it, just as I had seen it before in my mind's eye, just as I had told it in *The Sleeping Sword*.

All I had to do was believe in it.